PROPERTY
of the
STATE

PROPERTY
of the
STATE

KIKI
SWINSON

www.kensingtonbooks.com

DAFINA BOOKS are published by

Kensington Publishing Corp.
119 West 40th Street
New York, NY 10018

All Kensington titles, imprints, and distributed lines are available at special quantity discounts for bulk purchases for sales promotion, premiums, fund-raising, and educational or institutional use.

Special book excerpts or customized printings can also be created to fit specific needs. For details, write or phone the office of the Kensington Sales Manager: Kensington Publishing Corp., 119 West 40th Street, New York, NY 10018. Attn. Sales Department. Phone: 1-800-221-2647.

The Dafina logo is a trademark of Kensington Publishing Corp.

ISBN-13: 978-1-4967-2007-8
ISBN-10: 1-4967-2007-5
First Trade Paperback Printing: April 2021

ISBN-13: 978-1-4967-2009-2 (e-book)
ISBN-10: 1-4967-2009-1 (e-book)
First Electronic Edition: February 2020

10 9 8 7 6 5 4 3 2 1

Printed in the United States of America

PROPERTY
of the
STATE

1

TIME'S UP

"Misty, time's up," Agent Sims had said, his hand-cuffs dangling in front of him.

"No." I shook my head as tears sprang to my eyes. "I have to make sure my mother is okay. I can't just leave her like this."

"We'll take care of her. But, right now . . . 'You have the right to remain silent. Should you give up that right, any-thing you say can and will be held against you . . .'"

I opened my eyes after replaying one of the worst days of my life. My chest heaved and the air around me felt heavy. I felt like my body would collapse, just like my whole world had days before Agent Sims had taken me down and handed me over to the local cops for my ex-boyfriend Terrell's murder. On one hand, I was grateful that Sims had saved me from being taken by mafia guys that wanted to kill me, but on the other hand, facing down a long prison sentence wasn't ideal.

Damn! I had fucked everything up. Everything about my life had gone in a totally opposite direction than what I had planned. One seemingly foolproof plan to steal drugs had sent my entire life on a crash course with disaster. Murder, mayhem, and now my arrest had been the result of my plan, instead of making money and getting rich quick. Call it karma, or just straight bad luck—whatever it was, I was knee-deep in it now.

Goose bumps cropped up all over my body as I thought back to watching my mother scramble for her life. Knowing that it was all my fault she'd been kidnapped and held hostage made it even worse to bear. My whole plan to trade my life for my mother's had fallen apart, even though a small part of me knew that Ahmad, the bastard that had held my mother hostage, wasn't going to trade my life for hers as easily as he'd made it seem. Ahmad was ruthless and he was out to avenge the savage killing of his family, which he blamed on me.

I swear, this wasn't how my life was supposed to end. And now I was sitting in lockup, waiting to be arraigned for murder. *Murder! Me, a murderer?* I had worked so hard in school and struggled in life to be successful. And all for what? To end up in jail facing a real-life prison term.

I'd been racking my brain thinking of all sorts of ways I could get out of this situation. But Agent Sims had warned me that the local detectives had clear and convincing evidence against me. I was officially doomed. When I get convicted, because I am sure it will happen, I know that I will probably spend the rest of my life in prison while my mother is out on the streets alone. Who would protect her now? I was locked up. Carl was dead. My grandmother and cousin Jillian were gone. My mother was alone with a bag of money and an entire organized crime family out to get her so they could exact revenge against me. My mother's safety preoccupied most of my thoughts.

I had bitten my fingernails down to the quick and could barely keep still. I hadn't eaten since I'd been arrested.

Sleep was a thing of the past; I hadn't gotten one solid hour. Every time I closed my eyes, all of the craziness played out in my mind's eye, over and over. My life had turned into a real-time nightmare. One thing after another had me wanting to end it all, again. I thought about it and could actually see myself going through with it, all over again, but the thought that my mother would really be left with no one in life kept me from doing it. I let the tears that I'd been hiding run down my face this time.

As different officers moved me through the process, my head pounded with all sorts of thoughts. I had had enough of hurting people that I love and getting hurt as well. At one point, I even wanted to die myself. The whole plan was to trade my life for my mother's, but then that plan blew up in my face. I mean, I can't win for losing. Nothing I do ever comes to fruition. *Ugh!*

The time came for me to be moved from the holding cell in the precinct, where those backstabbing detectives dropped me off, to the county jail until my initial appearance and arraignment could finally be scheduled. When the police officer pulled me from the cell, he escorted me down to the first floor, where the inmates were processed in and out to be transported to jail. He handed me over to a white man and white woman dressed in regular clothing and a dark blue jacket, which told me right away that my case had been turned over to state authorities. I was handed a brown paper bag, escorted to a back room and was told to change. Without saying a word, I took the brown paper bag, which contained my belongings, and went about changing. Immediately after I finished, both feds, the man and the woman, handcuffed my wrists and placed shackles around my ankles.

"Ouch!" I bellowed as I looked down at the cuffs around my ankles.

"Are the cuffs too tight?" the female asked.

"Yes, but you already know that because y'all do this type of stuff on purpose," I answered with an attitude.

She didn't get rude back; she just smirked like she knew that I was going to have many more complaints ahead. Once she loosened up the cuffs, she stood straight up and placed her hand around my arm. She waited for her partner to give her the signal that they could head out.

"We're ready for the other inmate," the male fed told the precinct officer.

That alarmed me a little bit, because I thought I'd be in the black jail van alone. I'd heard horror stories about inmates assaulting others in those van rides. My stomach cramped up. This was going to be the worst part of my life; I could already tell. I had done a lot of things, but I was not cut out for the prison system.

"Opening doors!" the officer yelled out, and then the metal door let out a loud buzzing sound and the lock on the door clicked.

"Step out into the hallway," the officer instructed. I couldn't see who he was talking to, but I was still nervous. I heard chains slide across the floor as the other female inmate made her way out of the holding cell. And when she appeared from behind the beige painted metal door, I immediately looked at her from head to toe. She looked completely out of place. I had to admit she was pretty with delicate features and looked more like a celebrity than a prisoner. She didn't look like she belonged there at all. I could see the male officers ogling her, and I can't lie, it made me a bit jealous that none of them had had that reaction to me when I was brought out.

The male officer instructed the pretty female inmate to walk toward us. The second she got within arm's reach of us, she was told to walk side by side with me and follow the lead of the female state officer that was about to transport us down to county. This is what they meant by *chain of custody.* Even though the agents had taken me to the local precinct, as feds, they were still responsible for turning me over to county. Chances are I wouldn't stay in county. I was facing down state time, for sure.

While the female officer led the way down the corridor, all three of us followed. We went through several metal doors, and when one closed shut, we had to wait for the other door to open. The security at this place was in full force. I couldn't see anyone escaping if they wanted to. Trust me, I thought about all types of ways I could get out of there.

After the last metal door opened and closed, we ended up in an underground garage. While I was being escorted to a black van with darkly tinted and caged windows, I saw two uniformed police officers escorting a young guy toward the door we had just exited. He looked like he had been roughed up, given the fact that he had a black eye and blood all down the front of his shirt. I winced just looking at him. These officers didn't care. Police brutality was an issue in our area, for sure, and I was seeing it firsthand. That's exactly what I was afraid of too.

The guy they were moving whistled and catcalled us when he saw the other female inmate I was with. The officers holding him yanked him by the handcuffs and told him to shut his mouth. The guy laughed like he didn't even care. It was obvious he had given up after being beaten and held. He probably knew his life was over, just like how I felt.

Both of the cops that were moving us along chuckled at how rough the officer was with the guy. I personally didn't think that shit was funny or amusing. Like I said, police brutality was an issue, and I was praying I didn't have to endure any of it.

"I see you got yourself a fake thug with a big mouth," the male cop with us called to the other officers.

"You're right about the 'big mouth' part, but we busted

his stupid ass on weapons charges, so you might be making a trip back this way to pick him up too," the same officer said.

The male cop looked at his female partner and smiled. "The more the merrier. These people keep us gainfully employed with their stupid behavior," he replied, and then laughed.

He meant it too. The more black people they locked up, the more money they made off of cheap labor and off of their jobs. Locking people up was the new form of slavery, I was convinced. I knew all about it, which is why I'd always tried to keep my ass out of jail or prison.

Right after, the male cop with us turned his attention back toward me and the other female inmate with me. He opened up the side door to the van, grabbed a footstool from underneath the seat, and then told us both to climb inside. He didn't give us a bit of help and it took me a few times to get up into the van, since the handcuffs kept me from having good balance.

"Sit on either side and not together." The female cop droned her instruction like she had said that same line a thousand times a day.

After we both struggled into the van, we took our seats and were strapped down with seat belts. The male officer hit the side of the van to signal to the female cop that we'd been strapped. "Animals ready for transport," he said. I was screaming in my head, *Who the hell you calling an animal, you racist!* But I didn't dare say anything at all.

"Ready to get on the road?" the female called out.

"Ready," he commented, and then he smirked at us and slammed the side door shut. He used a key to lock the outside of the door and then he climbed into the passenger side of the van. I could see the backs of their heads and out of the front windshield, but other than that, we couldn't even see outside. I was hoping to see some trees and anything that might cheer me up.

I still couldn't believe I was strapped down in a fucking jail transportation van with metal bars protecting the window, handcuffed and shackled like I was a part of a freaking chain gang. I was definitely out of my element. The girl that sat across from me seemed super calm. A little *too calm*, really, for my liking. I started thinking about the way I'd gotten here, and I just chuckled under my breath at how stupid I'd been.

With a look of aggression, the girl turned her focus on me. "What's so funny?" she asked.

I stretched my eyes and looked over at her like she was crazy. "Nothing that has anything to do with you," I came back. I don't know who she thought she was with that question. I turned my focus to look out of the windshield as the van exited the precinct. I didn't want any problems before I even officially got locked up.

I turned my thoughts to the day and what I might be doing if I wasn't locked up. I thought about all of the people out in the world going about their daily routines. They were free to do whatever they wanted to do, and I envied them. Knowing that I may never be able to spread my wings again was a thought that began to cut me deep in my heart.

Thinking back to when I first fell into that trap of getting involved with the feds, and that prescription ring operated by my former boss at the pharmacy, brought tears to my eyes. I had had it good before that. My life had been turned upside down and now I had the very likely prospect of life imprisonment dangling over my head. I thought about how unfairly I would be treated once I went to trial. There was just no way I would get a fair trial based on the fact that the media had dragged my name through the mud as a killer. Terrell's family had made sure of that, especially his mother.

While I was in deep thought, I noticed the girl across from me fidgeting with her handcuffs. She tried to do it discreetly, but my peripheral vision was working overtime. She was moving her cuffed hands up to her face and back down and she repeated it several times like it was a tic. I looked directly at her and she looked at me. She didn't say anything at first, but I think she noticed that I was getting suspicious and might tell on her. Because of that, she started making small talk with me. I knew it was a distraction, but I went along with it.

"What's your name?" she asked. Then she smiled.

I guess it was her way of changing how she approached me a few minutes earlier.

I gave her direct eye contact. "Misty," I muttered, and quickly turned my eyes away and looked down at my hand.

"That's it . . . just Misty?" she asked.

"You don't need my whole government. You work for the FBI or something?" I asked, annoyed. I wasn't no punk and she needed to know it. And besides, I had too much shit on my mind than to be answering a whole bunch of questions. And especially by a chick that's in the same predicament as me.

"Nah, I'm just asking, that's all," she said.

"What's your name?" I asked. I figured why should she only know my name.

"Shelby," she answered.

"That's it . . . just Shelby," I came back at her with the same comment she'd given me. Touché.

Her eyes grew two inches wide at my little dig. "You don't look like someone I'd expect to see locked up, Misty. I like that name, by the way," she said, and then giggled.

Okay, this chick had to be high off something. I gave her an expression of disbelief. I know she wasn't talking. She looked glamorous as hell even locked up. I could look at the nail tips on her hands and see that they were done at one of those high-class salons and not by the Vietnamese ones in the hood. Even Shelby's eyelashes were the high-priced mink ones that were applied one hair at a time. Her hair extensions were laid so well they looked like they had grown out of her scalp. She was high-class, and there was no doubt about it. I knew a lot about how chicks looked when they had a little bit of money, and Shelby definitely had money.

"You talking? You look like you need to be in some-body's magazine or walking a runway, so the feelings are mutual. I'm just as shocked as you are. There is no damn way I expected to see someone like you sitting up in here. You didn't see how many men were staring at you as we got led out to this van? Shit, you could've probably got that guy up front there to set you free—he had so much lust in his eyes for you," I said. "So now you tell me, what the heck is a fly chick like you doing locked up like an animal?"

She let out a long sigh and hung her head a little bit. She knew damn well I was right. "Let's just say, it's compli-cated, and you probably wouldn't believe my story even if I told it to you," she replied with a forlorn look on her face.

"I'm sure. You'd probably feel the same way about my story because sometimes even I can't believe it," I replied.

"Well, it was nice meeting you, Misty," she said as if she was about to go somewhere.

"Huh? What do you mean 'was'?" I asked. "Looks to me like we going to the same place right about now . . . county lockup."

"You'll see," she replied, and then she smiled once again, like she knew a secret I would never find out.

Then she did that weird thing again where she held up both of her hands with the handcuffs and put them to her mouth. It looked to me like she took something out of or put something in her mouth.

I crinkled my brows, but I didn't dare ask her what she was doing. I just wanted to mind my damn business. I just wanted to go home, honestly.

"I'm glad you didn't ask any questions," Shelby said after a few long minutes.

"What you do is your business, I'm no snitch," I said nonchalantly. I wasn't about to let her drag me into anything illegal she was doing or about to do.

"Well, I appreciate that, and you'll find out soon enough what's going on," Shelby said cryptically. "Just understand that I don't have anything to lose. That's all I'm going to say about it," she said with a lot of mystery behind her words.

"What does that mean?" I asked. I wanted to know.

"I murdered my parents and I'd do it all over again," she blurted, changing the subject.

"Oh my God! Are you serious?" I asked her, feeling my eyes go big. This bitch was crazy. I thought what I was in for was bad, but at least mine was self-defense. This was crazy. Who has the guts to kill their fucking parents? Well, unless they're pedophiles or physically abusive. Other than that, you've got to be a very sick individual to commit a heinous crime such as that.

Instead of responding verbally, she nodded her head kind of somberly. Shit, she looked really sad, like her life was surely over, and I kind of agreed. I thought that murdering your own parents was as low as you could go. I immediately reflected on my crime and suddenly my whole mood changed.

"You all right?" she asked me in a weird tone.

I don't know exactly how she wanted me to react to her telling me she had murdered her own parents. I turned my focus back to her and said, "Not really. I can't imagine what would make someone kill their own parents. I'm in here dying to see my mother one last time, so I just can't understand it. I know people with terrible parents, and they wouldn't dare kill them. So . . . no . . . I'm not all right."

"I guess you'd have to know my story before you could judge me, right?" she said, and then shrugged her shoulders like she didn't care. "Every parent is not the same. I may look like I had it all, but you have no idea and neither do these people trying to keep me locked up for the rest of my life. I won't let them do it. I'd rather die."

I shook my head and then I turned my focus away from her. I was no longer in the mood to talk to her. I had enough problems of my own. And I had already made up in my mind that this chick, Shelby, was crazy as hell. The one thing I didn't need to do was get into it with anyone crazy.

I could hear the two cops up front having a conversation, but I couldn't hear exactly what they were saying. Periodically I noticed the woman look at us through the rearview mirror like she was making sure we hadn't jumped out, which would've been impossible, anyway.

After a long period of driving, I saw Shelby start to nod, her head jerking down and then back up. I just chalked it up to her being tired. I noticed that the van had slowed down. I leaned to my left and looked straight through the windshield and saw that we had come upon railroad tracks. The gates were down on both sides and the lights flashed on and off, but there was no train in sight.

I heard the female cop sigh really loudly while the male cop made a loud outburst. "Dammit, I thought we would make it around it. This could be like an hour sitting here," he snapped.

"You think it takes that long?" the female cop asked him.

"Hell yeah," he replied, annoyed.

As the van came to a complete stop at the railroad tracks, I went to say something to Shelby and noticed that she was hanging way over at the waist. The only reason she hadn't slid to the floor was the fact that she was chained to the seat in the van.

"Shelby?" I called to her in a harsh whisper. I didn't want to be loud and bring attention to us back there. She didn't answer. "Shelby," I called her again, this time a little bit louder. Still, nothing. Then, as I listened to the cops complaining, Shelby's body started to jerk. I jumped back.

"Oh my God!" I gasped. "Shelby!" I called out, this time louder and with more force. I didn't care if the cops heard us.

"What the hell is going on?" the male cop called back to me.

My body started trembling as I watched Shelby's body convulse and white foam started bubbling out of her mouth. "Fuck! Shelby! Oh my God!" I screamed this time. Now I really didn't care. Something was definitely wrong with this girl.

Both cops turned in their seats at the same time.

"What the hell are you screaming about, inmate?" the female cop yelled out.

"You better shut the fuck up if you know what's good for you," the male cop followed up.

All of a sudden, we all seemed to hear a strange sound at the same time. Shelby's body started convulsing even more violently, causing a loud banging in the van.

"Help! Help her!" I yelped. Not only was white foam bubbling all over Shelby's face, blood started to leak out of her nose. "She's dying! Help her! Oh my God!" I wailed. I started stomping my feet, the only power I had to make them understand that something was seriously wrong.

I saw the male cop scramble out of the driver's seat. I continued to scream, and so did the female cop, but only she was telling me to shut up and calm down. She tried to be the voice of reason, but I was too inconsolable to listen to her. There was a damn girl dying right in front of me, as if I hadn't seen enough death and destruction in my life. I watched in shock; and my heart was beating so fast, it hurt. I looked over at Shelby with a look of pure terror etched on my face.

"Oh my God . . . she's dead! I know it!" I screamed out. I was nervous as hell because we were helplessly shackled in the back of the van with no way for me to help her and no way for her to be saved. The inside of the van suddenly grew overwhelmingly hot and the air felt stiff. I heard another loud bang on the van, and I started saying a silent prayer that they were going to help her. This would be a fucked-up way to die for anyone, even an inmate that these cops cared nothing about.

The back doors to the van flung open. I jumped so hard, I almost pissed and shit on myself. The male cop was standing there, breathing hard with a beet-red face. "What's going on, inmate!" he screamed.

It was clear that he didn't believe me and thought maybe we were just trying to make a distraction. I mean, who could blame him? Convicts do it all the time in the movies. But this time was the real thing.

"See for yourself! She's dying!" I belted out. I was crying by then. Seeing someone die like that was a crazy experience. The male cop scrambled his ass into the van. He looked horrified. He pushed Shelby back up into a sitting position. I was in shock, to say the least. Her face was completely different. She had foam coming out of her mouth, blood out of her nose, and her eyes were all white. She looked like the girl in the movie The Exorcist. My heart dropped and I quickly closed my eyes. I knew that if I didn't, nightmares of her face would haunt me for months, just like Terrell's did.

"What happened here?" the male cop asked me.

"How am I supposed to know?" I replied with an attitude. "She was sitting over there one minute, and the next minute, she was nodding and then this. I have no fucking clue what happened, but I will tell you being in here with a dead person is not cool for me."

"Did you see her take something?" he asked, his voice getting a bit more frantic. He needed answers.

I thought about what I would say, and whether I should tell him about seeing Shelby fiddling with her hands and handcuffs, but I didn't want to be set up to be any kind of witness. The cops and the feds had set me up one too many times and I didn't trust their asses as far as I could throw them. And that wasn't very far.

"I told you what I saw! I saw her sitting here one minute, and the next minute, she was like that!" I screamed out. That was it, I almost fainted right there in that van. Sweat broke out all over my body. This girl was dead, right then and there, right in my direct line of vision, and we seemed to be in the middle of nowhere. How much more drama can I take?

"I feel a faint pulse. We need to call a medic!" the male cop yelled up to the female as he touched Shelby's neck.

A feeling of relief came over my entire body and my nerves kind of simmered down a little bit. I was hoping Shelby was still alive and it seemed that she was . . . for now.

"I'll call for one, but that means we still have to wait for this train to pass!" the female cop yelled back.

"Looks like you're going to have to sit in here with her until we can get a medic to come. If she dies . . . well, then . . . she dies," the male cop said, then shrugged his shoulders like he didn't give a damn about Shelby.

There was complete silence. If this was any indication of what I was in for, I didn't know what I would do with myself.

After what seemed like an eternity, an ambulance finally showed up. "One female, no pulse!" the first medic yelled out.

I wanted to scream, *Of course, she doesn't have a pulse now! You bastards took forever to come save her!* But I just sat there, shaking and looking at Shelby. Her lips had turned completely purple and so did her fingernails. They took another thirty minutes before they even unstrapped her from the van seat. This is how messed-up they treated inmates, like we weren't even human beings.

After what seemed like forever, they finally took Shelby's cold, dead body out of the van in a black body bag. They pulled it right past me with no regard for my mental state at that point. They left my ass, shaking, crying, and in handcuffs and shackles. No one even cared. To them, I was just another fucking criminal awaiting my fate for killing a nigga. It didn't matter that I was trying to defend myself. All they knew or cared about was throwing another black person in jail so they could throw the book at you.

"Hopefully, we make it to county with at least one," the asshole male cop joked with his partner.

"She looked spooked, so we better hurry up before we have a cardiac arrest on our hands," the female cop joked back.

I didn't find anything about what they were saying funny. I also didn't find anything about my situation funny. Little did I know, life had just begun to get interesting for me.

2

UP A CREEK

My arrival at county finally happened. I was completely shaken up by the time I got there, and being there didn't help at all.

"Open eleven!" a female correctional officer yelled at the command station.

She was one evil bitch. I had watched her push another girl down on the floor and kick her because the girl wasn't moving fast enough. That was an eye-opener for me. I tried to be as quiet as possible when she processed me, but it was immediately apparent that the wicked CO couldn't care less that I was crying and shivering after she'd stripped me of all my clothes and humiliated me by making me bend over, spread my ass cheeks, squat, and cough.

I could swear the evil bitch even had a tiny smile on her face as she violated me, forcing her gloved, sausage-shaped fingers into my mouth and roughly running them around the inside of my mouth until I almost gagged. I knew she took sick pleasure in lifting my breasts up and probing my scalp as if she was sure I had stashed something nefarious in those places. All of this so she could put me in a county jail uniform and give me an inmate number. They surely tried to dehumanize you. It was an inmate control tactic.

"Run the gate!" the CO yelled again. This time, her fat-on-the-bottom-skinny-on-the-top ass shoved me toward a cell. It was dark and dank. The acrid scent of piss and mold assailed my senses. The cell block wasn't pretty, but it was much quieter than the holding cell I'd been kept in at the precinct before I was transported to county to await court. The quiet around me didn't fool me, though; I knew this was the calm before the real storm. After the CO damn near threw me into the cell, the door shut behind me. The loud screech and clang of the metal caused my heart to drop into the pit of my stomach. Something about the sound was so final. If I hadn't known it before, I knew then that I was locked inside this jail and I wasn't getting out anytime soon. There is a different feeling of dread when you feel your freedom being snatched away. It was what I imagined zoo animals felt every day of their lives—trapped, captured, and hopeless. I shivered just thinking about it.

"When will I get a chance to make a phone call?" I asked the CO before she got a chance to fully walk off. I needed to call my mother. I needed to tell someone about what I'd been through so far. I also needed help.

"When the next shift says you can," she grumbled barely above a whisper as she undid the leg irons from my ankles.

"And when will that be?" I asked.

"When it changes," she continued sarcastically.

She was being a real asshole right now. I wanted to give that bitch a piece of my mind, but I decided against it and slumped my shoulders with disappointment. On the other hand, I wanted to ask her why she was so nasty. I didn't want to be there as much as she didn't want me to be there messing up her day. I also wanted to tell her I was an innocent victim and that there was a complete explanation for what happened. But I'm sure she heard that every day from every inmate she processed.

"Can you give me a time?" I pressed. I was kind of desperate to see if I could get in touch with my mother. At this point, my mother was the only person on the outside that could help me. Someone had to corroborate my story about killing Terrell in self-defense.

"Honey, you shouldn't be worried about the time. After looking at your arrest sheet, I see you ain't gonna have nothing but time, so sit your ass down and be quiet. The noisy ones get the noisy-one treatment, and the quiet ones get what we let them have. Remember . . . I told you that," the bitch CO warned. With that, she stalked off as if she needed to make a point with her body language.

I sighed loudly. This was going to be a long prison term if I had to judge what it would be like from that CO's behavior. County was only the first stop. It was where I'd be housed for the minimum of a year and a day, and after trial and conviction, I'd be sent to prison . . . real prison. I stood up against the cell bars as if I was expecting someone to come save me. I really wanted to cry.

"You might as well take a load off, because it's going to be a while before you see the next CO," a voice with a heavy Southern drawl said from behind me.

Startled, I let go of the bars and whirled around in the direction of the voice. My eyes popped open when I noticed a broad-shouldered, stout woman standing in the shadows of the cell. My heart galloped in my chest. She'd scared the shit out of me.

When the woman moved into the little bit of light, I gave her a quick once-over. She had a short, masculine haircut, a square chin, thick furry eyebrows, which seemed permanently furrowed, and muscular arms that made me think she did one hundred push-ups a day. If the stranger didn't have such huge breasts, I would've mistaken her for a man. She was what we called in the hood a *butch*.

Great! They had locked me up with a butch who was probably going to kick my ass every day until I got out of there. I played it cool. I nodded at her, but didn't say anything. The butch bopped in my direction. She walked just like a guy.

My stomach lurched and I felt like I had to vomit. I swallowed hard. I didn't want no smoke with this butch. I'd heard so many horror stories of how these types of women bully more feminine women like me while behind bars. I said a quick prayer. I didn't need to get on this woman's bad side. I started thinking that maybe if I was nice, she'd be a good ally to have if we ended up in the same place later on.

I took her advice and took a seat on one of the hard metal planks that extended from the cell's left wall.

"What you in for?" the butch asked, getting a little too close for comfort.

She smelled like hospital antiseptic and cigarettes. The combination went straight to my stomach and I felt nauseous.

"Murder," I blurted without thinking twice. I just wanted her to back up off me, and if confessing to a murder was what I needed to do, then so be it.

She seemed stunned by my answer, and her caterpillar eyebrows shot up on her face. "Me too!" she exclaimed.

A cold chill shot down my back. "Self-defense or intentional?" I asked. I wanted to make sure she wasn't crazy, but I also needed someone to identify with my situation and what happened with Terrell and me.

"They trying to say that I put out a hit on my girlfriend. But I didn't do it," the butch replied. Her facial expression was cold and blank. "I didn't do that shit, man," she followed up, still with no real emotions behind her words.

She scrubbed her hands over her face roughly. "I got set up. Somebody set me up to take the fall. I wasn't even fucking with that bitch no more." I couldn't tell if she was telling me the truth or not, but I wasn't about to make her think I doubted her, so I just stayed quiet.

"What about you? Who you killed?" she asked me.

"My ex-boyfriend," I said.

The butch jerked her head back slightly and smirked.

"But I had a reason," I added, hurrying up to clarify. "He was abusive, and I just got tired of him putting his hands on me. I was sick of him, but what happened was really an accident. I wasn't trying to kill him."

Saying it out loud in that moment made me sadder than I had expected. Up until that moment, and with so much going on around me, I hadn't really stopped to think about Terrell and everything that went down. I had always wanted Terrell to be a good man. I'd tried to do everything right, but he still shifted into a monster from time to time. The ass whuppings I took from Terrell weren't even fit for a man, much less a woman he claimed to love. I closed my eyes and thought back to the fateful night that put me in this predicament.

It had started with Terrell calling my cell phone like a crazy person when he'd seen Agents Sims and Montclair leaving my apartment. I had contemplated ignoring Terrell's calls, but after what had seemed like one hundred straight calls, I finally answered.

"Terrell, what do you want?" I had grumbled into the phone, feigning sleep. It hadn't worked. Terrell had demanded to be let into my apartment. When I refused, he'd caused a loud scene outside my door. Yelling and hurling threats. Anything could spark his menacing and jealous rages. I just wished that I'd taken heed to all the red flags in the early part of our relationship. *Damn!*

"If you don't open this fucking door, I'm gon' go up to

your job tomorrow and tell one of those Arab niggas that the feds is watching them!" Terrell had screamed.

His words had sent a hot feeling of fear all over my body, but I still refused to let him inside. I knew when Terrell got like that his behavior could escalate.

"Get away from my house, Terrell. You ain't shit!" I had barked, hoping he'd get the hint that I didn't want anything more to do with him.

Terrell had pounded the door with his fists and had kicked it so hard the entire apartment seemed to shake. I had contemplated calling the police, but I didn't want to bring any heat around me. It was bad enough those state agents had found their way to my house, to begin with.

"Leave me alone, Terrell! Go home! I don't wanna see you!" I had yelled some more, on the brink of tears.

"Y'all neighbor named Misty Heiress is an FBI informant! If you're selling drugs, she's gonna snitch on you!" Terrell had screamed out for my entire neighborhood to hear.

"Oh my God," I had gasped. My heart dropped into the pit of my stomach. I had had enough at that point. With fear gripping me, I had hopped out of my bed, raced to the front door, and snatched it open.

"What the fuck are you trying to do to me?" I had gritted at him, my eyes stretched wide. "You want these niggas around here to kill me? Is that it, Terrell?"

Terrell's nostrils were flared and his eyes were ablaze. He'd bulldozed into me and stormed into my apartment like a wild tornado. He'd slammed the door so hard, two of my framed pictures fell off the walls.

"I knew I'd getcha ass to let me in after I said that," he had chortled. "You like fucking with me, right? Huh, Misty?"

Terrell then accused me of being a snitch and we had argued heatedly. He'd gotten in my face and grabbed me roughly. That had been my first indication that one of his ass beatings was coming. I had already promised myself after the last time he hit me, I was going to fight back the next time. I was tired of being his punching bag. I deserved better, but for some strange reason, he wouldn't let me move on without him.

"Fuck you, Terrell! Don't put your fucking hands on me! Get out of my house!" I had screamed.

"I ain't going no fucking where," he had protested, holding my arm so tight, pain shot up and down like electricity.

Without thinking of the consequences, I had kneed him in the balls.

"Agh!" he'd screamed. "You bitch!"

He had doubled over and that's when I had grabbed his arm and tried pushing him toward the front door, but I couldn't move him. He was in pain, but he hadn't missed a beat with calling me all kinds of "bitches" and "whores."

I had threatened to call the police on him to get him to leave. That hadn't worked. Then I came up with a plan. I told Terrell I had slept with someone else while we were together. As soon as I said it, I knew I had broken his heart.

I had watched darkness come over him and knew I had gone too far. Terrell had gotten to his feet, his pain seemingly dissipating in an instant. He had stood there for a couple of seconds, like he was trying to process everything I had said. I thought I had said enough to make him leave. I was wrong. Terrell squinted his eyes, rushed into me, and backhand slapped me with so much force that I crumpled to the floor like a boxer who'd just been hit with a clean chin shot.

Immediately after I had fallen down on the floor, I'd scrambled to get back on my feet, but I couldn't because Terrell had crawled on top of me.

"Get off of me!" I had screamed while swinging at him a few times with balled fists.

"Shut the fuck up!" he had growled as he grabbed my

neck with both of his hands and started choking the air out of me.

I gagged, trying to breathe at the same time. I had even tried to use my strength to push him off me, but it didn't work.

"Somebody help me," I had rasped. It wasn't loud enough. Terrell applied more pressure to my neck. He was trying to kill me.

"Bitch, I said shut the fuck up," he had hissed. I looked up into his eyes and I saw fire. I knew then he wasn't going to stop until I was dead.

"You said I wasn't fucking you good! You said my dick was whack, you dirty bitch! You trying to attack my manhood? You gon' die today, bitch," Terrell had barked, still clamped down on my neck.

I had felt myself fading fast. I kicked and bucked my body because something on the inside of me told me to fight. I still don't know how I did it, but in my fighting, I had managed to force my arms out from under him and I reached up to his face and dug my fingers into his eye sockets.

"Ah! You fucking bitch!" Terrell had screamed.

I thought that would've made him loosen his grip on me, but it didn't. He started choking me even harder.

"You fucking bitch! You're gonna die!" he had growled.

Darkness started closing in on me. I had known then that I was losing consciousness. But suddenly a light had come on in my head.

Misty, you gotta stay alive. Your family needs you. You can't let this man kill you. Fight back, girl! You can do it. An inner voice had spoken to me.

And, with the last bit of energy I had left in my body, I had bucked my body so hard that Terrell fell off of me. I quickly rolled on top of him, and I dug my fingers deep into his eyes until I had felt gobs of blood and human tissue between my fingers.

"You fucking bitch!" he had screamed. He couldn't see me.

I frantically searched for my cell phone. That time had given Terrell a few minutes to gather himself. He grabbed me by my hair and snatched me toward him.

"I'm gonna kill you now, you fucking ho!" he had roared, slamming me against the wall. My body hit the wall and caused one of my paintings to fall off. Terrell and I had wrestled against the wall. "You fucking bitch! I'm gon' kill you!" he had kept saying.

As we fought, Terrell had dragged me against the wall, and that's when the nail from the painting had scraped my upper shoulder. I don't know how I did it, but I had dragged myself back over to the left side of the wall and grabbed that nail out of the wall. Terrell had been too busy choking me to notice. With the long nail in my hand, I had lifted it and stabbed Terrell right in his face. He had screamed out and let me go. A few seconds later, he had collapsed onto the floor. Blood had spurted out of his neck every time his heart pumped.

I had stood there shaking all over. I had saved my own life. I had waited for him to move, but he wouldn't budge. After I had kicked his foot, he still didn't move.

"Terrell, get up," I had said breathlessly. I had kicked his foot again. Nothing. Panic had engulfed me.

I had dropped the nail on the floor and stared at Terrell's lifeless body lying in a pool of his own blood. "No!" I had screamed, and dropped to my knees.

"So you had to kill him? There was just no other way out, huh?" the butch asked.

I blinked a few times, her voice snapping me out of the nightmare of reliving the murder.

"I wasn't trying to kill him. It was an accident," I said honestly, my voice shaking. "I swear it was all an accident.

There was just no other way. It was going to be him or me. Period."

"Did anybody witness it?"

"No. We were there alone," I said. I don't know why I was telling this stranger all of this, but it felt good to get it off of my chest.

"Sounds like you're going to need a good goddamn lawyer," she pointed out.

I let out a long windstorm of breath. "That's why I need to call my mother. To see if she can get someone down here to help me out of this shit. Because I shouldn't be here. God knows the truth . . . I had no choice. It was either me or him," I replied sadly.

"That's what we all say." The butch chuckled. "Didn't you know that everybody behind bars is innocent?" she commented, and then she chuckled.

I knew that after she laughed, she was pulling my leg. But I wasn't amused by her fucking joke. This was not a game. My situation was serious and I didn't see anything funny about it. Someone happened to have lost his life, and the other person had to sit in freaking jail because of it. So there were no winners in this.

"What's your name, anyway? I'm here talking all my business, but don't even know your name." I sized her up again from head to toe, wondering if I could take her on if she ever tried to come at me with some drama. *The butch would kick my ass* was the conclusion I came to in my mind. Her hands alone would probably crush me. She truly looked and carried like a man. She was probably a whole hundred pounds heavier than me too. Like I said, she would probably have crushed me.

"I'm Patricia, but everybody in here and on the streets calls me Pat," she replied confidently. That immediately told me that she had a reputation.

"So you've been here before?"

"Hell yeah, I've been in here over a hundred times. All

the COs know me," the butch bragged. I crinkled my face. Who boasts about how many times they've been in jail? This bitch was crazy. And I knew that if I wanted to keep my ass out of harm's way, I would either have to befriend her or stay the hell out of her way.

"How long have you been in this time?" I asked.

"I got here about six hours ago," she replied. "As soon as they put you in this little-ass cell, they close the doors and from there it seems like the clock stops. And don't knock on the door and ask them how long it's gonna take them to process you. 'Cause if you do, they're gonna really take their time. Most of these COs are assholes with chips on their shoulders. But I don't pay their asses any mind. I do what I do, and they do what they do."

"Have they allowed you to make a call yet?"

"Yeah, they let me use the phone probably like an hour after I got here. So don't worry, they'll let you do it as soon as the new COs clock in," she said.

"I hope so. I can't sit here with this anxiety much longer," I replied, my legs moving in and out.

The butch and I talked for another two hours until the shift changed and the new CO on guard called out my last name and allowed me to make my one phone call. A black female CO pulled me out of the holding cell and escorted me to the phone station. "Press zero to get an open line," she instructed me.

I called my mother like she was on speed dial. Thankfully, she answered my call on the second ring.

"Misty, is this you?" she said in a low whisper.

"Yes, Mommy, it's me," I replied, immediately breaking down. The sobs came so fast and furious, I could barely breathe, let alone get my words out.

"Baby, please don't cry," my mother said, her voice cracking as if hearing me cry so hard was crushing her.

"Mommy, you're going to have to get me a lawyer right away. The more time that passes, the worse this thing will get for me," I cried. I needed her to understand that what I was facing was serious. I was fighting for my literal freedom. And if I took this thing lying down, then I was going to be fucked.

"I know, darling. I've already started making calls. I've talked to a couple of secretaries and a paralegal. I told all three of them what you've been charged with and the jail where the cops said that they're gonna be taking you to."

"Did they say how much the attorney is going to cost?"

"I asked, but they said that they couldn't give me that information. But the lawyer could, so I'm waiting for them to call me back now."

"Well, did they say that their attorney handles cases like mine?" I continued, barely able to speak.

"Yes, baby. They all specialize in murder cases."

"Do you remember their names?"

"Thomas Schwartz is one of them. The second one's name is Patrick Cohen. And the third guy's name is Todd Murr. From the conversations I had with the secretaries and the paralegal, all of the lawyers seem like they'll do a good job representing you," she assured me.

"You have one minute left," an overweight red-haired white male CO announced from a few feet away from me.

"What are they saying?" my mother asked.

I let out a long sigh. "He said that I have one minute left to talk."

"Have they given you a bond yet?"

"No. And I don't think they're gonna give me one either. But I will see the judge in the morning. I'm so scared, Mommy."

"Don't be afraid, baby. The worst is over. Neither one of us is dead. God spared our lives, so we're gonna be fine, sweetheart," my mother said, trying to console me. But it wasn't working.

My mother was a weak woman. She has never been able to handle things life had thrown at her. And now that I'm here, and she's in that house all alone, God knows what could happen.

Not knowing how to respond to what she had said, I decided not to comment and instead said, "Mommy, I'm gonna really need you to watch your back because—"

I wasn't able to finish my sentence before the line went dead. My heart sank. I wasn't able to warn my mother that very dangerous people were still after her and after me. They weren't going to stop until they got what they wanted.

"I told you that you had one minute left," the CO reminded me. "Now go on back in that cell until we call your name." He pointed toward the chipped-paint metal door. I dreaded going back in that small-ass cell, especially with that loudmouth-ass repeat offender. But I had no choice. I was in jail. And in jail, you have no control over what you do, what you eat, or where you sleep. I was officially property of the state. Now, how fucked-up is that?

As soon as I walked back into the holding cell, that chick, Pat, had a windstorm of questions for me: Did you get to talk to your mama? Is she gon' get you out of here if the judge gives you a bond in the morning? Did you tell her that you're gonna need a lawyer? And did she say what y'all are going to do if you don't get a bond in the morning?

I mean, this chick went on and on and on, like I made the call for her. I guess, since we're locked up, nobody's business is off-limits. Go figure.

Not too much longer after I got my phone call, I was processed and given an inmate number and a cell on the fourth floor. When I was escorted on the block, I was greeted by a slew of black female inmates, whistling and shouting, "Fresh Meat!"

"She's pretty too," one female inmate uttered.

"You might as well forget it because she's mine," another

female inmate said, while the others chuckled and laughed at all the chaos.

Carrying a county-issued wool blanket, one dingy sheet, a plastic cup, a toothbrush, and a plastic spoon, I marched into the cell block with the CO by my side as she pointed to the cell I was assigned to.

"You're gonna sleep on the top bunk. The mattress should already be there," the female CO told me.

So I headed into the cell and was greeted by a white female inmate that was lying down on the bottom bunk. She was reading her book and only spoke after I spoke to her first. And she did it without looking in my direction. Talk about a warm welcome. She made it perfectly clear that she was not a part of the welcoming committee. So I knew at that very moment that shit was going to be different. I was in this place alone. And I was going to have to look out for myself. Period.

After I made my bed and set my plastic cup and toothbrush down at the head of my bed, I headed out of my cell and into the day room, where the phones and the TV were. Eyes were on me like white on rice. I took a seat at one of the metal benches and was immediately approached by a woman. She looked to be at least five years older. She introduced herself.

"First time in?"

"Yes," I replied, still trying to make sense of how I really got here.

"What are you in here for?" she continued, looking straight into my eyes. She gave me this look as if to say, *Don't lie to me. You better keep it real. I'm gonna find out the truth either way.*

"Murder," I finally said.

She smirked. "Who pissed in your bowl of cornflakes?"

"It was self-defense," I added.

"Can you prove it?"

"Yes," I assured her. But I knew it was going to be hard

to convince a jury that I killed Terrell in self-defense, especially since I had his body dismembered and tossed out in garbage bags like he was trash. In my mind, that nigga was a piece of trash because he treated me like shit.

"Well, then, you're gonna be all right," she said, and then paused. "Got a lawyer yet?"

"My mother is trying to get me one right now."

"Well, if she hasn't retained one yet, tell her she should get John Fletcher. He's a beast in the courtroom. And he has beaten a lot of cases for his clients too."

"Is he expensive?"

"He can be. But anybody trying to stay out of jail shouldn't care how much their freedom costs."

"Yeah, I guess you got a point there," I agreed. I mean, she was right. And, besides, my mother can definitely afford to pay a top attorney, even if it came down to her selling her house. Hell, my mother could sell my grandmother's house too, since it would be willed to her after my grandmother's death certificate was issued and filed by the estate's attorney. So we should be good. "Where is this attorney's office?" I asked.

"His office is off Laskin Road, in Virginia Beach. She can Google him and get his number."

I don't know how, but we instantly hit it off. Aside from giving me pointers and the dos and don'ts of how to navigate around this county jail, we even talked about who I needed to stay away from while I was in this cell block. She gave me the lowdown on every chick on this block. She even gave me the lowdown on the COs too. There was a lot to take in, in so little time, but I had no choice in the matter. It was either do or die. And it was as simple as that.

3

JUDGMENT DAY

The following morning, I was hauled off to court. My mother was front and center when the two court marshals escorted me into the courtroom. Immediately after I blew a kiss at her, I was placed next to the attorney John Fletcher, the lawyer that the inmate Sandra recommended should represent me. He whispered a few words to me, and then we both faced the magistrate judge, only to be told that I was going to be remanded until my trial. They could've left me in jail for this bullshit! The law enforcement system is screwed up. This justice system is set up to keep people incarcerated. It's all a fucking scam. I just wished that I could turn back the hands of time. I really don't know how much more of this shit, I'd be able to take.

While we stood there, I entered a not guilty plea. Mr. Fletcher also asked for a speedy trial. According to him, I have a right to a speedy trial. And the fact that we're gonna use that self-defense angle, he's confident that I could get an acquittal. My mother seemed optimistic, since we're going to play on the fact that I was an abused woman and that I acted in self-defense.

But I soon found out that I was wrong, because eight months later, my day of reckoning crept on me. My heart thrummed against my chest bone and sweat drenched my brow. The hum of people talking and mumbling sounded so loud in my ears as I sat in the stuffy, hot courtroom. It was the kind of sounds that probably wouldn't have bothered me if I wasn't so nervous and sick to my stomach about my fate.

I was on the spot. I was the main attraction and all eyes and thoughts were on me. My legs swung in and out, and I chewed on my bottom lip like it was a meal. The irritation around my ankles from the leg irons was suddenly more painful than it had been during my ride to court from county. I tried my best to ignore the hum of the crowd in the courtroom, but the longer I sat, the louder it got. It wasn't lost on me that everyone there was talking about me . . . a murderer. My story had shown up on the news and all over the Internet and social media.

Some people were there because they wanted a piece of me. Terrell's family wanted justice for the wrong I had done to them. I'd seen his mother and sister glaring at me when I was led into the room. There were other people there that just wanted to be nosy and see the monster the media had made me out to be. I can't lie. The nervousness I felt was literally making me sick.

I didn't think I'd ever wish I were back in county lockup. I had been in county for eight months, going back and forth over my case, before my lawyer had finally told me, "Pleading guilty is the only way out of this without facing life."

He'd explained that if I took responsibility for my actions, the court would agree to a deal where I'd get some leniency since it was an act of self-defense. I had refused at first, but Sandra and the girls I'd grown close to in lockup told me it was probably the only way out. That was just how our criminal justice system worked. I was cautioned that taking my case to trial would've been very risky. If I had done that, any deals I could've gotten by pleading guilty would've been completely off the table. That was pretty fucking sad, if you asked me. I would be forced to stand up in court and say I killed Terrell intentionally, when, in fact, I had done it to save my own life.

"They won't believe you, Misty," my attorney had warned. "If it was self-defense, you would've called the police right after or during. You wouldn't kill someone and dismember and trash the body."

"I was scared. I didn't know what to do, so I panicked and made a bad judgment call. I mean, I didn't think that anyone would report him missing, because he's a fucking asshole and everyone hates him," I whispered.

Instead of commenting or tossing me a rebuttal, he looked at me like I had lost my damn mind. And right now, if I could go back to that night, I would've, for sure. I swallowed hard and closed my eyes. I couldn't help but rock back and forth, something I did when I was in distress.

I replayed it all over again: what had happened after I knew Terrell was dead. I saw myself sitting on the floor of my living room for thirty long minutes, trying to process what had just happened between Terrell and me. Terrell's gouged and bloody eyes had stared straight, haunting me.

I had told myself to call the police, explain everything to them about Terrell attacking me and vowing to kill me. But I hadn't called the police at all. Instead, I had finally gotten up off the floor and dragged myself to the bathroom. I had tried to avoid looking at my face in the mirror, but I couldn't. I had to see what mess I was in. The bruises, scratches, and rings around my neck probably would've been a good defense for me at the time. I couldn't chance it, I had told myself. I couldn't get locked up if the police didn't believe me. I had been torn, caught in the middle.

"Oh my God!" were the only words I had uttered in that moment. The gravity of the situation had gut-punched me so hard, I had doubled over and dry-heaved for what seemed like hours instead of minutes. I had to think quick in that moment. With trembling hands, I had called my cousin Jillian. Thank God she answered on the first ring. Jillian was street-smart and levelheaded.

"Hello," she answered, her voice had been gruff with sleep.

"Jill! I need you to come over my house right now," I had said, my words coming out fast and shaky.

"What's wrong? Are you all right?" she had asked. I could tell she'd sat up in her bed.

"Jillian, I can't talk over the phone. So please come over here right now," I had pled. "Alone."

When Jillian had arrived, she'd taken a total of five steps before she had stopped in her tracks and gasped. "Oh my God! What the fuck? Is that Terrell? And is he dead?" she had huffed, clutching her chest.

"Sh!" I had scolded. "Yes, he's dead." I hated to say it.

"What the fuck happened, Misty? And why is he dead?" Jillian's questions had kept coming rapid-fire. I told her what happened and let her know that she wasn't there for details. We needed a plan, a solution to the problem lying in front of us.

"So, what are you going to do?" she had asked as she immediately started pacing the floor.

"I don't know. That's why I called you," I replied, bouncing nervously on my legs.

"Think anyone seen him come here? Maybe one of your neighbors?" Jillian had asked as she rushed over to the windows and peeked out.

"I don't know." I shook my head. "It all happened so

fast. He was acting the fool outside, and I let him in. He attacked me and I fought back. And here we are."

"With everything we got going on, we don't need this distraction right here," Jillian had said, pointing toward Terrell's body.

"So, what are we going to do with him?" I had asked, biting my nails.

"We're gonna have to chop his fucking body up and put it in trash bags and take that shit out of here," she had replied, dead serious.

Jillian had been so calm, it sent an eerie chill down my back.

"I—I can't do it," I had said, trembling.

The same chill shot down my back now. The courtroom was even more packed than it had been a few minutes earlier. Everyone wanted to see me get sentenced to life, I was sure. I knew the one person who had ever really loved me was in the back of that courtroom, though.

I kept seeing my mother's face behind my eyelids like I was watching a projector screen. I could picture her in all of the stages of our lives—when I was a little kid and she'd take me places; when I was a preteen and she took me to get my first bra and explained the birds and the bees to me after I'd gotten my period; when I was a teenager and giving her pure hell; and now, as women, both of us in pain and distress over my actions. My mother had been there through it all and it hadn't changed. She was a rider and I was lucky to have her.

The court officer's booming baritone interrupted my thoughts. "All rise! The Honorable Martin Mason presiding."

Just my luck! The judge had the same last name as Terrell. What kind of message was the universe sending me? Karma was definitely a bitch, and she didn't play fair. Thankfully, they weren't related. The courts wouldn't allow a relative of Terrell to preside over this case. It would be a conflict of interest. But as I said before, the fact that they had the same name gave me a blow to the chest.

The rustle of suits and dresses as the crowd inside the packed courtroom rose to their feet made me feel like I was listening to nails being dragged across a chalkboard. I wasn't going to lie, I felt dizzy. Thank God I didn't have anything in my stomach because I probably would've thrown it all up, right on the spot. Trying to eat breakfast had been a dead issue earlier. Who could eat when the fate of their life was about to be decided? This was a fucked-up situation I had put myself in, all because I was looking for more. I was greedy. I was ungrateful. And now, I was fucked.

My legs felt like two strands of cooked pasta as I stood up. The muscles burned in every part of my body like I'd worked out for hours without stopping. The result of the all-night tossing and turning I'd done back in my cell. My attorney stood next to me, clutching my right elbow as if he could sense that I was about to take a spill onto the courtroom floor. My lips curled from the wave of nausea that crept up from the pit of my stomach to my esophagus.

The judge took his seat. He looked like an evil character from a Marvel comic book. He wore what seemed like a permanent scowl and his bald white head gave him a sinister look. He waved his wrinkled hand and motioned for everyone to be seated.

"Except for the defendant and her counsel," the judge grumbled.

My lawyer gave my elbow a quick squeeze. I ignored him.

"Counsel, I am going to address your client directly. No sense in prolonging this with silly motions to prolong the inevitable. Your client pled guilty and I am prepared to sentence her today. Is that understood?" the judge announced.

My attorney nodded his agreement. I stared straight at the judge. My vision blurred a few times as I stared straight ahead. My thoughts were racing. My heart was pounding. Sweat ran down my back in lines. The sound of my own blood rushing filled my ears until I had to struggle to hear anything. My legs were moving, but I wasn't making them move. I also couldn't make them stop moving. I was swaying, like at any minute I'd lose the strength to stand and then drop.

"Ms. Heiress, the crime you have committed is a serious one. In my opinion, people like you, who murder for nothing, deserve the maximum sentence allowable under the guidelines. You had a relationship with the victim, and as the government alleged and you admitted to, you lured the victim to his death and then illegally disposed of his body, preventing his family from having a respectable and proper memorial," the judge was saying.

What? I screamed in my head. My jaw rocked feverishly because I wanted to tell this judge off so badly. They never even heard my side of the story about what had gone down. Just because I got spooked and had Jillian's friend Tedo dispose of Terrell's body didn't mean that I set out to kill him, nor did I lure him to my house to kill him. My chest heaved as I continued listening to that evil-ass judge. The whole courtroom seemed to be spinning around me.

"Under the Commonwealth's sentencing guidelines, this court is prepared to sentence you to life in prison without the possibility of parole. However, under due process of the law, we will consider that you've cooperated with the government in a case against a large organized crime syndicate, which significantly helped that case. Also, during your plea hearing, you took responsibility for your actions, which I may or may not consider in deviating down on your sentence. It is also your right under this court to have the opportunity to tell me and this court why I should not render the maximum sentence available to me under the guidelines. You can tell me why, in your own words, I might have leniency on you and maybe sentence you to twenty-five years to life with or without the possibility of parole. What that means is maybe one day some parole board will have mercy on your soul and let you back onto the streets.

"Before I render a final sentence, you will also have the opportunity to present members of society that can speak on your behalf, to tell me why they think I should have leniency on you during this sentencing. Ms. Heiress, I must say, that just as it is your right to bring forth others that can speak for you, it is also the victim's family's opportunity to tell me why I should put you away for the rest of your natural-born life. Under this process, it is their right as well. Do you have any questions?" the judge said loud and clear.

The gravity of everything he had said felt like a thousand-pound sack of bricks had just been hung around my neck. I realized that the small flash of light that fluttered at the back of my eyes was me getting dizzy. I could only imagine what my mother must've been thinking and doing when she heard what the judge was saying. She was probably crying, biting her lip, and wringing her hands so hard that her skin was raw. I knew her so well. I had seen a quick glimpse of her when I was first led into the courtroom. She never took her eyes off of me. Aside from the first quick glance, I couldn't look at her directly, so I lowered my eyes. I was too ashamed to be her daughter in that moment.

"Ms. Heiress, after I hear you out, I have the discretion to formulate a sentence as I see fit, according to the sentencing guidelines. Whatever sentence is imposed, you will be remanded and transported to state prison for the duration of your sentence. We are prepared to hear your statement. So, do you have anything you would like to say to the court or the family members of the victim who are present in the courtroom today?" the judge said with an eerie finality.

I sucked in my bottom lip and tasted the blood from where I had bit so hard it had split. I was prepared to recite the story of what happened, which I had replayed over and over again with my lawyer. But, now that I had the floor, I opened my mouth several times to speak and no words came out. Finally, when the words were about to come, I heard a familiar voice yell out.

"This is not over! You can't get away with everything you did and think it will be over!" It was Terrell's sister. "I got people on the inside and that guy you fucked over—he does too! You won't get away with this shit, Misty! I'll make sure you don't! Karma is a bitch, and so are you! You a dead bitch!"

"Your Honor!" My lawyer jumped to his feet. "My client is being threatened!"

I felt like somebody had hit me in the chest with a big metal sledgehammer. Suddenly I couldn't breathe. A flame ignited on my skin and my entire body felt like someone had set me afire. I didn't turn around; fear wouldn't allow my body to move. I was afraid of who else I might see if I turned around. My entire body shook. I couldn't stop my teeth from chattering. The court officers rushed over to Terrell's sister to remove her.

The judge banged his gavel wildly and screamed, "Order! Order in the court!"

"You killed my son, you grimy-ass hussy! You won't get away with this, Misty! I never liked you, anyway! So you are going to pay dearly! Mark my words!" Terrell's mother screamed.

I swayed on my feet. Tears burned at the backs of my eyes. The chaotic scene made the spot directly above my right ear throb with pain. I closed my eyes and immediately remembered the day I saw Terrell's mother on the news.

"My son, Terrell, would not get up and leave town without telling me or his family. We all have a good relationship. People tell me all the time that he was a mama's boy, so if he hadn't said anything to anyone else, he would've at least called and told me. But I do have a strong suspicion that his ex-girlfriend, named Misty Heiress, had something to do with his disappearance. The police tracked his phone and the last pinging alert was a cell phone tower only a mile from her apartment. Now I've talked to her a few times and she's done nothing but lie. So I'm standing here and pleading to anyone that knows his whereabouts, please call the police. You don't have to leave your name. Just call us if you heard or seen anything," his mother had said while tears had run from her eyes and flooded her face.

I remembered instantly seeing the pain in Mrs. Mason's eyes. She had been doing everything in her power to find her son. A few weeks after that, another encounter with Terrell's family told me they weren't going to give up. Out of nowhere, I was sitting on Mrs. Mabel's sofa and I heard loud knocking outside the front door. Then came the angry voices.

"Open up the door, bitch! We know you're in there!" a woman had screamed.

Alarmed, I had jumped to my feet, tiptoed to the front door, and looked through the peephole and saw four women standing outside.

"Open this door, bitch, and come out here and face us!"

I realized then that Terrell's mother, two sisters, and his cousin were standing outside my front door and banging on it. I had stood there for at least five minutes, listening to them berate me. I silently thanked God that they didn't try to open my front door, because if they had, they would've definitely had access to my apartment. I had quickly grown sick of their noise, so I had decided to call 911. As I waited for the police to respond, Terrell's family continued ranting and yelling.

"Everybody, this bitch that lives in this apartment had something to do with my brother's death," one of his sisters had yelled.

"She sure did, and we ain't going to let her get away with it either!" Terrell's mother had followed up.

"She better turn herself in to the cops, because if she doesn't, I'm going to beat her ass!" Terrell's other sister yelled.

"Could y'all take that somewhere else?" I heard a different voice say.

By looking through Mrs. Mabel's peephole, I couldn't see who the person was, so I raced over to the window to see if I could get a better look. I saw that my neighbor that lived on the opposite side of my apartment was the source of the voice.

"And if we don't, what's going to happen?" Terrell's cousin had challenged my neighbor.

"Yeah, what are you going to do? Call the police," Terrell's mother had interjected.

"Listen, lady, you guys are disturbing the peace," my neighbor had replied.

"The chick that lives in this apartment disturbed our peace when she murdered my brother."

"Yeah, what do you have to say about that?" Terrell's mother chimed in.

"Look, I'm sorry to hear about your brother. But the cops have been all over this apartment complex asking everyone if they seen that lady. And none of us have, so what you need to do is get behind the cops that're investigating your brother's case and take that stuff up with them. Hanging out in front of her apartment door isn't going to bring your brother back," he had said.

"We understand what you're saying, but you can't tell a person how to mourn a deceased family member," Terrell's cousin had said.

"You're absolutely right. But as a resident, I felt like I had to tell you guys that you're going about all of this the wrong way. That's all." His tone had turned sympathetic.

"We appreciate what you're saying," Mrs. Mason had responded.

I had peeped the sorrow in her eyes.

"Oh, no problem, ma'am! Now y'all have a nice day," my neighbor had said, and then he walked off.

A few minutes later, Terrell's mother, sisters, and his cousin all walked back toward the parking area of the apartment complex. I watched them until they climbed into a black Cadillac SUV and sped off.

My whole body had relaxed with relief. I literally had to wipe the sweat trickling down from my forehead. I knew then that as long as I lived, getting revenge for Terrell was all they would focus on.

I blinked away the nightmarish memories to the sound of the judge screaming. I was sick to my stomach and I didn't know how much more I could take with these nightmares and memories and threats.

"Order!" the judge yelled again as the crowd in the courtroom murmured about the outburst. "Order!"

Thank God things quieted down.

"Let's get back to the matter at hand. Ms. Heiress, do you wish to speak?" the judge continued, giving me the nod to speak my last words.

"Yes, Your Honor, I have something to say. Everyone wants to blame me for what happened, but I was a victim too. I didn't kill anyone intentionally," I said.

I could feel my attorney, shifting next to me.

"What are you doing?" he whispered harshly in my ear.

He knew, then, that I was not going to read the statement he had prepared for me. He also knew I was probably about to undo the guilty plea by now saying I wasn't guilty, after all.

My lawyer lifted his hand up to interrupt me. "Judge, I need a minute with my client—" my attorney started to say.

"Sit the fuck down! I have something to say," I boomed. I was not letting anyone else in the world speak for me. I had done that all of my life.

The judge seemed a little thrown off by the power of my voice. "Order!" he yelled, and banged his gavel again. "Keep it respectful, Ms. Heiress. Counsel, sit down. Now, go ahead, Ms. Heiress."

"I regret everything that has happened, but I want everyone to know that I am a victim myself. No one knows my story," I said, choking back tears. "No one knows the abuse I suffered and the things I endured. It was my life hanging in the balance, so I can be judged by all of you . . . but I know what I had to do. None of you were there in the moments when I saw my life flashing before my eyes. Nobody was there to save me, but myself. You can believe whatever you want to believe, but I know the truth and so does God. I can't be judged by any of you, and I will have to face my Creator one day."

It was so quiet in the courtroom, you could probably hear a mouse pissing on a cotton ball. I had everyone's full attention now.

In the end, my whole story about Terrell's attack and my defense of myself had fallen on deaf ears. The judge still sentenced me to twenty years to life, but threw me a bone when he said with the possibility of parole after ten years' consecutive time served. I was to begin my sentence in a maximum-security state prison immediately.

My mother had screamed and cried at the end, but there was nothing that I could do, except pray. I had heard all sorts of things about those maximum-security prisons, and none of it was good. The court officers moved to my side to take me out of the courtroom, and reality finally hit me. I dropped and my whole world went black.

4

STATE PROPERTY

The day had come, and I was set to be transferred from county to the maximum-security state prison. I'd heard so many things about parts of the prison being privatized, and using inmates for slave labor and other things. My nerves were on edge about it all.

I approached Sandra. The thought of me getting cool with someone in jail made me feel worse than the sentence I had received. No one liked to be locked up, but to make friends made it a bit easier to do your time. I had no idea what I would encounter in a new facility. It just all gave me anxiety, if I was being honest.

Sandra was sitting on her bunk when I walked into her cell, which I wasn't supposed to do. That's one of the rules imposed on all the inmates in the county jail. But this was important.

"I'm about to be out of here," I said sadly. "Thank you for everything you did for me, especially the protection you provided me while I was in here."

"Don't mention it. I'm never going to forget about you, Misty, so don't be sad. I got a few more weeks in here.

They had to drop the charges against me . . . again," Sandra said proudly.

"Damn, you're one lucky bitch, I'll tell you that," I replied.

I don't know how someone who used jail like a revolving door kept getting off, and this was my first time and I got the entire criminal justice book thrown at my ass. The Commonwealth of Virginia's justice system was crooked as hell. They let who they want out of jail and keep the ones that may want to turn their lives around. No shade to Sandra, but she's a liability. And I'm the one that the cops and the judges want to keep behind bars because they're afraid that if I get the chance, I wouldn't come back to this shit box.

"Yeah, I am! So I'm sorry that you had to take the fall for that shit that happened to that no-good–ass nigga. You're a good person, Misty. Keep your head up," Sandra said. "They can try, but usually they can't keep a good bitch down. I speak from experience. You'll have your day. Wait and see."

I fought back tears. I didn't realize just how much I was going to miss Sandra. She had really looked out for me and had become a good sounding board when I needed to vent and talk about shit that had happened in my life. She was a good person, despite her coming in and out of the system like she had for most of her life. It's apparent that she was dealing with her own demons. But when it came to me, she kept it one hundred from the door.

"Look, don't fret. I know you're worried about your mother out there. Whatever you want me to do for you when I get back in the world, you know I got you," Sandra said, smiling. "Commit my digits to memory and never forget them. I'm always going to be around and I want to hear from you too. Don't make me come looking for you," Sandra said sincerely, followed by a little chuckle.

I knew she was dead serious. We had really gotten tight.

"That is so sweet, thank you," I said, truly touched.

"The one thing I want you to do is be smart, Misty. Here, read this whole shit right here. Take your rec time and go to the law library, whatever you have to do. This is what helped me and a few bitches I know beat cases, get early release. It's the key to finding holes in the system. The only way to beat this corrupt-ass system is with knowledge. Knowledge is power, you hear me? Nothing else works. You have to beat them at their own game. Don't waste this! Read it and understand it," Sandra said, tossing a thick packet of papers at me.

I picked them up and could tell they were legal papers as soon as I read the first few words. *So this is how this slick chick been getting off,* I thought. From day one, I could tell Sandra was like the jail lawyer. She was always spitting about cases getting overturned on illegal searches and lack of rights, but I always just figured Sandra was like the tons of other inmates who thought they knew the system. Obviously, judging from the fact that she had already beat a murder charge, I knew she was on to something. I had better get like Sandra and start researching how I was going to get myself out of this mess I was in.

"Don't just throw that shit away, Misty. You better read that shit. I'm telling you, there might be something between them pages that will save your ass one of these days," Sandra said, her tone serious and motherly.

"You know what, there is something you can do for me when you get out. I want to know it's done, so maybe we can write to each other after I get settled. I just need a good address for you."

"Sounds good. I got you. Just say the word and it's a done deal. Shit, especially if it's something that'll put your mind at ease while you do your bid," Sandra replied.

"Promise," I said seriously.

"Promise," Sandra said sincerely. "Anything you need, I got you for real. Just keep my number, and like I said, remember it, because chances are they're going to take all your shit from you and you won't have the paper later. And I just wanted to thank you too. Misty, you was one of the first chicks I ever met locked up that didn't judge me at first and make me feel like some freak. You have no idea how many bitches I meet that judge me and think I'm some devious chick."

"Aw, thanks for saying that," I said.

Sandra jumped down and pulled me in for a hug. We held each other in a long embrace. I whispered in her ear what I needed her to do for me. I was sniffling back the snot that threatened to escape my nose, but Sandra's face was dry. I knew she would miss me, but she was the type that did not like to cry. Plus, Sandra was happy as hell she had beat her case and would be released into the world to get into more mischief. Boy, what I would do to be in her shoes. To have a chance to leave prison and go back into the world. My life would be so different this time around.

"C'mon, don't be crying and shit. You making me sad, when a bitch like me supposed to be jumping for joy. I told you, you gon' be all right. If you would just listen to me and read that shit I gave you, you will be joining me soon," Sandra mentioned.

We let each other go and I swiped at the tears on my face. "I'm sorry for being emotional. This jail and prison shit is not for me. I don't know if I'll ever meet a person like you while I'm doing all these years of time. I'm going to miss the bitch that made my days doing this time easier," I said, smiling at Sandra. "Just be good out there and don't end up back inside. You seem to have nine lives, but as we all know, even those run out," I said.

"I hear you. A bitch like me gon' always be good. I'm not new to this, I'm true to this," Sandra said, chuckling. "You know the first thing I'm going to do when I hit the world is take care of what you asked me. I'm not going to let you down, Misty. For real, I never had a female friend before I met you. I never got along with chicks unless I was trying to fuck them, but you were different from day one. I'm your true friend," Sandra told me.

That touched my heart. Outside of my cousin Jillian, I never really had female friends either. I never trusted anyone, but for some reason, there seemed to be something more genuine about Sandra. I guess doing time together could make the most unlikely of people formulate a bond.

"Heiress! Get out of this cell. You know better! Y'all must want to get violated!" a male CO screamed.

Sandra smiled at me one last time. "She's coming, fat ass!" Sandra snapped at the CO. We both laughed.

"Make sure you stay in touch and don't make me have to come looking for your ass," Sandra called over her shoulder. "Remember that damn phone number. I ain't never changing it."

I nodded in agreement. Although I felt sad, I was excited about the possibilities of what Sandra could do for me on the outside. I walked back over to my cell with the paperwork Sandra had given me. I finally took her advice and began to read the thick stack of legal-sized papers. After the first couple of lines, and before long, I was enthralled with what was contained in those documents. The wheels in my brain had already started turning with ways I could make my case fit. If Sandra could do it, maybe I could too.

5

MY WORST NIGHTMARES

*T*edo, Jillian's cleanup man, walks into my apartment, looks at Terrell's dead body, and lights his cigarette like nothing. "Fuck happened to his eyeballs?" Tedo asks dryly.

Jillian chuckles evilly. "Somewhere down there."

"Please just get him out of here," I say, trembling. The smell of blood and human bodily fluids makes me sick as shit.

"After we get him in a bathtub, it shouldn't take us longer than forty-five minutes," Tedo says, still with not an ounce of emotion in his words.

The first thing I see is a black body bag. I'm talking about the ones you see on the TV series NCIS. Then a small handheld saw. I immediately gag. They are about to cut Terrell up.

"Hey, wait, you're going to cut him up in pieces?" I ask, my teeth chattering.

"How the hell else did you think we were going to take him out of here?" Tedo asks me. "Come on, let's put him in the bag," he instructs his partner.

Jillian and I stand in awe. "I ain't ever seen nobody do this shit in person. It's always been on TV."

We tiptoe around the blood on the floor and head into the kitchen.

"Tedo and April are the best that ever done it. After they leave here tonight, there's not going to be a trace of Terrell's blood in sight," Jillian says to me.

"I don't care how good they clean up my place, they could still rat me out," I whisper.

"Misty, Tedo and his people ain't into that snitching shit. That's a code that they live by," Jillian tries to assure me. But doubt looms in the back of my mind. There is nothing Jillian could say that would ease my mind.

While we sit in the kitchen, we hear the saw buzzing from the bathroom.

"No, hold it like this," Tedo says.

"I wonder how far they've gotten?" Jillian asks.

"I was just thinking the same thing."

"I'm going to go in there and check." Jillian stands up from the kitchen chair.

A few minutes later, she screams, "Oh my God! I can't do this!" She runs back into the kitchen and buries her face in her hands.

"What happened?"

"I couldn't stand there and watch them with all the damn blood, with the legs and arms and shit. My stomach couldn't take it," she explains after she removes her hands from her face.

I then walk to the bathroom and all I see is the blood everywhere.

Terrell's arms and legs and head roll toward me, and from his severed head his mouth is moving. He is screaming my name. "Misty! Misty!"

"Agh!" I scream, and take off running!

*   *   *

I jumped out of my sleep, my body trembling all over. I was jolted by the same nightmare I'd been having every night since my sentencing. I couldn't shake it. The disposal of Terrell's body was haunting me, day after day, and night after night. I guess it had started because now I had nothing but time to think about it. Before, I was so busy running for my life, I didn't have the time.

The loud sound of clanging metal was noticeable as soon as I was fully awake. The noises were constant in the new prison. I used my forearm to cover my eyes from the bright lights that had come on. The first thing I felt was the sharp stab of hunger pangs. I hadn't had a real appetite since I'd gotten there. It was hard to eat that nasty-ass food and I didn't trust sitting down with any group. This new prison had many cliques of women. I could tell that as soon as I arrived. I wasn't interested in being in anyone's clique, but I knew if I didn't join one soon, I'd be open to anything with no protection.

There was more clanging sounds and the lights over my head seemed brighter than they usually were. I hated this fucking place. And, as many times as I had to say it, I still couldn't believe I was locked up.

"Rise and fucking shine! Let's rock and roll, ladies!" a fat female CO screamed out as she passed my cell. I squeezed my eyes shut and prayed that I was dreaming and would one day wake up in my own bed in my own house with my mother in the kitchen cooking me a good home-cooked breakfast of her famous biscuits, grits, and slab bacon.

When I opened my eyes again, I realized it was real: I was still in prison. The pungent smell of disinfectant from the little silver sink/toilet combo seemed to be more noticeable to me than before too. The scent went straight to my empty stomach and immediately made me nauseous.

More screaming from the COs forced me to finally sit up. I couldn't understand why they had to be so loud and dysfunctional. My head was spinning. I don't know if it was lack of sleep or just stress, but I had woken up with a headache every single day since I'd been sent from county jail to state prison two weeks prior. The pain in my back from the hard bed with its thin, worthless mattress told me it was very real.

"Heiress! Time to lock out! Why I gotta tell you the same shit every day! Get up for breakfast and let's go! Ain't no sitting in the block at mealtime no more. Y'all bitches be scheming too much," the same short, fat, female CO yelled at me through my cell door.

I looked up and sucked my teeth. The hunger pains were really the only things that made me move. *Fuck them COs* is what I was thinking. They were bullies with a badge, but not when it fucking mattered. They didn't protect people when we needed it, but they were here to harass us every step of the way, otherwise.

Inside my cell, I washed my face and brushed my teeth at the little sink, but I had to go to the communal shower to bathe, which I absolutely hated. I gathered the horrible-smelling soap, shampoo, and lotion I had been given at intake and headed to the showers. I entered the shower stall and there were three other women inside already. They obviously knew each other because they were talking and laughing. Another corny clique. I hadn't been in the mood to make friends since I'd been there, so I basically kept to myself. I spoke when I was spoken to; otherwise, it was silence. I had actually been doing a ton of reading about possibly changing my plea and having my case reexamined. I mean, it was clear self-defense and I still thought I stood a chance of getting everything reversed. Thank God for what Sandra had put me on.

The sound of the other inmates in the shower laughing immediately grinded on my nerves; I couldn't figure out what could be so funny or why they would be so happy when they were in prison, just like me. I just shook my head in disgust. Since I wasn't trying to make friends, I had made up my mind that I wasn't going to speak to them or join in their girlish banter. I missed the friends I had made in the county jail, though, especially Sandra.

When the women noticed that I had come into the shower room, they stopped talking and eyed me up and down.

"That's her," one of the women whispered, turning back to her little group of friends after rolling her eyes at me.

I heard her immature, high-school-acting ass, but I ignored her. I wasn't up for the drama. I knew they knew who I was. Everybody in Virginia probably knew of me now, after I had such a public plea hearing and sentencing, and since my arrest had made the headlines in every newspaper.

The inmates continued to snicker and whisper about me as I took off my clothes and got into the shower. *Stupid-ass, childish bitches.* I was thinking those chicks were all probably locked up for some dumb shit, or because they were strung out on drugs and out there committing crimes to get it, which also made me think of Jillian real quick. Her pill habit had walked us down a long road of bullshit. It didn't matter, though; I still missed my cousin like crazy.

Anyway, I considered myself different. This incident was a fluke. An accident. A onetime thing that just went all kinds of wrong. I had been living a pretty good life before shit went awry. Yes, call me stuck-up, or whatever, but I considered myself different from the bitches I was locked up with. In my mind, I was above them, and that's how I planned to keep it. Although, right then, just like them, I was behind bars with nothing and no way out.

The cackling bitches finally left the shower area, leaving me relieved to be alone. It would be the only sliver of privacy I got anytime soon. I finished and prepared to go back to my cell block so I could go to breakfast and hopefully talk to my mother. My mother was still trying to find a work-around for my case too. It may not have made sense to everyone else, but to us, we had to keep fighting. The thought of it not working out made me anxious.

I dried my body and then wrapped my towel around my hair and slipped back into a fresh prison jumpsuit. There were no mirrors and I was glad. I was sure that by now, I probably looked tired in the face and my skin was irritated with stress bumps. Just as I prepared to leave the showers, three women came rushing in. It wasn't the same ones that had been in there earlier whispering about me, so I didn't think anything of it. I got a good look at all of their faces this time and thought to myself they were all ugly as shit. I rolled my eyes and stopped, to let them go pass me before I tried to walk out. I wasn't trying to bump anyone and get into any altercations. I was banking on good behavior to help me down the line when I had to face a parole board.

These women clearly had other plans. One of them—a tall, very light-skinned, skinny girl, with a natural ash-brown Afro—stopped in front of me and blocked my path. She was an albino and ugly as shit, so I couldn't blame her for being mad at the world.

Not fucking today, I thought as I let out an exasperated sigh and stood holding my ground.

"Yo! Your name Misty, right?" the tall chick asked, her face drawn into a tight scowl.

I could tell she was supposed to be the tough one out of the group. She was so skinny I could see bones sticking up at her collar like they were out of place. The other two women—one that was so fat I doubted I could take her, and one that was obviously not as down with whatever was about to go down, because she looked more scared than me—stood flanking the ringleader.

I crinkled my face and gave my own tough-girl look.

"Yeah, I'm Misty and . . . who wants to know?" I snapped, dropping my stuff and balling up my fists. My street smarts told me to be ready for anything. I was outnumbered and probably outpowered, but I couldn't show weakness.

"I got a message for you from Terrell's family," the light-skinned chick snarled.

I felt a sense of dread wash over me and my heart started to pump with pure fear. "What the fuck—" I started.

Then, *wham!* Something slammed into my face with so much force I felt like my skull had cracked. I felt my teeth click and I thought I had swallowed my own tongue. Right away, the metallic taste of blood filled my mouth.

"Ah!" I gurgled, and stumbled backward as another punch landed directly in the center of my face. The bridge of my nose cracked, immediately sending a stabbing pain up the center of my face that reverberated through my entire skull. I swear it felt like my brain had been knocked loose.

"Ow! Help!" I wailed. Another fist slammed into me. This time my nose sprayed blood all over.

A follow-up bevy of punches and slaps from the women made me see stars. At first, I moved my arms wildly like a windmill, but I couldn't see clearly, so it was all for naught.

"Ah! Somebody help me! Please help me!" I screamed again, throwing my hands up to my face as the blood leaked through my fingers. "Fucking bitches! Help!" I screamed, gurgling blood.

My screams were for nothing. It was like I was alone in the entire prison with my attackers. There was no fucking CO in sight. I swear, this felt like a planned attack. I mean, when correctional officers want to harass me, they're lurking around every fucking corner. So, where are they now?

"Guards . . . somebody help!" I continued to scream for my life.

"Nah, bitch! You're gonna wear this ass kicking," one girl gritted.

"Yeah, you're gonna die today, just like you killed Terrell!" another girl threatened through clenched teeth.

Another close-fisted blow to the top of my head made me feel like things would go dark at any minute. I tried to fight, but I had no wins. My breathing was so labored, I thought my lungs had failed. Then I felt myself being dragged down by my hair. My defenses were up, but I had to face the fact that I had no wins over these wild bitches, who were now on me like a pride of lionesses on small, easy prey.

I fell to the floor and immediately curled up into a fetal position so I could protect my vital organs. Kicks, slaps, and punches rained down on me like a hailstorm. The women punched and kicked me without mercy. I was bleeding from the side of my head and could feel blood filling up in my right ear. I kept my legs curled in and my arms over my chest in an attempt to keep them from hitting me in the heart. I knew that the right blow to the heart could cause it to stop on the spot.

"This is for Ahmad too! Him and his family send their regards, you snitching bitch!" the ringleader of the attackers spat.

"Yeah, and Ahmad also sends a great big 'fuck you' and said he hasn't forgotten about you either!" the other chick snarled; and with that, she lifted her foot and kicked me with all her might, right in my head.

The pain rocked through my skull like what I imagined a volcano erupting within me would feel like.

"Agh!" I let out a bloodcurdling scream that felt like fire searing the back of my throat. I immediately felt shit closing in on me and then my world went black from the shock.

* * *

My eyes fluttered open as the sound of voices around me filtered through my ears. I had no idea where I was or how long I'd been there. I attempted to lift my right arm, but something prevented it. I moved my eyes to the side and noticed silver handcuffs glaring back at me. I looked around to see where the voices were coming from.

There was a group of doctors standing at the foot of the bed I was in, but it wasn't my cell bed. There was a CO posted up in a chair near the window in the corner of the strange room. I looked up and saw a monitor with numbers flashing. Then I became aware of the oxygen mask covering my nose and mouth. I was definitely in the prison hospital. I lifted up my free hand and saw the IV stuck in the top of it. The doctors were still talking, but none of them had noticed that I was awake.

Trembling and feeling weak, I slowly moved my free hand and touched my head. I ran my fingers over the rough ridges of stitches on my head. It was so painful. I tried to lift my head and immediately felt darkness closing in on me. I knew then I had a bad brain injury, probably more than just a concussion. Panic quickly set in and my heart started racing fast. The machine I was hooked to began beeping loudly.

One of the doctors whirled around, his eyes wide. "Ms. Heiress, you're awake," he said, sounding a bit surprised that I had made it.

"Where am I?" I rasped, my throat dry as dust. I used my free hand to pull the oxygen mask from my face.

"We are so glad to see you awake. You suffered some pretty serious injuries, especially to your head," another doctor said, stepping closer to my bedside.

"Where am I?" I raised my voice as much as I could, given my condition. The doctors all looked at one another like they were trying to concoct some story before they told me where I was. I eyed each one of them. My voice had stirred the CO and he stood up with a look of horror on his face.

"You should rest, Ms. Heiress . . . really," a female doctor said, trying to push me back down onto the bed pillow.

"I want to know what happened and where I am!" I strained to scream. The veins in my neck and at my temple were raised and pulsing against my skin. The heart monitors were going wild with loud, rapid beeps. A piece of gauze on my head began to soak through with blood. I had busted a stitch or two and the pain made my eyes tear up.

"Listen, calm down. They'll tell you what's going on when you *calm down*," the CO said, moving closer.

The doctors looked at each other as if they were trying to figure out who would be charged with giving me the information. Finally the petite female doctor stepped closer to my bedside. She was clearly nervous.

"Ms. Heiress, the injuries you suffered during the assault were pretty serious. The blow you took to the head could've caused permanent damage. When they got you here, we had to work to get you better. We don't think it's safe for you back in general population. We have brought you here to a protective medical area for your own safety," the doctor said.

I flopped back onto the pillow. "So . . . you're saying . . . I've been transferred?" my voice cracked. Blood soaked the head gauze again. "To a different prison?"

"No, just to a different area, where you'll be safer. There are only a few conditions to your stay in this area," another doctor said.

Conditions! What fucking conditions? I thought.

Sandra had told me about state prisons where they used inmates as human guinea pigs to test drugs. She said she had read up about them and the ones where they used inmates as slave labor for big corporations. I had thought she was crazy, but maybe she had been right. I wasn't letting them keep me here, safety or not. I'd rather take my chances than be given some disease they couldn't cure, like Sandra said they did to several hundred inmates that she'd read about.

"No! Take me back! Get me the fuck out of here!" I screamed, thrashing on the bed. The handcuffs dug into my wrist. Pain rocked through my skull and all of my muscles burned, but I didn't care. They stood there and looked at me like I was speaking another language. But I wasn't. I was speaking English so they understood me perfectly well.

"Get something to sedate her!" one of the doctors yelled to a nurse who had come busting into the room to see what was going on. The nurse turned on her heels and raced out of the room.

"Get the fuck away from me!" I howled, making the heart monitors go berserk.

The doctors all looked horrified. Finally the nurse skidded back into the room and handed a syringe to one of the doctors. I was kicking so hard it took all of them to hold my leg still enough to be injected. The doctor was finally able to plunge the needle into my left thigh muscle. And he did it with ease, it seemed.

"Ow! No! What the fuck are y'all trying to do with me?" I wailed. "Get off of" were my final words as the medicine in the needle immediately took hold of me.

My body went slack, and my head lulled to the side. The doctors all looked at each other in relief.

"That was the saddest thing I've ever had to do," the female doctor said to her colleagues. "How do we just take away people's rights like this every single day in the fake name of science?" she continued.

"I guess somebody gotta sacrifice for sick people to get better," the CO answered as he made sure I was really knocked out.

"Yeah, but somebody also has to have some damn ethical responsibility too," the female doctor said, sounding disgusted.

I could hear them. And I could hear the sorrow in her voice, but I couldn't react or respond. I was trapped in my own body. Buried alive. And, little did I know, that was just the beginning of a hell for me.

6

INFIRMARY OR TRICKERY

The clanging of doors slamming shut snapped me out of a hard, drug-induced sleep. It had been more than a week since the episode in the hospital room and I was still not able to think straight. My stitches had mostly healed, but the headaches were still rocking through my skull randomly. They'd get so bad, I would have to hide from the light. There weren't many hours I had been awake and conscious since I'd been in this new place, but in the moments I was lucid, my constant worrying made the pain worse.

I wondered if my mother knew I'd been transferred to this so-called medical protective unit. I couldn't stop worrying about her every time I gained the slightest bit of consciousness. My mother wasn't cut out for this bullshit. I could just imagine how crazy she was going, being on the outside without me. I had no time to write Sandra either. I didn't even know where they'd taken my personal things, which is where an envelope and money receipt with her address was located. This was some other type of shit these people had me going through.

More noise around me told me I was fully awake this

time. I leaned over on the bed and dry-heaved. My stomach wasn't feeling right this morning and I knew right away that the queasy feeling meant they'd probably doped me up on too much shit. It wasn't lost on me that the prison system had gone hand in hand with the big pharmaceutical companies. I'd heard from Sandra that they used inmates to test out drugs that they couldn't get good results from testing on animals. In other words, treating humans worse than fucking rats and monkeys in labs.

They tried to tell me being on this new unit was for my protection, but I knew better. Something else was up. Something serious. I dry-heaved for the tenth time. My gut was never wrong. I felt like I had landed myself in a serious situation with no hope. Isolation was how they made inmates fall to their mercy. I hadn't had a visit, a phone call, pen and paper—nothing that would allow me to contact someone outside of this place.

I closed my eyes and tried to calm the bat-sized butterflies jumping around in my stomach. I had no idea what to expect today, but judging from the way they had doped me up days earlier, I wasn't hopeful that it would be any different. All of this was my fault. From sneaking around stealing pills for Jillian to killing Terrell, I felt like karma or some shit was catching up to me.

More clanging, screeching metal and what sounded like a stampede of rapid footsteps caused me to open my eyes. I crumpled my eyebrows and stood up slowly. My eyes moved rapidly, scanning from left to right as if I was watching a moving train pass. I moved closer to the little window in the door as a phalanx of COs stomped past in a frantic line.

"The fuck?" I whispered, my face folding into a frown. "Somebody probably tried to escape," I grumbled.

This was how they acted in the regular jail and prison cell blocks when they were preparing for a total lockdown. Just as I turned my back to get back into my bed, my door slid open and I heard my name being yelled like it was an emergency.

"Heiress! Misty Heiress!" a tall, dark-skinned, fish-eyed CO yelled out. At first, I was going to sit quietly and see if the ape-looking officer passed by. However, that feeling in my stomach already had me so jittery, I just spun around on my legs after he called me for the third time.

"That's me. I'm Misty Heiress," I said apprehensively, my eyebrows scrunched in confusion. Six more officers stepped up behind him.

"All right, Ms. Heiress, I'm coming in there to cuff you. Then, nicely as you can, you will come with me. Quietly and without a fight, if I were you," the ugly officer said as he signaled for the backup officers.

Before I could put my wrists out on my own, two COs grabbed me and damn near dragged me toward the doorway.

"Agh! Get off of me! I can fucking walk on my own. I don't desesrve to be treated like this. Where y'all taking me? What the hell is going on?" I shouted as they handled me way too roughly.

"You need to close your mouth and do as we say," one of the COs said smartly. "Down to solitary you go—step one," he continued. The mouthy CO was quickly shushed by another officer.

My eyebrows dipped low on my face as I tried to figure out what the hell he was talking about. I hated it when I was in the dark about something that concerned me. So it was in my best interest to find out what they were talking about.

"Why don't you just fucking tell her everything and then have her acting the fool before anything can get started," another officer whispered harshly, more like being sarcastic.

My heart immediately began racing and my stomach turned over in my gut. *Step one? Anything get started? Anything like what?* I was screaming in my head. I wanted to scream, kick, jump, or do anything to deal with the overwhelming feeling of fear I was experiencing. I knew, though, that would just get me an ass whupping from those COs. I decided to play it cool until they got to wherever they were taking me. I wasn't going to get any answers, and that was clear to me in that moment.

With wide, stretched eyes, I looked around the dimly lit hallway we finally stopped in. On each side of the hallway, there were two rows of black metal doors with tiny windows and rectangular slots. I could hear women screaming from behind the doors. Screaming like someone was killing them or torturing them at the least. I was scared shitless. I felt like my bladder would involuntarily release. Finally the COs opened one of the doors and I was tossed inside a dank, musty room that held only a cinder block platform with a thin mattress on it. There was a lone silver sink/toilet combination that was built into the wall, and also a slim, rectangular slot in the heavy metal door. It was the inside view of what was behind the doors I had just seen.

I thought being on the medical unit was supposed to be like an open area with beds or hospital-type rooms. This shit was solitary confinement, like I had committed some heinous crime in prison or something. My mind raced in a million directions. I walked up and down the small cell, my fear and confusion almost palpable.

"God, if You have any mercy left for me, please protect me. I don't know what is going on, but I don't like it at all," I prayed out loud as I moved back and forth in the tiny space. I wanted to be with my mother. Or with Jillian and my grandmother, even if it meant that I had to die. Anything would be better than this. It felt like my whole life was at a standstill. I wasn't making any progress whatsoever.

Finally exhausted from pacing, I sank down on the cold cinder block bed that would be my new sleeping place and hugged my knees up to my chest. I closed my eyes and bit down into my bottom lip. I couldn't help but think about the love and the bonds with my family that I was missing now. I thought about all of the people that had been hurt behind my actions. When the thought popped into my head, immediately what happened that fateful day to my sweet neighbor, Mrs. Mabel, who'd let me hide out in her house, played out like a movie in my mind's eye.

I had been dumb enough to open the door for a little boy selling candy right before Mrs. Mabel had come into the kitchen holding a new door lock. We'd been standing there talking when her doorbell had rung. I stopped and turned toward her. We'd both exchanged surprised and nervous looks.

"Are you expecting someone?" I had whispered, my voice shaking.

"No. I'm not," Mrs. Mabel had whispered back. "Go to my bedroom and close my door. I will come get you when they're gone."

"Okay," I had replied, my heart slamming against my chest.

Mrs. Mabel had watched me until I walked into her bedroom and closed the door.

"Who is it?" she had yelled through the door.

I couldn't hear the person on the other side of the door, but when Mrs. Mabel had asked the person to repeat himself, I heard a man's voice, but I couldn't decipher his words.

"How can I help you?" she had continued, and that's when I cracked her bedroom door a little.

"My name is Officer Kahn and this is Officer Pax and we would like to ask you some questions," I had heard a male voice say to Mrs. Mabel.

I couldn't get a look at the guy talking at the front door. At this angle, all I could see was the police patch stitched to the arm of the uniform.

"What kind of questions do you need answering?" Mrs. Mabel had asked him. "Are you looking for something?" she followed up.

"Is there someone else in this apartment?" I had heard the other person ask. The sound of the voice had immediately alarmed me.

Peeking, I had caught a glimpse of the second man. "Oh my God, it's Ahmad," I had gasped. Fear and anxiety had consumed my body all at once. I immediately ran to the window and opened it. I punched the screen out of the window and watched it fall down on the ground, but I didn't leap out of the window.

Confused and scared to death, I went into Mrs. Mabel's walk-in closet and closed the door. "Fuck! Fuck! Fuck!" I had whispered as I cowered in the small ceiling space inside. I began to sweat profusely and I hadn't been in that space for two minutes. My heart rate went from fifty to one hundred miles per hour in three seconds flat. And I knew that at that very moment my life was about to end. Then the sound of the bedroom door crashing into the wall behind it terrified me.

"Fuck! She climbed out of the window!" I had heard Ahmad bark. "Go get her before she gets away. Kill her. I want her dead," he had yelled at his men. I had known then that Mrs. Mabel didn't stand a chance of making it out alive.

Ahmad had stayed behind and searched Mrs. Mabel's bedroom.

"She got away," I heard his partner say breathlessly.

"How the fuck did we let her get away?!" Ahmad's voice had boomed again.

I could tell that he was furious. And if he knew that I was still in this apartment, he'd definitely torture my ass without thinking twice about it.

"I told you we should've gotten her after we sent the kid

to sell her the candy bar the first time," the other guy had replied.

I had been set up good. In the end, Mrs. Mabel had paid for my misdeeds with her life.

How will I ever forgive myself for that? That shit will probably haunt me for the rest of my life.

"Heiress, stand center for bed check," a CO's deep baritone snapped me out of reliving the day I had put Mrs. Mabel in grave danger.

The slot in the door slid open.

"Step up to the window," the CO demanded. His voice wasn't as annoying as most correctional officers', maybe because he wasn't screaming like the rest of them usually did.

I got up and reluctantly stepped in front of the door slot and peered at him through the small, scratched-up plastic window. The officer was looking at his clipboard, scribbling something down. He finally lifted his head and looked at me. He did a double take.

I could tell he saw something that he liked. Maybe I didn't look as bad as I thought. Either that or he was just a pervert. Yup, I could tell he liked what he saw. Although I thought I looked like shit, and probably did, I could tell he had some lust in his eyes.

"What—what . . . what's your inmate number?" the CO stammered. His yellow face immediately flushed pink.

"I don't know. I just got here. I don't even know why I'm here. I went from being injured to placed in the hole. It makes no sense. Maybe you can help me understand," I rambled like it was my first and last chance to speak.

The CO exhaled loudly. He looked a little annoyed and surprised at the same time. He still looked like he was interested in me, though. At first, that gave me pause, because I knew a lot of COs raped female inmates they thought were vunerable. Then I started thinking, maybe I could befriend this CO and get to the bottom of this place. Maybe I could get him to get me the fuck out of there too. All sorts of crazy thoughts entered my head causing it to pound like crazy.

"Okay. Bed check done," the CO droned, still unable to take his eyes off of me.

I knew right then that he found me attractive underneath all the state-issued hospital garment.

"What's your name, Officer?" I asked, deciding to shoot my shot. "If I'm going to be all alone down here, at least I'll have you to talk to," I said as seductively as a bitch who was locked up could be. I was not trying to miss out on this opportunity, if it was going to be my best shot.

"Anderson," he answered like he was a little winded.

He was clearly unnerved. You would've thought I was standing there naked. The CO swallowed hard, but couldn't keep his eyes from wandering down to my breasts. I noticed, and he knew that I noticed.

"It's nice to meet you, CO Anderson," I said; then I walked away from the door.

Teasing had worked best in my years of experience. Had I thrown it all out there too soon, I knew I would've spooked the CO and then he would've been of no use to me later.

"Same here, Inmate Heiress! I'll be assigned to you from now until its time for you to go to testing," the CO yelled at my back.

"Wait? What's *testing*?" I asked, and my voice rose a few octaves. I wasn't being sexy and seductive anymore. "If you would please just explain all of this to me, I would be so grateful," I pled.

He never turned around to look back at me, but I knew he had heard me but chose to ignore me.

When I heard the slot in the door close, I exhaled and dry-heaved, again. My mind was moving like the cars on the lanes of the Autobahn.

"I have to find out what the fuck I'm in for, in this place," I whispered, running my hands over my face in exasperation. Even when locked up, I had to think on my feet. I couldn't afford to keep getting caught slipping because my life depended on it.

7

SOLITARY CONFINEMENT

It had been two days in the hole and I had already figured out that Officer Anderson was the regular guard on duty down there. He was awkward and kind of shy, but I could tell with the right prompting, I might get him to tell me what I needed to know and even maybe sneak me a cell phone to call my mother. Or maybe one better, help me get the fuck out.

"What's up, Heiress? It's time for some fresh air. Get into movement position," Anderson said.

I got to my feet and rushed over to the door, happy as shit to be getting out of there after having no human contact and being extremely uncomfortable. I had already started to feel like I was losing my mind. I had even started hallucinating a little bit. I'd seen Jillian and my grandmother right in the tiny room with me. I had started talking to myself, laughing at nothing, and contemplating ways I could end it all.

In the time I had spent alone thinking, I had decided that I would have to put a plan into action. All I could do was hope that I was as good at the art of seduction and gaming as I thought I was. It had worked while I was out on the streets, but being in prison was a totally different ball game.

I turned around with my back facing the heavy metal door and put my hands through the bottom slot. Anderson put the cuffs on me and I gently pulled my cuffed hands back inside.

"Opening door twenty!" Anderson called out.

I heard loud alarms sounding and then the locks clicked to release the door. I told myself that if I played things correctly, maybe this could be my last day in solitary. Especially since I didn't know why I was there.

I bit into the side of my cheek and started moving out of the cell.

"Ay! Heiress!" a loud scream from behind one of those black doors jolted me. I couldn't tell which door it was coming from, but it was loud. And how did the inmate know my name?

"Don't give in to them! If you let them break you, they'll have you where they want you! You have to stay strong! This is all part of their plan!" the female voice screamed out.

I paused. I wanted to hear if this inmate was going to give me any more nuggets of knowledge about this godforsaken place.

"Keep it moving or stay inside," Anderson said, pushing me forward. He sounded a bit nervous, like he didn't want me to hear what the inmate was saying. There was something definitely up about this creepy-ass place.

I turned slightly and found myself face-to-face with him. He had something in his eyes that I sensed as maybe a mixture of weakness and fear. I immediately thought those were the two things in a CO that might work to an inmate's favor. That might work to my favor particularly.

I locked eyes with Anderson and we both stared at one another for a few seconds. Shying away, Anderson broke the eye contact first. He wasn't that cute, but I didn't care if he looked like a gorilla. Whatever I had to do to get him on my side, I was going to do it.

"You moving too slow. You only get forty-five minutes," Anderson warned me.

"I thought it was an hour when you're in solitary," I replied, repeating what I'd heard about the hole from when I was in jail.

"Oh, you must think you're on the regular prison side," he answered. "Nah, this ain't the same. This is a different type of setup," he continued cryptically.

"Well, can you explain to me what it is? Because I'm starting to go crazy with nobody to talk to, and nobody to answer my questions. I don't know how it was decided to send me here. I don't know why I'm in the hole or nothing. I was assaulted, in the infirmary, and then next thing I know, I'm in solitary with no explanation," I said in the most pitiful voice.

"I can't get into all that. I'm restricted. But I'll keep you company while you walk the square and get some air," Anderson answered, averting his eyes from mine.

I could tell he was just shy and probably was a sweet person. I wondered what had made someone like him take such an asshole-type job. Most COs were true dicks, and Anderson didn't seem like the norm. He was trying real hard to be professional, but I kind of could tell he liked me. I sensed that he had a decent spirit about him.

"I think you're a nice guy. Most of these guards in here are over-the-top mean for no reason," I said, trying to game him.

I saw Anderson kind of smile a little bit, and I think he was even blushing. Just that little sign gave me a bit of hope. Now all I had to do was keep talking to him and wearing him down.

"Maybe one day while you're out here keeping me company, you'll finally tell me what this area is all about."

"Maybe," he said.

Anderson led me into a small fenced-in area that had nothing but a dying patch of grass, gray cracked concrete, and an open top. When I looked up, I could see the blue sky, white clouds, and not one other sign of life. After I walked the square plot about six times to stretch my aching muscles and work the kinks out of my stiff back, I stopped and walked closer to where Anderson stood guard, waiting for my time to be up. I leaned against the fence and stared straight ahead, but started talking to him.

"I can tell that this is not the job you saw yourself doing in life, am I correct?" I asked, hoping to play on that little glint of attraction I thought I saw with him. This was classic get-in-his-head-type shit. Leave it to me to come up with a new plan. I just hoped it worked. Anderson looked at his hands. I could see they were shaking a little bit. *The first sign of weakness! Yes!* I was getting to him.

"I must be right," I said. "See, I could tell you were too good to be working as a CO. So, what did you really want to be when you grew up? Wait—let me guess! A lawyer? Maybe a doctor? You look like you're super smart. It's so obvious that you're wasting your talents here. This dead-end job ain't stimulating for a highly intelligent person like you, Anderson," I said, laying it on thick. I knew with men that flattery was an ego stroke that could lead to more things later.

"Um . . . you—you're not supposed to . . . ," Anderson stammered, his head moving around like it was on a swivel. I saw his eyes dart up toward the tower and then I noticed cameras hanging from the sides of the building. The cameras roved back and forth.

"Oh, what? You can't really talk to me? Okay, I'll just keep it moving, then," I said, quickly catching on.

"No, um, wait," he said, sounding like he didn't want me to stop. "Just, uh, cover your mouth when you talk so the tower and all those cameras won't know we are chatting. I can't hold conversations with inmates. They're scared of fraternizing," he explained.

A pang of excitement flitted through my chest. The fact that Anderson told me how to break the rules was a good start. It was a great sign.

"Thanks for talking to me," I said.

Then I sat down and covered my mouth, like he'd told me to do. I kept talking to Anderson. By the end of the hour, I felt like I'd gotten to know him enough to know he was a little more simple than I thought.

To my dismay, it was another four days before I got another day out of the hole. I hadn't slept. I barely ate the shitty food they put in the slot. And I had paced so much; my feet were raw on the bottoms. My eyes were swollen from the long bouts of crying and my throat raw from screaming. They had even made me spend one whole day in total darkness and another night with the lights flickering until my eyes ached from it. I started figuring out that this system was in place to somehow break me down. This way, by the time they let me out of this shit, I would be so desperate they could probably get me to agree to anything: even being a human guinea pig for drug testing. At this point, I'd do anything to get out of here.

When I heard Anderson's voice at the door tell me to get ready to come out, I thought I would piss myself with happiness. I didn't think I had ever been that happy to hear a nigga's voice in my fucking life. I was in bad shape, though. My legs were weak from me barely having enough strength to use them. I knew that I looked and smelled like shit. I hadn't brushed my hair or my teeth, or taken a shower in days. They were breaking me down, all right.

I could tell as soon as Anderson saw me that there was a difference in his reaction. The glint of lust in his eyes had faded. He even seemed a bit angry, like I had done something to him personally.

"Where you been?" I whispered, my voice scratchy from underuse.

"Move out, Inmate Heiress," Anderson said, all business.

He ignored my question. He wouldn't really look at me either. It seemed as fast as I had gained a little bit of in with him, I had lost it and any chance of getting him on my side. He seemed like a totally different person, and not in a good way.

Once he got me out of that fucking tiny room, and was leading me down the hallway, I heard that same strong female voice again yelling from behind one of those black doors.

"Sis, stay up! I heard you screaming the other night. That's what they want. They want you to lose your mind so they can justify the shit they about to do to you. Don't give them the satisfaction! Hold on to your sanity. Hold on to your safety!" the female voice called out to me.

"Be quiet!" Anderson scolded the screaming inmate. "Just shut the fuck up!" he boomed.

I jumped when he yelled at the inmate. It was the first time I'd really heard him raise his voice in an angry way and it shook me inside. He was definitely different. Maybe he'd gotten in trouble for being too nice to me, or maybe someone had figured out we'd talked too long on the yard. He led me outside, and after I painfully stretched my legs for a couple of minutes and inhaled and exhaled the outside air, I did what he'd told me to do the last time I was out there. I sat against the fence and spoke into the material of my jumpsuit.

"How come you haven't been here in days?" I asked.

At first, he sighed loudly, as if I was annoying him. My heart sank. I was convinced then that I had lost my only possible ally. Tears welled up in my eyes. But then, so the tower and the cameras wouldn't see his mouth moving, Anderson turned his back and spoke with me.

"I didn't know you killed someone. You were trying to game me, I can tell. You're like the rest of them. You want to get in my head," Anderson said, like his feelings were hurt or something.

My heartbeat sped up. *Dammit! Now he's not going to help me!*

"I didn't exactly kill someone just like that," I lied, trying to see how much he knew and how much he'd reveal.

"Well, that's not what I heard. I heard you murdered this guy Terrell Mason. And Terrell was involved with some very dangerous people. People he owed a lot of money too. So, by you killing him, you killed the deals he had with those people. And I hate to say this, but you could be at risk for their retaliation because we live in a small town." Anderson relayed.

My head shot up with shock. Holy shit! Anderson was right too. I needed to be extra careful about death threats coming from Terrell's family *and* associates. Terrell was more valuable alive than he was dead, so my life was going to hang in the balance from this point on. What the fuck had I gotten myself into? I didn't ask for this. I just wanted to live a normal life. Now look at me.

I was trembling. This whole thing with the assault and sending me to this unit was a setup from the beginning. I didn't know how I would get myself out of this. Terrell's family and street affiliates probably had everyone in this town on their side. I was fucked!

"Please don't let this affect the arrangement you and I have. We can get around it," I said. "Listen, you wanted to be my friend, I could tell. You like me and I like you," I said, grasping at straws now. "Don't let that worry you."

"I'm sorry but I can't be associated with you, Heiress. I will lose my job and possibly my life," Anderson replied, his tone serious.

He sounded so weak, but I couldn't let him know that I thought that about him, although it made my insides crawl. I wanted to scream at him and tell him, *Man up! Stop being a pussy!*

Fuck! The one person I thought I could get on my side was flaking on me now. I had to think fast. And right away the bag of money my mother still had came to mind. If I could just get Anderson to check on her on the outside with the promise of some money, I'd kill two birds with one stone. I just had to hope that he went for it.

"Listen, I know you think you know, but you have no idea. I got a proposition for you, Anderson," I said flat out, wasting no time. "I think it'll benefit you in more ways than one, and it will surely help me out," I told him.

"What?" he asked. He seemed somewhat interested.

"I got a plan that will help us both . . . a whole lot," I said.

"What is it?" he asked.

Now I knew that he was interested. I just hoped that he would take my bait.

"What they saying about me is not true. They want to set me up because they think I was down with this organized crime group. The big medicine companies want me out of the way so they can control the information I got in my head. I know a whole lot about what they were doing in the hood and a black-market pill mill they had going on," I began to explain. "I know a lot of dirt on them, but if they kill me, the feds will know right away it is them. But I got some money and I'm willing to share it with you, *and only you.*

"But I have to know that I have your help first. I need to get up out of here. I don't know what they do to inmates down here, but look at me. I'm being reduced down to nothing, and I can't understand it. It's like they want me to lose my mind or get really, really sick. This is inhumane, and I won't last if you don't help me. I know you are feeling something toward me. I feel it toward you too," I continued, rushing my words out in a pleading tone.

Anderson didn't reply. I could tell that he was contemplating what I was saying. But he gave off no expression on his face that would indicate if he wanted to help me or not. I instantly started regretting that I even brought this proposition to him. I mean, had I stuck my own foot in my mouth? I knew I needed to go into damage control. I needed to say something to make him talk.

"I will give you the contact information of the person on the outside who can give you a significant amount of money. But first, I need your promise that you'll help me get out of here."

"Wait! You mean escape from the prison altogether?" Anderson asked, his voice quavering. "I—I could nevnever . . ."

Shit! I cursed to myself. This guy was really a weakling. I had to choose my words wisely if I was going to get his help. If he got spooked at all, it wouldn't go down at all. My stomach churned. There was nothing worse to me than a weak-ass man. He was a man that needed direction. He needed to be told what to do, which seemed impossible at this moment. But I had to stay focused on the prize in dealing with this sucker-ass CO.

"You can make a good amount of money, Anderson. Much more than the pennies you make working here, locked up all day in this place, watching the horrors of this stupid system. I can tell you how to get your hands on some of the money right away," I said, although I hadn't spoken to my mother since they'd thrown me in this dungeon. But I wasn't going to tell him that. I knew he'd crumble into pieces then.

He was quiet again and then he walked away from the fence and stopped talking to me. Then the time bell rang. My time outside was up. Anderson immediately moved back into business mode.

"Stand for lock-in, Heiress," he said, perfunctorily.

My heart sank. "Dammit!" I grumbled under my breath. Anderson didn't seem to be fully convinced, and now I had to lock back in, which meant I didn't know how many days would pass before I'd see him again.

My chest got tight with angst about being locked up days straight again. I needed a proper shower too! I didn't know what torture tactic they were trying on me, but I definitely felt myself slipping into some sort of dreadful, gloomy depressed state. I understood all of the horrors I'd heard about solitary confinement in prison now. The system was literally trying to drive inmates crazy. I believed this was the new form of slavery.

I actually felt like the walk back to the cell was the walk of death inmates take before they go to the electric chair or lethal injection. Anderson handcuffed me and didn't utter a word. I was whispering, "Please, please help me" as he led me back. He remained stoic and didn't say a word.

It would be God knows how long before I could try to execute another plan. Each day that passed, I felt myself slipping more and more. These bastards were trying to make me go insane.

Anderson put me inside, and as he went to lock the door, he said, "I'll make sure you're all right."

My stomach jumped at those words and each syllable wrapped around me like a warm blanket. I wanted to run to him and hug him. My mind started running. *Does that mean he will help me? Does that mean he's going to get the contact information and go see my mother?*

Shit, I couldn't keep still, so many questions ran through my head. Whatever it meant, it gave me a litte bit more hope than I'd had a few minutes earlier.

"Come on, Misty. You've been through worse. You got this," I told myself as the cell door locks clicked into place. For some reason, I had a tiny bit of hope, something that was truly hard to come by in prison.

* * *

The next day, Anderson showed up at my cell door, and although I felt weak as shit, I jumped up and got ready to lock out. This time was different. Anderson didn't instruct me to put my hands through the slot, instead the door just opened up.

I froze as Anderson and about five other people walked into the cell. I backed up, feeling like a scared, dazed animal. A bright flashlight was flashed directly into my face. I threw my hands up and shielded my eyes.

I didn't know whether to feel scared or relieved. I shivered all over and my bladder felt like it would release by itself.

"Inmate Heiress, these are the doctors in charge," Anderson announced.

Anxious, I backed up farther. My legs were shaky and jerky. I was confused as hell.

"Inmate Heiress, I'm Dr. Stanley," a tall white man announced without looking up from his clipboard.

I squinted, still seeing black spots in my eyes from the flashlight being put directly in my vision. I think that was the plan; they didn't want me to see their faces clearly.

"What do you want? Why am I down here? I need to get out of here," I said in a rush of words, which came out all in one breath.

"Please turn around," a female doctor said as she stepped up.

"What? Why?" I questioned. She didn't answer, and Anderson stepped up and forcefully made me turn around.

"She's still not ready," the female doctor said. "The mind still has solid cognitive differentiation," she droned. "The new ones won't work, unless it's completely diminished."

"Okay. More days, then," another doctor said. "The deterioration needs to be readily seen, or the test subject won't be viable. Let's exit. Record the date and time. Give it another thirty days."

"What! No! I can't be locked in here like this for another thirty days! Just ask me! I'll agree to whatever!" I screamed, and lurched forward. I needed her to reconsider what she had just said, because there was no way that I could last another thirty days in this room. What was wrong with these fucking people?

Anderson clamped down on my arms. "Calm down, Inmate Heiress. Calm down or you'll lose your rec and shower time," he warned, and then flashed me a look. Something about that look told me to comply and I might have his help. I backed down. The doctors filed out of my cell and Anderson handcuffed me as usual.

A few hours later, I was finally allowed to take a shower. There was a female CO watching me the whole time. The water felt strange on my skin after so many days. I scrubbed my skin almost raw. I let the water run over my face and it mixed with my tears. Everything was painful—the water, my thoughts. My entire body and soul ached in ways I had never experienced. I sank down to the shower floor, curled my body into a ball, and sobbed.

After the quick shower, I was handed back over to Anderson and led into the fenced-in recreation area. I did my usual—took a seat up against the fence so I could hide my face and talk to him. I was usually the one who initiated the conversations in the past, but today, I was uneasy because I had no idea if I could trust him anymore. He'd shown up with a gang and it threw me off. One minute, he was Mr. Nice Guy; then the next time, he was back to regular CO type of behavior.

"I'll help you. You know, um, with the thing you asked," Anderson mumbled.

My head shot up.

"But I need to get the cash first—like right away—so I know it exists," he said with his face turned away from the cameras and the tower.

I was about to say something.

"Sh!" Anderson scolded. "Cover your fucking mouth . . . you crazy," Anderson snapped nervously. "You better remember where you're at, or they'll change me out and you'll have someone else to deal with," he warned.

I snapped my lips shut and lowered my head again and spoke into my shirt.

"How can I be sure that if I tell you where the money is, you won't take it and fuck me over? What kind of assurances will I have?" I asked him. He had the upper hand.

"All you have is my word, just like all I have is your word that you actually have money to give me in the first place," he answered.

"Right," I agreed. "So tell me the plan to get me moved out of solitary."

"I'm going to slip something into your hand when I lock you in today. You need to make surface cuts on your wrists and then scream at the top of your lungs. When the other CO comes, smear the blood on the small glass in the door. They'll have to open the cell and get you out. They'll take you back to the infirmary and then they'll think you're ready to be in the medical-testing unit.

"I'll make sure you get put under a nurse named Lisa Sanders. She's my sister. She will look out for you and I'll help. Around here, shit is run real tight, because of the inhumane shit they're doing, but I'm going to do my best to work with Lisa to help you. You just have to be real careful. There's a lot going on, and Lisa and I can do the best we can, but you have to do your part too," he said.

I was disgusted by the idea of cutting myself, but what choice did I have?

"Just make sure you don't actually cut the vein in your wrists or they might not get to you in time," Anderson warned.

I guess it was my only hope. I felt like crying, smiling, jumping, and cheering, but I knew that nothing could be celebrated until it was all said and done. Besides, on the inside, I knew that Anderson was a weak-ass man. He'd fold in an instant. But if all went well, he might just come through for me. All I could do was my part and keep my fingers crossed.

"Even though you will get money, I also want to thank you for helping me, since you're taking a huge risk for me. So know that I am truly grateful," I said as tears rolled down my face.

"Don't cry. Stay strong," he told me, and then he left.

The thought of me finally getting out of this godforsaken place gave me hope. Anderson's tone of voice gave me hope too. Now all I had to do was pray that my mother still had the money. If she didn't, this plan was going to blow up in my face.

8

BE CAREFUL WHAT YOU ASK FOR

The plan Anderson told me to use to get out of solitary worked. In fact, the shit worked too well. It wasn't even ten minutes after I put my bloody wrists up against the door before at least five COs busted into the cell to get me. Anderson had also told me to act very crazy when they came in so that they knew it was time to move me the hell out of that cell.

"Get off of me! Get the fuck off of me! Just let me die! I want to die! I have to die!" I screamed, dropping myself to the floor and then kicking and flailing my arms. "Just let me die!" I flailed so wildly, both of my wrists leaked blood. My wrists ached with pain, but I didn't care. I needed them to believe I was losing it.

"Agh!" I growled, trying to bite one of the COs. Then I felt a punch to the side of my head and I fell to the ground.

"Call the medical unit. She's bleeding all over the fucking place!" another CO screamed.

A few minutes later, a bunch of people dressed in white coats and scrubs ran in. It was like a scene from a horror film. Never thought that I'd be in one either.

"We need sedation! Somebody get me a fucking needle over here!" a tall man in white scrubs barked just before one of my wild kicks landed right in his crotch.

"Ouch! This little bitch!" the man shrieked, then fell to his knees.

I tried to kick him again, but I wasn't able to get any more kicks in before at least ten men rained down on me. I felt hands all over my body and they weren't gentle touches either. This is the part Anderson hadn't warned me about. Between the COs and the doctors and orderlies, I was being manhandled.

"Get off of me!" I squealed so hard and loud, the back of my throat burned.

When it was all said and done, it took twelve white coats and so many COs I couldn't count to finally get me into a position that they could stick me with the needle filled with some drug. I tried screaming from the pain of the needle prick, but the medicine took effect so quickly, my mouth just hung open with no sound coming out of it. I felt my body relax within a few seconds and my head lulled to the side. I could hear footsteps around me and see slivers of light, but I couldn't react or control my body movements.

"Ready? One, two, three, up." The voices sounded robotic in my ears.

I was hoisted up and then slammed down onto a stretcher. Tears drained out of the sides of my eyes; I was in pain. I felt them roughly wrapping my wrists with gauze. I looked up and saw a woman huddled on the side. She was watching everything that was happening to me. The woman had a look of genuine concern etched into her facial expression. In my fading moments of consciousness, I wondered if that was Lisa Sanders, Anderson's sister that he'd told me about.

Suddenly I felt them moving me, but it felt more like I was floating on air. Right before my eyes closed on their own, I heard the screaming female voice that had been talking to me for weeks.

"I thought you were going to stay strong, sis! Now you probably won't make it out alive! They're going to pump you up with shit! I'm going to pray for you!"

With that, everything suddenly went dark. I couldn't even process fully what the woman had said.

I don't know how many hours or days it had been when I awoke in a straitjacket locked in an all-white padded room. I can't count how much time passed before I was let out to mix with the other inmates or patients, whichever way you wanted to look at the people there. I guess we were all property of the state and had at some point become patients. The area I had been moved to wasn't set up like cells; it was dormitory style, but it was clear we were still in prison. COs guarded the doors, and there was a command center located at the back of the room, and the windows had crossbars.

"Let's go, Inmate Heiress. I ain't got all day. Move it or go back to the room," a CO screamed as I shuffled my feet trying to keep up.

The odor emanating from my body was making me sick. I hadn't had a shower since they had moved me from solitary to the padded room, where I had been locked down for the self-inflicted cuts on my wrists. I felt like I had to learn to walk all over again. My body ached in places I didn't even know existed; pain even crippled the spaces between my toes. I had been drugged up and tied down for so long, it was as if my brain wasn't sending signals to the rest of my body parts. A few times, I even stumbled, nearly spilling to the floor flat on my face.

"Stop here," the CO demanded. "This is your bed. Stay

on your side and on your bed and there won't be no problems. Got it," the CO told me, dumping a blanket roll and a small basin filled with toiletries onto a tiny, unmade metal spring bed that had a thin striped mattress on top of it.

I could feel a hundred sets of eyes on me. I didn't connect with any of them. I collapsed onto the bed and closed my eyes. I didn't move an inch. Suddenly a deep, comatose sleep overcame me before I could fight against it. I bet it was because they'd given me something again.

"Please . . . no! Please . . . not tonight! I'll do anything! Just don't take me!"

I was jolted out of my sleep, thinking I was having a nightmare. The sound of a high-pitched, screeching, pleading voice coming from my left told me I was awake. Although it hurt my head to open my eyes, I did, anyway. My eyes almost popped out of their sockets when I noticed two men in white coats dragging a woman from her bed. I sat up, my head throbbing. It quickly registered with me that the girl was fighting and crying, asking them to leave her alone.

"What are y'all doing to her? Where y'all taking her?" I croaked through cracked, dry lips. My throat burned with every word.

One of the men rounded on me and glared at me with the evilest light of fire in his eyes. "Shut the fuck up and mind your business before you get thrown back in the hole," the white coat growled. He was serious too.

"Please! Please!" The girl they were dragging out continued to cry as the men pulled her past my bed and off the unit.

I struggled to my feet and rushed as fast as I could to the door, but a CO stepped in front of me and obstructed my view and movements. I started to push him out of the way, but I decided against it. I knew that I wouldn't win this fight.

"Go back to bed, inmate. Don't be a troublemaker. It's for your own fucking good," the CO said, pushing me in the chest until I stumbled backward. I turned around in the darkness and began moving back toward my bed. It seemed like I was walking in slow motion. Walking on air.

"Don't worry. You'll find out where they took her real soon, and then you won't be so fast to want to know," said a female voice in the darkness. I jumped; the eerie tone in the voice gave me chills.

"What?" I squinted.

The source of the voice moved closer to my bed.

"I'm Shanta," the mysterious voice said. Then she boldly flopped down on the end of my bed, which wasn't allowed, I was sure.

"The girl they just dragged out of here is Lena."

I looked at Shanta tentatively. I didn't trust many people, especially other females in prison. I didn't think there were any inmates more ruthless than the women. They were probably more dangerous than some men who were locked up for serious crimes.

"When people introduce themselves, you usually follow up by introducing yourself?" Shanta said sarcastically.

I could tell that she was a feisty one. "Misty," I answered back.

"Wait? Misty Heiress?" Shanta asked like a lightbulb had just gone off in her head. "I watched your story on the news," Shanta said in an eerily cheerful tone, which I didn't think was healthy. It was like she admired me. "You don't look exactly the same, but I could surely tell it was you. Wow . . . I'm locked up with the infamous Misty Heiress."

That statement made me uncomfortable, but if it was going to sell the story that I was dangerous and shouldn't be fucked with . . . then so be it.

Shanta moved so that I was able to see her face in the

faint light. I surveyed her up and down. She was average at best from what I could see. Her face had quite a few scars on it and her hair looked like it hadn't been combed in a while. I guess you could say she looked just as rough as I did at that point.

"So I guess you're here for trying to commit suicide too?" I asked, nodding toward the old, dingy, blood-stained gauze on Shanta's wrists.

"Something like that," Shanta replied, touching her wrists like she was discovering her bandages for the first time. "And so did Lena. That's why we were chosen for this area and everything that happens here . . . ," Shanta said. Her voice seemed to trail off, and she turned her head away, as if she didn't want me to see the emotions in her face.

"Chosen for *this* area? What do you mean? What happens here?" I asked. I wanted answers.

"Chosen to be in the medical-testing area. You don't know what happens here? Well, I'll tell you. Torture happens here," Shanta replied, shaking her head. "They fucking torture—"

"Inmates! Get in your own bunks!" a CO barked, cutting off Shanta's words.

Shanta jumped up from my bed and got ready to rush away to her own bed. Before she left, she turned back toward me. "We all got chosen because they think we don't have people that can protect us or care about us on the outside. Whatever they know about you, they will use against you. You'll see. Good night, Misty," Shanta said cryptically.

I tried to keep the conversation going, but Shanta didn't say another word. She just scrambled back to her bed. I wasn't awake when Lena was returned to the dorm-style room, but even in my dreams, I felt like I could hear Lena sobbing like her entire world had just ended. It wasn't until I got up the next day that I saw the blood droplets leading from the door to Lena's bed. *Yeah, those doctors were definitely poking her with all sorts of needles last night. Damn!*

Every day after that, as soon as my eyes opened in the morning, I could not control the tears. I hadn't heard from Anderson since I'd given him the information to contact my mother. That worried me to all hell. All I could think about was that he might have betrayed me. He might have gone and found my mother, and then took all of the money from her, knowing damn well there would be nothing I could do from inside the prison.

Thinking about my mother being put in danger all over again because of me was enough to send me into a lifelong depression. The worst of it, though, was being stuck and powerless because this system was so corrupt and fucked. That shit made me boil inside from anger. I regretted ever cooperating with those fucking agents because it hadn't done me any good. I was still kicking myself for that move. I had taken the full fall for the murder and then, on the urging of my stupid lawyer, pled guilty.

Somewhere deep down inside, I had held out hope that I would get some help getting out of here. It never happened. I started thinking it was never going to happen for me. I was going to be here until I turned old and gray, or until they killed me with whatever it was they did in this place.

I lay back down on my bunk and just cried. What I had found out since I'd been moved out of solitary was that the unit I was on housed women that were at high risk for either being injured in general population or at risk of harming themselves. The open-style dormitory was part of the infirmary unit inside the women's prison. Most of the inmates said that it was a front for the unit where they tested out drugs on humans. So far, it had been three days and I hadn't gotten pulled yet. I knew that once I did, shit might get very hectic for me. I just hoped that Anderson came through and I would see his sister soon. She hadn't come and identified herself to me yet.

"Misty, what's good?" Shanta called out to me.

This chick was a bit more cheerful than you could imagine an inmate being, but I guess maybe she figured there was no use in being down and out. We were here and that shit wasn't changing, so we might as well make the best of it.

Shanta had interrupted my negative thoughts. I watched her approach from the other side of the room. I wasn't in the mood for anyone with a bubbly personality. As Shanta got closer, she could tell I had been crying.

"What's the matter, Misty?" Shanta asked, sitting down on the end of my bed. She knew that she was breaking the rules, but she didn't seem to care much about rules. I could tell that already about her.

I sat up. I didn't really feel like talking, but I did, anyway.

"I just feel hopeless. They won't let me do shit! They won't even let me make any phone calls. Nobody is explaining shit to me. I thought I had a friend who would help me, but I haven't heard shit from him," I said in an almost inaudible whisper.

Shanta listened intently, her head moving up and down as she looked me in my eyes. Suddenly her face softened. "This is what happens to us all when we first get here. You'll feel hopeless, but it will wear off, Misty. They will wear you down and drug you up until you forget all your worries. You just have to be strong and pray that one day . . . something gives. Or that someone comes in here and saves us," Shanta said in a calming voice, which did make me feel better.

"I don't want to wait for one day. I can't live like this. I have to do something about this," I told her.

"Do what? What could you do to change your situation? We're outnumbered," she continued nonchalantly.

It was as if she'd already given up, so I knew that I couldn't count on her. Then I looked around the room at the other inmates lying in their beds, looking oblivious. Most of them were so out of it that they'd burst into laughter or start singing without being prompted. It was their *La La Land*. So I figured that Shanta was right about us being outnumbered. But then my gut feeling rose up in me and told me not to give up. I could still get out of here.

9

ENEMIES ALL AROUND

It was my fifth day on the new unit, and I awoke to a piece of paper on my bed. My face immediately crumpled into a confused frown when I saw it. I picked it up and it was a note.

Misty,

> *Don't think you got off easy with what you did. We are everywhere and we won't rest until you get what is coming to you. Life always has a funny way of bringing karma to those who deserve it. You've fucked over a lot of people in your time, and that is going to be returned to you one thousand times over. We have eyes everywhere. We see and hear everything. You thought you had an ally in Officer Anderson, but guess again. We find out everything. Good luck with trying to survive everything we have in store for you.*

My entire body felt frozen like someone had injected my veins with ice water. My heart throbbed so hard, it threatened to choke me. I read that note, over and over again, and each time, a different emotion grabbed hold of me. I finally looked around the dorm to see if anyone was watching me read, but I didn't notice anything different. All of my housemates were just waking up or busy doing their routine to get ready for the day ahead. My stomach swirled with nausea.

I didn't know if that note was from Terrell's family or Ahmad and his crime syndicate. What I did know was they had gotten to Anderson. I could only pray that he was still alive. And my mother too! *I'm so stupid! I could've led them straight to my mother through Anderson!* The thought made me lean over and dry-heave. *Oh my God!* I trembled.

I didn't know what to do in that moment. It took me almost an hour to get myself together before I left my prison bunk. I made sure I took out that note and read it a couple of times. It had now become fuel for my fire and my daily motivation to keep going, although I wanted to give up totally. I needed my enemy's words to remind me that I had been through worse and had gotten out of it. This time wasn't going to be any different.

I had learned a long time ago from my grandmother that faith could bring you through anything. Being locked up like this, I wasn't always convinced that faith was a real thing. I had started giving up on God, and maybe that's why things hadn't improved. I don't know, but there was no scarier feeling than being trapped inside the prison and unsure who your enemies were. I felt like a sitting duck at all times. I also felt like I didn't belong there at all.

I looked at myself in the scratched prison bathroom mirror and shook my head in disgust: Misty Heiress, former fly girl, was standing in a prison bathroom looking like complete shit. I had unkempt hair, which looked like dried tumbleweed, chipped and bitten-down nails, ashen pale skin, and without a person in the world who could help me out of this shit. My mother was God knows where by now. The thought made me bend at the waist over the sink, this time stomach bile came up.

My life had changed so drastically over the past six months, and for damn sure, it hadn't changed for the better. Sometimes I think the fact that I was in this predicament—sitting in prison, with no hopes of getting out—was karma for what happened to Jillian, my grandmother, and Mrs. Mabel. Yeah, I fucked everyone's life up, and people I really loved lost their lives behind my actions.

Like I said, I think my situation is karma, but at other times, I think this is just a temporary situation to teach me something—a situation I will bounce back from and come out even better than before. I have to admit that wasn't the thought I had most, though. Most of the time I was thinking I'm doomed and I'm going to die in prison with no family to even claim my body for a proper burial.

No matter what, though, I couldn't help but obsess about my past life. Sometimes it made me smile, but other times, it made me want to cry to even remember it all. I had the type of life people worked hard for. I had gone to school and got my degree. Gotten a good job in a pharmacy and was living the life that sometimes seemed impossible when you've grown up in the hood. No one expects any of us to actually put our minds to something, especially school, and then actually achieve it. Every person in my family, including Jillian and my grandmother, was proud of me. I was one of the first to do it in my family. I just knew I'd be the example for everyone else around me.

Yeah, my life was on the right track and going smoothly. I had gone from being a have-not to being a somewhat-have. And that doesn't mean I was, by any means, rich, but I was working and could get myself whatever I needed without depending on the system or my family or a no-good man, for that matter. I was living as an independent woman and loving it.

In fact, the day my life changed for the worst, I had been

on my lunch break when I got a call from Jillian—who, by the way, is dead now and partly to blame for the way shit blew up.

It all started the day she first asked me to grab more than a few pain pills for her, after her car accident. This time, Jillian said something to me that would change everything forever.

"I've got a homeboy who will pay top dollar for twenty to twenty-five Vicodin pills."

I had balked at the idea, and at first, I told her, "Hell no!" But as things go, I ended up being a major part of a black-market pill mill, anyway.

Ain't that about a bitch? I had gone from trying to be a square, on the straight and narrow, to wearing prison-issued clothes, white half-size-too-small Keds tennis shoes, and sleeping on a metal bed with a paper-thin mattress. That was a far cry from my apartment, which I had been so proud of, which I had worked hard to furnish and decorate all by myself.

I closed my eyes and fought back the round of tears that threatened to fall every day when I woke up facing the dank gray walls surrounding my bunk and the crowd of women I had to rub arms with, all day, every day. Reality was a bitch, but so was reminiscing over the past.

Two days after I received that crazy note, I awoke to my name being called frantically from a distance. I looked in the direction in which my name was coming.

"Misty . . . Misty Heiress! Girl, get up!"

I heard her voice before I could fully see her. Shanta was huffing and out of breath as she rushed across the dorm toward my bunk. Her eyes were all bugged out and sweat was wetting her hair line.

"Listen, I gotta tell you something," Shanta said, winded.

I was still rubbing sleep and tears out of my eyes when she had rushed over. It was an alarming way to be woken up.

"What? What could it be, this early in the morning?" I growled, seriously annoyed that she was bothering me.

Shanta huffed and took a minute to catch her breath. We had grown close over the time I had been there. She seemed more loyal than most, and she seemed to be able to hold her own. I had learned from Sandra while I was in county that you could make connections in prison, but not friends. And you could use those connections to your benefit if you needed to, kind of like how I did with Shanta.

I had only gotten close to Shanta because she seemed to know shit about everything that was going on. I don't know who gave her the information, but she was usually right. My first few days there, I was weepy and real sensitive, because I wasn't ready to accept my fate and because I couldn't come to grips with the fact that Anderson might have betrayed me. But I learned from her real fast that bitches are ruthless, and if I didn't stop with all the weak shit, I would get eaten alive—even on this unit where everyone seemed to be much calmer than in general population.

So I got with the program real quick and gave up on all the crying shit. Once that happened, I had solidified myself as someone who could be strong. I had also solidified my connection to Shanta. I still wasn't ready to call it a full friendship, though.

With sleep still clouding my judgment, and an attitude that could, I cocked my head to the side and glared at Shanta through squinted eyes. My growling stomach made it easy for me to be mad and agitated that early in the morning.

"I—I—I just heard something going around." Shanta put her hand over her heaving chest like she was about to faint. She could see that the look on my face was clearly telling her to get to the point.

"They—they saying that they heard that there is a hit out on you. They even offering chicks in here some money to take you out. It's serious shit and dangerous for you," Shanta gulped.

I let out a long, exasperated breath. "What?" I asked, alarmed. "There would be no reason for anyone to have a hit on me," I lied. I threw my legs over the side of the bed and stood up. I needed to pace, because that made me feel better when I was nervous. I started moving in circles in the tiny space around my bunk. First the note, and now this. It was a lot to think about and handle at the same time.

"They saying that it might be as soon as tonight. They said some real dangerous people out for blood when it comes to you," Shanta finished breathlessly.

I let my tense shoulders fall. I rolled my eyes and inhaled, feeling like I had just gotten kicked in the pussy, for real.

What the fuck? I thought. What Shanta was saying wasn't really news to me after I had gotten the note, but damn! I knew the day was going to come that I would have to face the wrath of either Ahmad and his people or Terrell's people. Still, when she said it, the reality was just like a splash of cold water to my face.

I stopped pacing and exhaled. I decided no matter what, I was not going to let them see me sweat. There was still a good possibility that maybe even if Anderson had been derailed from helping me, he had gotten the message to his sister, the nurse. He said that she might be able to help me get out of here before anything bad could happen. Acting tough was 100 percent of what got me through each day inside, so I wasn't about to change it now.

I looked Shanta dead in her eyes. "Shanta, don't worry about me. I ain't worried about all them threats. It ain't about shit and I'm getting used to it. I've already seen the worst, so at this point, let them bring it on. Those threats are coming from the outside, and I know exactly who it is," I lied, playing it off.

Shanta was looking at me like I was crazy not to be scared shitless. I sat back down on my bunk and she did too.

"I already been assaulted in the last place I was at. I ain't worried about dying, for real. I don't know if living is worth it if I got to keep living like this. Honestly, that's the one thing I might not be afraid of anymore—death," I said calmly, although my heart was drumming against my chest bone.

I could've won an Emmy Award in that moment. The entire time I spoke to Shanta and acted calm, it was all an act. Inside, I was a shaken, scared little girl dying to go home and get a hug from my mother before somebody murdered me like an animal in prison.

As Shanta and I got ready to leave the dorm, I could feel my stomach churning with a mixture of anger and fear. I knew that anything was possible. At any time, the threats from Terrell's family or Ahmad could materialize into some crazy inmate attacking me in the shower again while I was wet and helpless, or while I slept, or when I had my back turned in the library, researching my case. I had seen it happen to other women, and, trust me, I hadn't seen any of them return once they were carried out by the medics.

"I think this will all blow over and it may just be talk. I'm going to get out of here before anything bad can happen. Don't you worry," I said seriously, hoping that would make Shanta finally feel better about my potential threat.

Shanta shook her head in agreement, but I could see in her eyes she didn't believe it. She had seen a lot inside the prison, so it was harder to convince someone like her. It pained me to know that I had to watch my back. I had my head on a swivel, and every move I made, I did it carefully. A damn shame, if you asked me. Paranoia and anxiety had been regulars in my life since this whole debacle started. The fact that I couldn't catch a break was really starting to get to me.

"Either way, I got your back, Misty. I feel like there is

something good about you, no matter what they say you
did. It's the same for me. They say I'm some heinous bitch,
but I just call it survival. Anything I ever did out in them
streets, it was to survive . . . ," Shanta said, her voice trailing off.

"I hear you. I feel the same way," I agreed. It felt like
she was finally coming around and this gave me hope.

Shanta smiled. "Enough of the serious shit. Let's go get
something to eat," Shanta said as we moved into the line
for our meal.

I had no choice but to eat the food the prison provided.
In this unit, there were no commissary privileges. I had
heard it was because sometimes they wanted to control the
food so they could systematically starve inmates at certain
times in order to test certain drugs out on them. It seemed
logical to believe. There were days we had all stayed
locked in the dorm and only allowed to have crackers that
they brought around. Those were the days I had seen the
worst come out in the women I was locked up with. Those
were the days fights broke out and some serious injuries
happened. Those were also the days you'd hear more than
one inmate screaming in the night as they were being
taken away by strange men.

Shanta and I sat down in the chow hall. I looked down
at my tray of cold powdered eggs, which they tried to pass
off as scrambled eggs, a rotten banana, and a piece of stale
institutional bread, which was rough enough to be used as
a scouring pad. Shanta seemed happy to have her meal,
but I didn't have an appetite at all. Not only because of the
food, but because I felt like a target. I don't know if I was
bugging or not, but it seemed like all eyes were on me.

I kept telling myself that the threat wasn't real, but the
idea of it was nagging at me like mosquitos buzzing in my
ears. All of the inmate voices seemed super loud to me. I
couldn't make out what they were all saying, but I just
knew they were talking about me. I even thought I saw

some of them pointing at me. Their laughter seemed more pronounced too.

"You good?" Shanta asked, noticing that I wasn't eating and my eyes were darting around nervously.

"Girl, yes. I'm good. I told you, I ain't scared," I lied, waving my hand like it was nothing.

I couldn't stop thinking about the nerve of Terrell's family or Ahmad to put a hit out on me. After all I had been through at Terrell's fucking hands? I had stuck by his worthless ass through prison bids, him being broke, cheating, and him beating my ass whenever he felt like it. I think they all must've forgotten that fact.

And as for Ahmad, he knew what it was when they got me involved in crimes for their own selfish reasons. Ahmad acted all gangster, but it was just the fact that he couldn't stand that he had been bested by a woman. He wasn't a real fucking man, anyway. He hid behind his henchmen and his guns.

I would never forgive Terrell for the shit he put me through, especially, because I ended up in prison behind his ass. All the years I had spent with him, riding with him through it all. I deserved better than this bullshit. I had to shake my head as I thought about how many times I had to fight off chicks and fight off Terrell himself. It was always a constant battle being with him, and then when I finally cut it off, he couldn't take it. I shuddered now, thinking about all the times he had put his hands on me.

One time, I had opened my apartment door and immediately a bulb of lightning had flashed behind my eyes and a force beyond my control had taken hold of me. With a scream stuck in the back of my throat choking me, and a brutal force pulling me down, I had scrambled on the hardwood floor of the small foyer, still not aware of what had hit me. Another blow caused an unbearable pain in my head.

"Ah!" I had finally been able to let out a bloodcurdling scream. I could hear Terrell's animalistic breathing. I had known what it was then. Instinctively I had placed my hands up in defense, but to no avail. Another blow to the top of my head had caused me to see stars. I felt myself stumbling backward.

"Terrell, please!" I had finally managed to scream.

"Where the fuck you been, Misty!" Terrell had growled as he wound his hands around my hair.

I had been there before, so I let my body go limp. I knew the results of Terrell being like this. I'd get my ass beat.

"Where have you been?!" he had screamed again. Then he reached under my bowed head and slammed his balled fist into my face.

Blood had sprayed from my nose like a lawn sprinkler, sending my blood onto Terrell's pants. That had just seemed to infuriate him even more. Blood from my nose had dripped into the back of my throat as he yanked my head back to look into my eyes. I could tell then he'd been getting high. I could hardly breathe.

"You're a lying bitch," Terrell had spat.

"Terrell, please!" I had gasped, huffing out each word.

I had continued pleading as he dragged me across the floor farther into the apartment. I could feel the skin on my knees stinging from carpet burns. An open-handed slap had landed on my cheek. I saw small squirming flashes of light out of the side of my eyes. I said a silent prayer that Terrell didn't kick me, like he had before.

I was sure my ribs hadn't fully healed from the last time and I feared that another kick or blow would surely send bone fragments into my heart and kill me instantly. The pain had pulsed through my head and had become so unbearable, I had placed my hand on top of Terrell's hand, which was embedded in my hair.

"You be trying to play a nigga. I know you out there doing shit, Misty!" he had roared, continuing his assault.

"You fucking niggas behind my back, right? Right?!" Terrell had boomed like a maniac.

It didn't make a difference if I had answered "no" or "yes." He had been blinded by anger at that point. I had known that he would beat me until he got tired. Then he would help me up off the floor and force me to have sex with him. It had been a cycle that, unfortunately, I had become familiar with.

As Terrell dragged me through my apartment, I had kicked and screamed, but that didn't deter him. In fact, he had punched me in the chest so hard, it caused me to involuntarily emit a loud cough. He'd literally knocked the wind out of me. Urine had run down my legs and I could hardly stay awake. When Terrell had finally gotten finished that day, he stood me up and helped me to the bedroom.

"I'm sorry. I just love you so much," he had whispered as he placed me on the floor of the bathroom so he could clean me up. His mood had switched so far that I knew he was the living and breathing Dr. Jekyll and Mr. Hyde. I had struggled to breathe because every breath hurt. I felt like all of my ribs had been broken. My knees burned from the friction burns I had suffered from being dragged. As bad as I had wanted to scream out or even moan, I hadn't wanted to take a chance on making him angry again.

"Come here, let me help you clean up," Terrell had consoled in a low, soft voice that was completely different than the booming, maniacal voice he'd been using just a few minutes earlier.

I had struggled to open my eyes, since blood and tears had dried and crusted around them, almost sealing them shut. I had lain in a fetal position, every inch of my body aching. Terrell had gone to the linen closet and gotten a hand towel. I heard the water running. Then I felt a warm rag against my battered skin. I had shrunken away from his touch, but I was careful not to piss him off.

"I am so sorry," he had said, wiping more blood from my face and neck.

Never again. I will never stand for this again, I had vowed silently as tears danced down my face. I had promised myself that day I wasn't going to take any more beatings from Terrell without fighting back.

Even after all of those beatings, I had tried to forgive him and believe him when he had said he wouldn't do it again, but what happened? He would turn right around and do it again. All of this on top of the fact that he was always cheating!

I had a right to fight back. And when he attacked me the last time, I had a right to kill his ass. I had a right to end his abuse.

As for Ahmad, I knew he was dangerous. I should've never gone along with the stupid-ass plan about getting involved with the federal investigation that my former boss was under. If I had known that they were dangerous kingpins and illegal businessmen, I would've told the feds to kiss my ass and taken that little-ass pill charge that they threatened me with. But, no, I had to be a chickenshit and let them talk me into it. Now look at me. I went from potentially getting federal drug charges to getting a murder charge. That's what happens when you get involved with shit on the black market.

I swiped roughly at the tears cropping up in my eyes. I couldn't afford for anyone to see me having a moment of weakness. Anyway, in the end, after the Ahmad setup, there was no getting out of it. The fucking feds were on that shit and they didn't give one fuck about me helping them.

I'm telling you, money and power will make niggas kill their own family, so I should've known that not one of them would be thinking about saving my ass. They were all out for self, and I got caught in the fray.

I was shaking my head in disgust. It was all me when it

came down to it. The planning and takedown of Ahmad and his crew was all my handiwork. I didn't think I had all of that conniving in me, but, apparently, I was more talented than I thought.

Still not talented enough to save myself from sitting in prison, though. No way. I lost this battle.

10

THE TIME HAS COME

Just like Shanta had warned, my time had finally come. I was asleep in my bunk when I felt a big, rough hand slam into my face. It covered my nose and mouth, which caused my eyes to pop open in shock. I opened my mouth and tried to scream, but the sound was muffled by the massive hand. My chest felt like it would cave in from the jackhammer of fear slamming into it. I just knew my heart would explode. This had been one of my worst fears all of my life—being woken out of my sleep by an attacker.

The hand belonged to a huge man, who breathed hard like an animal. He smelled like shaving cream and cigarettes. Grunting like he was struggling, he grabbed me up out of my bunk, like I was a rag doll, and threw me over his shoulder. He started carrying me away, like this was something I should've expected.

"Get off of me! What are you doing? Get the fuck off of me! Help!" I screamed out, and started kicking my legs frantically. I punched the hulk of a man in his big back and squirmed my torso, trying to cause him to drop me. It didn't matter that the way I hung, caveman style, over one of his huge shoulders, would've caused me to crash to the hard concrete floors and probably crush my skull. At that point, I wasn't thinking about anything but getting away.

Oh my God, I sucked in my breath because I could barely breathe. I was in a state of shock. "Put me down! Let me go! Get the fuck off of me!" I hollered, slamming my tiny fists into his back. I moved my head and tried to bite the hulk in his back, but I couldn't get a good enough angle to really sink my teeth in. He held on to me so tight, I felt like he had me in a vise.

I had no idea what was happening, but I knew it wasn't going to be good. As I fought, I caught a glimpse of a CO that I thought could be Anderson. I wasn't sure if it was him. My vision was too blurry. The gorilla-sized man was moving so fast with me, I couldn't be sure if who I was seeing was actually Anderson. But I decided that I was going to try, anyway.

"Anderson! Help me! Anderson, is that you? Help me! Don't let them do this to me! You know me!" I screamed. I could feel the blood rushing to my head as I flailed and kicked and screamed for dear life.

The CO that I thought was Anderson didn't say a word. He just kept following behind the mysterious man as he carried me. I knew I would see Anderson sooner or later, but I thought it would be when he was helping me get the hell out of this place. I guess the note I received was true. Anderson had betrayed me. I couldn't be sure, but since everything else in my life seemed to be headed straight to hell, him betraying me wouldn't come as a surprise. I was used to people fucking me over and abusing me for their own purposes.

The big guy carried me down a long, sterile white hallway. But not without a fight. The whole time I continued kicking, punching, and screaming. All of my efforts were for nothing, though; I was no match for the guy. In fact, he acted like my hardest punches felt good, instead of hurting him. All I had served to do was make myself tired as hell by the time he stopped moving with me. I was winded and my head pounded. Every nerve ending in my body was standing at attention. I must say, I don't think I had ever been that afraid in my life. I felt like I was being held by one arm while dangling over the edge of a cliff that was hundreds of thousands of feet up in the air. It was a spine-chilling fear that could send anyone into cardiac arrest.

The big brute finally took me into a brightly lit room at the end of the long hallway. From his shoulders, I could see women all over the room. Some were in beds; some were strapped in chairs; some were standing against the walls. They all seemed to be in different stages of consciousness. Some looked like they were experiencing hysteria, flopping around in chairs and fighting against restraints. I swallowed the huge lump that had formed in my throat and managed enough air to scream again. I felt like I was suddenly thrust into a scary TV show, like *The Twilight Zone* or *Black Mirror.*

"Help me! Somebody help me! What the fuck is this!" I hollered with every ounce of power I had in my voice box. Some of the women looked at me, and some seemed like they were too spaced-out to even notice me. The big man finally lowered me from his shoulders and onto the floor.

"Be quiet. If you know like I know, you will just stand still and be quiet," the man hissed in my face.

I noticed he didn't wear a uniform like a CO, nor did he wear scrubs like some of the men who worked in the infirmary unit as orderlies or whatever they were. Instead, this gorilla of a man wore a polo shirt and jeans, which in a prison setting was odd to see. I hadn't seen anyone in street clothes in months, so it was a bit alarming. Did he even work for the prison? Had someone from outside sent him to get me? I had no idea who he was, and it didn't seem like I'd get my questions answered anytime soon.

"What the fuck is this place?" I asked through my chattering teeth. I hugged myself and looked around some more, astonished.

I kept looking around and around. My mind was racing with a billion crazy thoughts: *They're about to kill me. I'll never see my mother again. They are going to steal my organs and sell them on the black market. They're going to give me some incurable disease.*

I looked over and squinted at that CO that I thought was Anderson. His back was turned this time, though. The lights were so bright, I couldn't tell if it was actually him. He was standing there like a statue, not saying shit. I jumped when the door to the side of me swung open and five people filed into the room like soldiers ready to do their bidding. I could tell the people were either doctors or scientists because of the way they were dressed: white coats, holding clipboards, and most of them in glasses. Telltale nerd shit. And a bad sign for me. They all just looked like they were ready to experiment on somebody. I shivered as I thought about a scene from a mad-scientist movie I'd seen.

"This is Inmate Heiress, the last one requested," the man who'd carried me there said to the group. "Everything has been done to get her ready for incubation and then testing. All four phases have been completed, according to plan. She's ready on the scale of one to ten."

"*What!* What the fuck are you talking about? *Incubation?!*" I screamed.

Just as I did, the hulk bastard grabbed hold of my wrist, bent it at an angle, and twisted it. That shit made me drop to my knees. The pain rocked through my wrist and traveled up my arm so fast, I swear to God it hit me in the brain. He had done a pressure point hold on me. I'd heard about those being used in prison. *Damn!* That shit *hurt*! It actually made me dizzy.

"Ahh!" I shrieked, blinded by the pain.

"I told you to be quiet and stand still," the man said as he finally turned my wrist loose. I let out a long breath and used my good hand to hold on to my aching wrist. I stayed on the floor, shaking and ready to pee on myself.

"Back to what I was saying . . . African-American female, in the thirty-year category. Good health upon entering the program. No known history of diseases. Prime candidate for injection with K1250992, and pre- and post-testing of B1250993," the man told the group.

I could not believe my fucking ears. I was completely flabbergasted, to say the least. These motherfuckers were actually talking about giving me some unknown disease to test some unknown drug! The big man stepped closer to me and I shrank farther down to the floor. My body was curled into a ball. He didn't care. He grabbed me under both of my arms like I was a toddler and picked me up.

I finally got to see his face. He had a huge scar on the right side of his face that ran the entire length from his temple to his chin. His right eye was white and glassy, like he'd lost it in a fight or got it poked out. He looked like he'd been in one hell of a battle and had come out of it pretty fucked-up. His nostrils were large like an animal's, and they opened and closed every time he breathed. He was the ugliest person I had ever seen. He looked like a bad guy from a movie or comic book.

My heart sank into my stomach. This couldn't be good. Clearly, he had bad intentions and so did everyone in the room. In the hood, no one would believe me if I told this story. We always spoke conspiracy theories about shit they did to people in prisons, but I was living it.

"She's a prime candidate," the man said.

Another man stepped forward from the nerd group. He was a short white man with red hair. He wore thick oyster-shell glasses and had a red handlebar mustache, like the ones you'd think you'd only see in movies from the past. Although he was short, I could tell he was muscular. He had a thick neck and his white coat was tight on his thick arms. He reached out to touch my face and I immediately cowered away.

I turned my face away as tears slid down my cheeks. I wanted to run, but it was like my feet were stuck there. Besides, where would I run? I was in the belly of the prison or somewhere that was on lockdown and there was no escaping it.

"I see that she is in decent condition. Despite it all. Eyes look clear," the redheaded white man said, flashing a small pin-light in my eyes like I was a specimen being examined. This was the craziest thing I had ever seen. I felt like I was having a bad dream or like I'd gotten stuck inside a Stephen King novel.

"Okay—well, then, my work here is done. She's all yours to do whatever you see fit. But our company paid good money for this one, so make sure you get more than one use out of her. In other words, try not to kill her on the first try, like the last couple of disasters we had," the man who'd carried me there said.

When he said that, something inside me snapped like a string inside my brain had popped loose. I didn't know if it was the finality of it all or if it was just my natural-born instincts to survive. But I lifted my foot and kicked that big bastard in his balls so hard, I was surprised at my own strength. I kicked him so hard, I hurt my own foot and I almost fell doing it.

"Argh!" he growled, crumpling to the floor.

Then I stomped on the white doctor's foot, whirled around, and pushed through the group and beelined for the door. I made it out into that long-ass hallway and started hauling ass like my life depended on it, because it fucking did.

I could tell a bunch of them was chasing me, because even without looking back, I could hear the pounding of feet. I don't think I have ever run that fast in my life.

Whether I'd make it out of the area or not, I didn't have shit to lose at that point. I needed to get the fuck out of there. I was finally at another door and I heard a loud bang. I knew they couldn't have been shooting after me.

I felt something whiz past my face and then I felt a sharp pain in my back. My body lurched forward, and I became lit up with an electric jolt. I had been tased. Now I had a general idea of how people who got electrocuted in the electric chair felt. Even my brain buzzed with the shock of the electricity.

"No!" I screamed out as I crashed to the floor in what seemed like slow motion.

There were about twenty-five people running toward me now. I finally gave up and just lay down on the floor, crying. My body couldn't move. It was like I had no control over my limbs. I was fucked. The big guy was over me in no time. He grabbed me on the top of my head by my hair. I guess he was pissed I had kicked him in the balls and had run, which apparently wasn't part of whatever plan they had for me.

"Get the fuck up!" he growled. "You little stupid ass. You can't get out of here, no matter what you try."

I looked up into his face and he seemed more like a monster than he had earlier. I swore I saw demons dancing in his eyes. He dragged me back down that ominous hallway. Once we were back in the room, I noticed that the redheaded doctor was huddled with the others.

"She still has a lot of strength and cognitive ability, I see," the doctor commented. The other doctors were scribbling wildly on their clipboards. "We usually don't test on this type of subject. You told me she was ready."

"I'm sorry. That won't happen again. She was just losing her fucking mind for a minute," the hulk said. "She's definitely ready. I made sure of it."

"Our test subjects need to be in more of a weakened state. I don't know if she is right for this. We can't afford to have her corrupting the other test subjects who've been broken down," the doctor said.

"No, no. She's good. She will be perfect. That was just a fluke, I'm sure. We did everything by the book with this one," the big man said, sounding almost like he was pleading.

He sounded like a wimp all of a sudden. If I could have just put my hands around his throat, I would squeeze him until all of the life left his body. I hated him and I didn't even know him. The feelings were instantaneous, and they made my insides rage like an inferno.

"Okay. Let's get her undressed and tied down. We don't need another episode of that," a different man in a white coat said.

Still weak from the Taser shot I'd taken, I started weakly flailing and kicking again. *Fuck that! I am not going down without a fight.* That's when I got a look at the CO and it was Anderson! I could see him clear as day now. He was moving toward me with a stick in his hands.

"I'm not fucking taking off my clothes for nobody! I fucking cannot believe you, Anderson! You bastard! Why didn't you just let me die in solitary! You fucking traitor! Karma will catch up to you!" I screamed at the top of my lungs. I saw Anderson and the big guy coming toward me. I knew whatever was going to happen next wasn't going to be good.

"Shut the fuck up and take your fucking clothes off!" the big man gritted, grabbing me roughly.

"Fuck you!" I screamed, and I spit right in his fucking face.

He wiped my spit from his face and looked at me. His one good eye seemed as if it had turned completely red; he was so mad.

"I'm not taking—" I started to say, but my words were cut short.

The next thing I felt was a sharp pain in the back of my head. Somebody had definitely hit me, I was sure. Next the room started closing in around me and my ears were ringing. I had been knocked to the floor. I knew this because although my eyes were kind of out of focus, I remembered landing on the floor with a loud thud. Then darkness overcame me. All sight and sound had ceased for me.

I had definitely been knocked out, because I didn't remember a thing after that. And one thing was very clear and for sure, I wasn't leaving this place unless some kind of angel or miracle came through for me. I was laid out and not aware of what would happen next.

11

IN A LOT OF PAIN

When I opened my eyes, the pain that shot through the back of my head was crazy. I winced as I tried to get my eyes to focus on my surroundings. I started moving my arms and legs, and that's when I noticed I was tied down by my wrists and my ankles. It was a strange feeling and I was alarmed, to say the least. The restraints were painfully tight, and each time I flexed, they dug into my skin.

"What the fuck? Help!" I screamed out, fighting against the restraints.

But when I did that, the pain in my head just intensified and I was kind of forced to relax my ass back down on that bed. Every inch of my body ached like I'd been in a twelve-round boxing match with the old Mike Tyson.

"Hello," I heard a soft voice say to me.

I moved my head and looked to my left and then my right. I saw a petite black woman dressed in scrubs.

"I'm Lisa, a nurse, and I'll be here with you for a while." She was soft-spoken and had a calming smile on her face. "If you calm down, it'll make it easier on you," she said, smiling again. "It's the only way to make these days easier . . . not fighting."

I didn't know whether to curse her out or be nice, since she was being so nice to me. She was the first friendly face I'd seen in hours. Her name was familiar too, but I couldn't remember why. With my mind still so fuzzy, it hurt to even try to remember where I'd heard her name before.

"What are y'all doing to me?" I cried out as I tried to pull my arms and legs out of the restraints again. My skin felt like it would rip apart—that is how tight they had those things pulled.

"I'm not doing anything to you. I'm here to make sure you get what they want you to have, and that you don't vomit in your sleep and choke to death, or that your heart doesn't stop . . . things like that. You know, to keep you alive and thriving," Lisa said, and she went about taking my vital signs.

I can't even front. Although I was in a fucked-up position right now, that woman's voice was so soothing to me. She wasn't aggressive or mean at all, and she looked like she wouldn't harm a fly, because she was so small. If I wasn't so weak, in so much pain, and tied the hell down, I probably would have gotten up and tried to make a run for it, knowing damn well Lisa wouldn't be able to take me down.

"You should calm down and relax. There's really nothing you can solve by being upset, except you will make yourself sicker," she said.

"*Sicker?* I wasn't sick when they brought me here. So, how am I sick now? I need answers. I have rights. I'm a prisoner, but I know that I have rights!" I exclaimed.

"I understand," she said. "We'll need to get you cleaned up. I just want this to go easy. Can you cooperate with that?" she asked, her voice still level like I wasn't just screaming at her ass.

I sighed loudly. "I guess I have no choice," I relented, relaxing back on the bed. I closed my eyes and said a silent prayer. Then Lisa moved around the bed. She unlocked the arm restraints first. Of course, I was thinking about punching her and trying to escape, but I quickly changed my mind. First of all, my legs were still strapped down, and second of all, that hadn't worked out so well for me the last time.

Instead of fighting or trying to escape, I let Lisa help me get out of the dirty, disgusting hospital gown that I had been wearing for days after those bastards stripped me, probed my body like I was a lab rat, and knocked me the fuck out. She helped me sit up and get off of the bed. When I looked around at the place we were in, I was in awe. It was some kind of high-tech, *Back to the Future* type of laboratory.

There were ultramodern hospital beds, with all sorts of machines connected to them, and also computers and monitors and machines built into the walls. There didn't appear to be any doors, just glass windows that resembled observation decks. I could see through the glass in front of me and there were huge silver tanks behind the glass. There were people in white lab coats inside the room with the tanks, moving around them, jotting down information from small rectangular computerized boxes on the tanks. To the left of the beds was a table filled with syringes, gauze, pill bottles, and small bottles of liquid.

The inside of this place immediately reminded me of something from a science-fiction movie or book. It definitely was clear that this was some sort of testing laboratory. It wasn't something that I'd ever think I'd see inside a prison. It also wasn't someplace I had ever envisioned myself ending up.

"Where are we? What is this place?" I asked.

Lisa didn't answer, but she wore an eerie smile, almost a smirk. She was being weird. It was like she hadn't heard my question clearly.

"I'm not smiling or laughing. What the fuck is wrong with you? What is this place, and why am I here?"

Lisa's face got serious, but she still didn't answer me.

She continued getting stuff prepared for me to use for a bath.

My insides warmed up. I was getting angry. Forget being scared. I hated to be ignored. It made me feel like she was trying to play me like I was lame.

"I'm supposed to be in prison, not in a fucking lab, like a monkey or rat. This is not right. How are they getting away with this?" I kept talking, although she wasn't saying a word. "I know that I have basic human rights. I didn't consent to any of this. Whenever I get out of here, I'm going to sue, and I'll take it to the media. This shit is not right."

"Are you ready to get cleaned up now?" Lisa asked, ignoring my rant and still wearing a partial smile. There was something very scary about her, in a *Stepford Wives* type of way. Why was she just smiling like that? It was like she was high on something, because this was definitely no smiling matter. Lisa's eyes were vacant too. It made me wonder if they had programmed her in some sort of way. I thought that I was starting to sound crazy as hell, but I knew what I was seeing, and it wasn't normal.

Lisa led me into the bathroom, and it appeared to be out of place in the facility. There were regular old tiled prison shower stalls and old-fashioned sinks that had separate spouts for hot and cold water. There were scratched up Plexiglas mirrors above the sinks. The walls were supposed to be white, but as with everything else in prison, they were faded, old, and dingy until they appeared the color of yellow stomach bile.

The draft inside the bathroom felt like every window in the place was open. I was freezing and the goose bumps and chattering teeth gave that away. I looked around for anyone else, but it was just Lisa and me. I thought about trying to overpower her, but I changed my mind. I didn't even have the strength to fight a baby in that moment.

"Take all of the time you need. Just be sure to use the disinfecting soap that is in the pump in the shower. It may burn your cuts, but they'll heal, and they need cleaning," Lisa said.

When she said that, I looked down at my body, particularly my arms and legs. Sure enough, my arms and legs were covered in small cuts and scratches. I imagined I got those while I was fighting to escape from the bastard who'd snatched me out of my bed and brought me to this place. The memory of exactly what had happened to me was still very fuzzy in my mind. It hurt my brain to even try to remember every detail.

Lisa stood while I walked slowly into the shower stall. Clearly, there would be no privacy, as the stall did not have a curtain or any barrier to keep her from being able to see me. I inhaled deeply because the water was so hot, but it was also soothing. I exhaled and let the water run all over my body. With the way things had gone since I'd been whisked away to this crazy place, only God knew when I'd get another chance to take a shower.

"Be sure to use the soap," Lisa reminded me while she stood like a weirdo and just watched me.

She made me feel very uncomfortable, so I closed my eyes and just imagined that I was back home, in my old apartment living my old life. I pictured my mother and I thought about my grandmother and my cousin Jillian. It was a false sense of security, though. After about fifteen minutes, Lisa cleared her throat to remind me she was there.

"You need to wash good. Be diligent with every part of your body," she said.

I was thinking, *How is this bitch going to tell me how to wash? What business is it of hers whether I am clean or not?*

Ultimately I did as I was told. I washed my skin, over and over again. Not because she'd said so, but because I felt filthy.

"You have about six more minutes," Lisa said, peeking down at her watch.

She was getting on my nerves. I mean, even though she spoke softly and was fairly nice, she seemed nervous and was all of a sudden rushing me for some strange reason. Whatever she was on earlier looked like the shit was wearing off.

When I was done cleaning myself up, I went to get out of the shower. Lisa rushed over with a towel and damn nearly wrapped me in it like I was a toddler getting out of the bath. She helped me until I said I could do it myself. I swear it was like she thought I was a precious commodity that she was afraid would break or something.

Lisa led me back into the room where the bed was. I noticed that there was a fresh white hospital gown laid out on the bed.

"I'm in prison. I don't understand why I have to put on a hospital gown," I said, suspicion evident in my voice. "I'm not sick. So, what happened to the jumpsuit? This is just way too fucking weird for me," I grumbled.

"This is just what is worn in this unit," Lisa said in the blunt way she answered questions when she didn't want to elaborate. She'd responded like that a few times now. She wasn't always all smiles, which was weird. I wasn't sure if she switched up because of me or because she knew in certain places someone might be watching and listening. Either way, it was weird.

I had no clue what kind of shit I was about to endure. After I dressed in the gown, Lisa told me she was taking me to another room. She said it flatly, with no emotion.

"Where are we going?" I asked. "I think I have a right to know where I'm being taken and why."

Of course, she didn't want to answer the question or respond to my little rant about my rights. She was busy writing something down after looking at the huge digital clock that hung on the wall. She had done that every step of the way. She'd look up at the clock, jot something down, then look at me and jot more stuff down.

Don't ask me why I just went along with everything Lisa asked me to do, when I surely could have beat her ass and made a run for it. But I knew hitting her over the head and kicking her ass would be short-lived, because I was probably in the belly of the beast with no way out of there on my own. My head still hurt a little bit.

"Let's go," Lisa said. Then she nodded to the bed.

My eyebrows shot up into arches. I looked from Lisa to the bed and back again. I didn't understand what she meant. If we were moving to another room, why was she nodding at the bed?

"I can walk," I clarified, my face still folded into a confused frown.

"Not today," Lisa said. "It's not allowed during this time. You have to be transported on the bed. It's for everyone's safety."

She had her bullshit-ass response ready. I knew what the fuck she was doing.

"Well, I'm not going on the bed. This is crazy. I'm fine. If anything, y'all are making me leery about my safety with all of this shit," I replied.

She knew I wasn't trying to hear anything she was saying.

Lisa let out a long sigh. Then she walked over and pressed a button on the wall. My eyebrows dipped in the middle of my face as I watched her. *What the hell is that supposed to do?* I thought, but not for long.

With that, the door swung open and three men barged in. I whirled around, my eyes stretched wide and my heart started hammering. They immediately moved toward me like they were about to devour me. I knew what this meant. Since I wasn't trying to cooperate, then shit would be forced upon me. So I braced for impact.

"Transportation to room A, third subject," Lisa said to them in a flat, routine tone, as if she did this all day, every day. She carried herself like the head bitch-in-charge, all of a sudden. Gone was the smiling, meek, soft-spoken nurse that I had woken up to.

"No independent movement," Lisa said with finality. "No freedom."

At that, my ears perked up even more. What did she mean by "no independent movement"? I didn't have a chance to complete the question in my head before the men moved in, surrounded me, and forced me down onto the bed.

"No! Wait! Lisa! Wait!" I yelled out. "I can walk on my own. Please, I'm tired of being locked down and lying down. I need to stretch my legs."

She ignored me. Her face remained stoic. I don't think I had ever seen anyone shift personalities quite like that. She handed one of the men something.

"Hold and ready," he droned like a robot. Then he plunged a needle into my right thigh.

I opened my mouth to react to the sting, but it just went slack. My body and brain relaxed so fast; I couldn't control it. I felt tingly all over and I felt warm inside. I could see and hear, but I couldn't fight. It was as if whatever they'd given me gave them a remote control to my muscles, including my brain.

My body felt heavy, like it was full of lead. I watched the men move adeptly, working to strap me to the bed. I could follow them with my eyes, but nothing else was working. In my mind, I flailed and kicked, but in reality, my legs were lead pipes that couldn't move. When my ankles and wrist and midsection were secured to the bed with thick leather straps, I tried to move my head to the side, but I couldn't get my mind and body to cooperate. I was only able to move my eyes, and barely even those.

I watched Lisa pull out a cell phone and make a call. She spoke in a low murmur, so I couldn't hear exactly what she was saying. Plus, my mind was fuzzy as if cotton had suddenly sprouted on my brain. Damn, how I wished Lisa stood a few inches closer. I was eyeing the cell phone. That is what I needed to get my hands on. I needed to call my mother. I needed to call anyone who might help me. Maybe Sandra. Anyone on the outside that might come and bust me out of here, or at least get me a civil liberties attorney and fight for my basic human rights.

As I was being wheeled out of the room on the bed, I noticed all of the armed guards around. They seemed to be everywhere in that section of the prison facility. That was strange. This was definitely a different type of prison. Usually, COs didn't have weapons. I'd heard that was for their safety and for the safety of the inmates. This was different. I immediately felt sick. I was in an entirely different realm of the prison.

Fighting the sleep that was trying to take over me, I was wheeled through what seemed like a million mazes of corridors, elevators, and more corridors. We seemed to be moving for a long time. I could tell we were going deeper and deeper into the bottom of the building, because it got colder and darker. It smelled like funeral home flowers mixed with pungent disinfectant.

Finally I was wheeled into a door. That's when shit got crazy. My eyes roved around, and although I couldn't scream or talk, I could see clearly. There was a line of beds like mine with women lying on them. They were all dressed similar to me in hospital gowns, not prison jumpsuits. Some were awake, and some were knocked out. Some were strapped down, and some appeared too weak to move. Some cried. Some moaned. Some lay perfectly still, like maybe they were dead.

I wanted to scream, but the paralytic drug they'd given me wouldn't allow it. This was another room similar to before, but this room wasn't high-tech at all. It was more prisonlike and less laboratory-like, but it was in the same part of the prison. I could only wonder how many thousands of helpless state inmates were going through this same thing. And they couldn't do anything about it.

"Move her into position," Lisa said.

The men went about unstrapping me so I could be moved. I felt like a paraplegic, my body was heavy and numb. They dragged me over to an oversized chair with wires, probes, and monitors around it. They dumped me into it. There were different sounds filtering into my ears and I could hear the murmur of voices, but I couldn't see right away where they were coming from. It didn't take long, though.

Soon Lisa was joined by a huddle of doctors. The redhead with the handlebar mustache was back. He examined me, using his light again.

"Can you move, Ms. Heiress?" he asked. "Can you lift your hands or wiggle your fingers?"

In my mind, I was moving, but my body was stock-still. He reached over and pinched my arm. I felt the sensation of his pinch, but I didn't feel the pain. My eyes darted around, but I could not get my brain to cooperate with the rest of my body.

"She's ready," he said. "Bring me the specimens. Let's make this quick. I have several more of these to get done. I don't want to spend a lot of time on this one."

Ready? Ready for what?! I was screaming bloody murder in my mind, but only a series of short grunts came out of my mouth and nose.

Everyone in the room did as they were told. I noticed Lisa had fallen back. She seemed to have a glint of sympathy in her eyes now. I couldn't figure her out. It was strange. She had gone from smiling, to serious, to sympathetic. Something about her gave me pause. I was more and more convinced that she was being given drugs to make her act a certain way.

Probes were placed on my head, neck, and chest. My

arms were secured to the chair arms and my legs to the chair legs. There were bright lights shining down on me and I could feel the heat from the lights on my face. I looked out into the gathering crowd of doctors now filing into the room. It was crazy to me. They all seemed to be ready to see the spectacle. It looked just like some sort of science or premed class. When I looked up and over at the other women, some were watching. I could only wonder if they were trying to warn me with their eyes.

"Test subject ready. Record day one, first injection," the redhead boomed loud enough for the group to hear.

That's when all of the gathered people hurried to take notes and put their full attention on the doctor and me. I was suddenly grabbed on the top of my right arm. I fought to twist my head sideways, but, of course, I couldn't move. My eyes stretched painfully wide.

"Keep your face straight and eyes forward," a voice whispered to me from the side.

I felt a gun pressed up against the side of my head. It was one of the armed guards. But I couldn't understand why they'd need to do that when I was in a helpless position. It was a scare tactic that was over the top, and for no reason at all.

Or maybe it was to serve the purpose of scaring the holy shit out of me so that I would be compliant for the rest of my time here. It worked. I was scared shitless.

I immediately closed my eyes. Then I felt the excruciating pain of a huge needle being plunged into my tiny arm. All I could do was scream inside. I was buried alive in my own body. The numbness I was experiencing on the rest of my body was no match for the needle they used. I could feel my body straining because of the pain I was feeling, but with no way to let it out.

My heart felt like it would explode. My insides churned as if all of my organs were being put through a meat grinder. My head pounded and I felt my eyes roll up into my head. I sucked in my breath because I felt like I was going to suffocate. I don't know what the hell they had put into my body, but I knew it was serious.

What happened next amazed the fuck out of me. Some of the other women in the room started screaming as if they could feel my pain. My eyes came back down, and I looked around strangely, eyes wide like a trapped animal's. Out of the corner of my eye, I noticed that one of the girls had jumped up from her bed and dashed toward me.

"Help her," the girl said robotically. "Help her. Help her. Help her," she kept repeating. She was running toward me one minute and crumpled on the floor the next.

One of the armed guards had handled her real quick with a crack to the head with the butt of his gun. I screamed inside my head, but that did me no good. I was feeling faint. This was some sick shit, for real.

Whatever they'd injected me with felt like it was spreading over my body like a black massive blob. It was thick and slow and oozing into my organs like a plague. I wheezed for air and tried to suck in as much breath as I could, but I knew there was nothing I could naturally do. They had probably injected me with some terminal disease.

As I sat there suffering, I saw my entire life flash before my eyes. The mere fact that they were experimenting on human beings told a lot about my fate. I was officially these people's guinea pig. A fucking lab rat.

So I'd lost all confidence that I would make it out of this place alive.

12

DEATHBED

I awoke convulsing on a bed. My body jerked and flopped, and there was nothing I could do to stop it. Blood leaked out of my nose and ran down my face, neck, and chest. I couldn't stop my body from violently thrashing, and I felt like my bladder would explode at any moment. Wherever they had me now, it was freezing cold, like I was lying on a block of ice. When my body finally stopped involuntarily bucking, I felt extremely weak. I heard voices around me, but it sounded more like buzzing than talking. The room spun as if I had just gotten off of a high-speed ride at an amusement park.

"She's conscious," a man's voice sounded off. I braced myself because I didn't know what was coming next. I had been injected several more times over the night—that much I knew. I felt like I had the worst flu you could imagine—body aches, fever, chills, and, now, convulsions with stabbing pains all over. Sweat drenched me, and maybe that's why I was so cold. I felt like I was dying. I couldn't imagine making it out of this. I hadn't ever been this sick in my life.

"Please," I slurred, but that was for nothing. It was clear

that these very dangerous people were not going to have any mercy on my body or my soul. Whatever experiments they had in mind were more important than my human rights. That much was clear to me. I saw the redheaded doctor approaching my bed. He represented danger in my eyes. Every time I saw him, something terrible was done to me afterward. He was the Devil, if you asked me. He terrified me.

"Ahh." I let out a weak scream as the doctor got closer to me. "Please don't," I whimpered, my words sounding like I was intoxicated. My tongue felt heavy and my head ached.

I didn't know how much more my body would be able to take. My face was scrunched and fear played out across it. Sweat poured from every pore on my body and danced in jagged lines down the sides of my face. I gagged, but nothing came up from my stomach. The waves of nausea were so strong that I was sure my entire gut would come up out of my mouth.

My heart pounded painfully against my weakened chest bone and my stomach churned. At that point, I prayed for death, because nothing else seemed fitting. Another syringe filled with poison, and I was sure I'd be dead.

The redheaded doctor ran his hand gently down the side of my face. "Seems like it is working," he said eerily. "The disease is progressing quickly, as we suspected. I see the symptoms, and soon the test subject will be fully incubated. I think this one will implant successfully. Now let's just hope we can find the right medication to reverse it," he continued, smiling slyly.

When his fingers got close to my mouth, I moved my head, opened my mouth quickly, and tried to catch hold of his finger. I wasn't fast enough. I would've bit his shit off, I swear to God.

"Oh!" The doctor jumped. Guards rushed over. "She tried to bite me," he grumbled, seemingly unfazed. "Another dose should take care of that," he said. "She won't have the strength of a newborn baby soon. That's when this gets fun."

"But Dr. Clemons, wouldn't that be overdosing? The medicine only has the capacity to maybe cure . . . ," Lisa said, stepping up.

I was glad to see her. She appeared to be a reasonable person. She wore a look of genuine concern.

I finally learned the name of the redheaded doctor: Dr. Clemons, the equivalent of the Devil himself. Even his hair was red—red like the Devil.

"Lisa! Help me!" I struggled to get the words out as my body jerked fiercely from another painful shot in my arm muscle.

"Please let me go," I mumbled, my words came out labored and almost breathless. "Just kill me and let me go in peace," I whispered through dry, cracked lips.

Suddenly I had that feeling in my lungs again. I began coughing and wheezing as everyone stood on, watching. It was almost unreal what I was going through. I was in a position of total helplessness. I was weak and useless. My eyelids closed on their own, and I saw my mother's face. She was crying. She was calling out my name. She was surrounded by men in suits, carrying guns. She was in grave danger. Then suddenly she was starting to fade away, fast.

"Mommy," I panted. "Don't let them kill me. Please save me."

I spoke as if my mother was right there. I squinted my eyes and swore I saw my mother standing right there, but the bright lights the doctors were using brought me back to reality. I was hallucinating. I figured that I would probably never see my mother again.

I could hear the voices around me clearly, though, so I knew I was still in prison. Suddenly I heard another familiar voice. I jumped and whipped my head to the left. Then it seemed like the voice moved to the right. I whipped my head that way.

"You betrayed us, Misty. You and your cousin thought you could outsmart us. I should have never trusted you. I should have known that such a ghetto bitch would turn on us. You dishonored my family. You got too big for yourself. I would've let you have a good life, but you didn't know how to act. You thought the feds were your friends. Now look at you! Look what they've let happen to you," the voice said.

Finally, it hit me. It was Ahmad's voice.

"Help me! Don't let him get me!" I screamed, shivering all over. "He's trying to kill me! Don't let him kill me! Help me!"

Ahmad had stepped around the bright light and I could see every feature of his face. He had a gun to my mother's head and she was sobbing. He cocked the hammer of the gun and pressed it harder to my mother's temple.

"No! I didn't have a choice. I was always loyal to you. I didn't have a choice. I didn't kill your family. It wasn't me. I did everything you asked for. I was prepared to trade my life. What more could I do, Ahmad? Now you have my mother. You can't kill her! She's all I have in the world! You can't kill her!" I cried, saying the words, pleading over and over again. I had worked myself into a frenzy. More coughs erupted from my chest and out of my mouth. "Help me!" I cried out. "I'm going to die!"

"Enough!" Lisa screamed. "She is hallucinating to the point of hysteria. Give her the medicine, or you'll send her into cardiac arrest. This is a lot on her body. You've overdone it! Stop it, right now!" she demanded. "You have taken things too far, too many times now, Dr. Clemons. You're bordering on inhumane and unethical practices, and I'll not stand for it anymore," she gritted.

The doctor squinted his eye and rounded on Lisa, like he was about to snatch her voice box out.

"You listen to me, Nurse Sanders. This is my test subject and my test. *I* say when it's enough. You do as I tell you to do, and you shut your mouth. I am the boss here," Dr. Clemons gritted. Then he came beside my bed and flashed his light in my face again. "If I want to kill her right now, it is my prerogative. When these nobodies are sent here, I get to do as I please with them. Who is going to care? All of a sudden, you have so many morals? Yeah, right. If you did, you wouldn't work here. I get to do as I please. Nobody can stop me, and with them, nobody cares," he said with a hint of sick satisfaction in his tone.

I heard his words, but I couldn't believe my ears. It was a lot to handle. I had never thought of myself as a *nobody* or someone who would ever be in the position where I had no one who cared about me. My heart was breaking. It was worse than any pain I had ever experienced.

"She is still a human being," Lisa challenged. "You still have standards to work by. You can't do all of this. I don't care what you say! This is wrong."

"Nurse Sanders, you can be excused if you can't stomach what we do here. We've spoken about this before," Dr. Clemons said. "You can also be released. I don't have a problem with either. Or you can get on board and do your job in silence, which is what we actually pay you to do. Now I won't hear another word from you, or you'll be locked out of here and I'll have your nursing license in my shredder by morning."

"Mommy! I'm so sorry! I just wanted to make things better. Just kill me, Ahmad, and let my mother go! It is me that you want! I was the one who brought all of the heat to your door and pulled the lid off of your business!" I cried out. The images of Ahmad and my mother faded in and out. "Mommy! Don't go! Please stay!" I screamed.

"Shut her up. Administer more heavy sedation before the drug dosage. She is ready for the next phase immediately," Dr. Clemons said, nodding toward his flunkies.

The orderlies, or whatever they were, immediately surrounded me. My heart rattled in my chest, but there was nothing else they could do to me that would hurt me more than I'd already been hurt. I gave up at that moment. Whatever was going to happen must've been my fate from the beginning, I reasoned with myself. I kept screaming out for my mother. I kept asking for God's forgiveness.

After a few minutes, one of those huge guys grabbed me by my hair and yanked my head.

"Agh!" I screamed. I felt like my neck would pop. I don't know how after all of those hours, I hadn't gone into shock.

"Get off of me! Get the fuck off of me!" I screeched so loudly that my throat itched. It took every ounce of strength I had to get those words to come out. "Fuck all of you! You're all going to burn in hell for what you're doing!"

I felt blood rushing to places on my body that I didn't know even existed. I mustered up all of the strength I could—and trust me, it was not a lot. I managed to buck my body wildly. All of my fighting efforts were to no avail.

Of course, they were stronger than me. Of course, I wasn't going to be able to break free, but it just made me feel slightly better inside to try.

The man holding me finally let go of the fistful of my hair he had been roughly grabbing. He released me with so much force that my head slammed to the bed. I was dazed for a few seconds, but not for long. I was brought back to reality when I felt the last syringe plunge into my thigh. The force was so great that I swore it broke off in my muscle.

"You don't have such a big mouth now, huh?" the orderly hissed. "This time, we get to enjoy you as a reward."

"Please don't hurt me anymore," I slurred. I had no idea what he meant by that, but I was certain they would make sure I found out.

"It is too late for that. You are here for good, and there's only one way out of here," Dr. Clemons whispered next to my ear. "The only way out is through me. I say when, or you'll be mine forever."

The next thing I knew, blackness engulfed me. I couldn't tell if I was dead or alive.

13

MY MIND PLAYING TRICKS ON ME

The ticking sound from a clock somehwere in the room seemed loud in my ears.

Tick. Tock. Tick. Tock. It was like my senses were hyper-sensitive because I would swear that clock was right up against my ear.

I hadn't heard that sound before. A ticking clock was something I would've remembered. Most of the clocks I'd seen since I'd been snatched into this nightmare were big digital ones, with glowing green numbers. A clock with a second hand was odd, and it was different from anything I'd seen here. It was the first sign that something was drastically different.

A chill shot down my back. I knew instinctively I was in a different place than I'd been when I blacked out . . . again. My eyes fluttered open and landed straight on the bright white paint on the ceiling. It was so bright, it stung to look at it. I turned my head slightly and, through caged windows, I could see the sky outside.

That was a first. I hadn't been in a place with windows in weeks, or maybe it was months by now. I'd lost count of days and times. I'd lost count of the last time I'd actually seen my mother or had spoken to her. I'd lost all sense of who I was and where I belonged.

"You're awake," Dr. Clemons said, with a sly smile on his lips.

I jumped at the sound of his voice. I wasn't expecting him, nor had I seen him lurking. I darted my eyes around frantically.

"Where am I? What—what is going on?" I asked. My voice was gruff and shaky with apprehension.

There was no one else in the room. That was a first. Usually, he had a group of doctors with him, or Lisa would be there, or even the armed guards or a CO or two. When I realized we were alone, I grew suspicious right away.

"No need to worry," Dr. Clemons said. Then he moved closer to me.

"No," I said, but it was too late. He stuck me. I was so sick of being drugged, it wasn't even funny. I had huge purple marks on my arms and legs from all of the injections. The shit was out of hand now.

"Ms. Heiress, you're a beautiful woman," Dr. Clemons said, smiling like he'd been friendly all of this time.

I heard the lust in his voice. I was very adept at picking up lust in men's voices. As a child navigating a family full of perverted uncles, I knew the tone right away. It was the first time Dr. Clemons had changed from all scientific and business to this. I was high from whatever he'd given me, but I wasn't so high that I couldn't tell this was different. He wasn't doing any medical testing.

"Your skin is so soft," he said, running his hand down my face.

I whipped my head to the right and shrank away from his touch.

Dr. Clemons grabbed my arm tightly and moved his face closer to mine. He held on to my arm like he could sense that I wanted to run away.

"If you fight, it just turns me on," he said. He wore a wicked smile. Then he let out a sick laugh, which caused every hair on my body to stand up.

"Please don't," I slurred, barely able to get the words out.

"Aw, you want to be nice now? This is all part of the punishment for what you did," Dr. Clemons said, smiling like he'd actually said something funny.

When he smiled, I saw how the evil played out over his face. It was like I was left alone with the Devil.

"I am here against my will," I said, my eyes going low. "I have rights and you can't do this to me. I know my rights. I will have you arrested," I continued.

Of course, it got me nowhere fast.

"Your *rights*? You gave up all of those rights when you committed murder, and when you murdered the wrong person. No one cares about your *rights* anymore, Heiress. You're mine now, and that's that," he said in an irritated tone. "I run this show, so you just better get used to it."

With that, Dr. Clemons pulled off the sheet, licked his lips, and began groping my titties and then my legs and ass as he stared at me. I swear, it was grossing me out.

"Don't!" I said, but that just seemed to spur him on even more.

He stuck his hand up under the hospital gown and fiddled with my pussy. After a few minutes, I could feel his fingers penetrate me. I instinctively snapped my thighs shut tightly. That didn't stop him, though.

"No sense in fighting," he said when he felt my resistance. "There's a million ways I can make you give me what I want, but I will try the easy way first. I like the easy way, but the hard way turns me on too." He continued acting and sounding like a freaking rapist.

I swallowed hard, but I wasn't budging.

He forced my thighs apart and rammed two of his fingers inside me.

"Oww! I swear, you won't get away with this." Tears

drained out the sides of my eyes. I wished that I could spit fire at his disgusting ass.

"I always do. No one cares that you're here. You're lost to the system now. You're all mine to do as I please, when I please," Dr. Clemons reminded me again.

He probed my insides like the sick fuck that he was. He grabbed my hand and placed it down into his crotch. I closed my eyes and willed my brain to take me to another place mentally. Dr. Clemons used my hand to rub his dick through his pants. I swear, he was rubbing for about ten minutes and I could barely feel even the least little bit of anything. That meant he had the smallest dick I'd ever felt.

He was grunting like a bear or some sort of animal as he forcefully groped himself, using my hand. I was so disgusted and angry. I could feel a knot growing in the pit of my stomach. I was fuming inside. I swore right there that if I ever got out of this, I would find a way to kill this sick bastard. I had nothing to fucking lose, anyway. Some people really deserved to die, and I decided in that moment that he was one of them.

Dr. Clemons's grimy hands moved all over my body. All I wanted to do was take a long, scalding-hot shower right then. As I rubbed his dick, I felt his cell phone in his pocket. My mind immediately perked up. I worked my hands until I made it fall out of his pocket and onto the bed. He was so into being a pervert that he didn't even notice that it had fallen.

I made a mental note to grab it before he saw it. I knew that phone was my only hope of an escape at this point. It was the only hope of getting some contact to anyone on the outside.

"You ready for the next phase?" Dr. Clemons asked.

Like he really thought I'd answer: *Yes, baby, I am.* He was truly sick.

I looked around and I still didn't see another soul. No Lisa. No guards in the room. No other patients. It was clear he'd brought me there to do his dirty deeds in secret. I wondered how many others he did this to in a day.

Dr. Clemons climbed off of the bed and walked to the other side of the room. As soon as he did, I grabbed his cell phone and stuck it into the pillowcase. My heart was racing. I was scared he would miss his phone and start looking for it, and then he would figure out I had it and I'd be punished. There was no telling what he'd do.

It looked like Dr. Clemons was feeling around in his pockets, like he was trying to find something. My teeth started chattering from my nerves. *Shit! I hope he doesn't realize it's gone!* I knew he was looking for his cell phone, so I hurried up and tried to get his mind off of it.

"Somebody is going to find out about this," I blurted. "You'll be arrested and your cover will be blown. You can't get away with what you're doing. We have rights."

I was hoping I could distract him. It worked.

He turned around on his heels, with a mean scowl on his face. He was distracted by his immediate anger over my threats. My plan had worked like a charm. He rushed over to me; his eyes squinted into dashes. In my head, I was screaming, *Your dumb ass fell for it!*

"You need to shut your mouth. You talk too much, Heiress," he growled. "I'm the boss around here and what I say goes. So it doesn't matter who finds out about it. No one is coming to rescue you. Don't you understand? Neither the system nor society cares about your black ass. Obviously, neither does your family, because we haven't received one call from administration saying your family is looking for you. What does that tell you? You're a nobody, and I can use you up and no one will care."

"You're evil. And, like my grandmother always said, you can't get away with evil without being repaid for it by karma. White devils always get what they deserve," I shot back.

At that point, it didn't matter what he did to me. He

couldn't demoralize or dehumanize me any more than they already had in every way possible—and now he was taking it to an even lower point.

Before I knew it, Dr. Clemons slapped me across the face. My head jerked incredibly hard; I felt like it would separate from my neck. My hand went up to my cheek and I tried to rub away the pain. It throbbed.

"Take off everything," he breathed, panting like a fire-breathing dragon.

I closed my eyes, but I didn't comply.

"Suit yourself. We can do this the hard way," he said. Then he moved closer to me. He leaned in and inhaled deeply, sniffing my hair, then moving to my tits and my groin.

It was just sick. I felt myself gagging. The only thing keeping me sane was the fact that one good thing had come out of this: I had his cell phone.

I could not understand his need to sniff me. I felt like bugs were crawling all over my skin. I was numb from all the shit I had been through, so I just lay there—motionless and emotionless. I thought about the cell phone in my pillow. Then I began picturing my mother's face or something more pleasant so that I wouldn't start screaming.

After a few more minutes of groping, Dr. Clemons walked to the door and tapped on it three or four times, like he was summoning someone.

I was confused and crinkled up my face. As if they'd been waiting all along, two men, dressed like the regular orderlies, came into the room. They were scrambling frantically to get to where I was lying. One of them grabbed my left arm and the other grabbed my right arm. I started flailing. *Not again!* I was so sick of this shit. I was living in a constant torture chamber in this place.

"What are y'all doing?" I cried out.

They didn't answer. Instead, they stretched me out and then they tied my arms above my head. I got a good look at one of their faces and his name tag. It read: BARKER. I was going to remember him too. I was going to start compiling my revenge list for when or if I ever got out of here.

"What the fuck? Get off of me!" I let out an ear-shattering scream.

I knew it was all for nothing, though. I knew not a damn soul on the outside would hear me. They kept manhandling me and I could hear chains jingling. There was no way I was going to let them chain me down. They were going too damn far now.

"What the fuck are you doing?!" I shrieked. I could feel my face filling up with blood. My temples pulsed.

Then Dr. Clemons's flunkies put my legs in some sort of leg irons. One thing I hated was to be tied down. I had a fear of restraints, so this position and constantly being tied up and strapped down was making me absolutely crazy.

Tears ran down the sides of my eyes. I kept looking all around, and then I noticed that there were bondage and sadomasochistic tools on a little table. This bastard was obviously into pain, bondage, and torture-type sex. No wonder he had to use helpless prisoners.

Now it was clear why that girl Lena had come back dripping blood after she'd been gone. I couldn't even imagine what he had in store for me. I couldn't imagine the atrocities he'd committed against women in the prison.

My stomach churned and I fought against the restraints when I saw that stuff. I was pulling my hands and trying to kick my feet. My efforts were futile.

After a few minutes, those orderlies got it done. I was secured tightly to that bed. My mind was running a million miles a minute. I had no idea what to expect from this sick fuck now. When the men all left, Dr. Clemons undressed himself.

At first, I watched so I would know when he was coming for me. However, the more I looked at him, the more I was spurned to turn my eyes away. His body looked worse naked than it did with clothes on. He had a layer of red hair on his chest and stomach that resembled a nasty carpet. The hair was shaggy and straight. It covered him, and he looked like a caveman or a monkey. His stomach was a hard six-pack and his arms were full of thick, defined muscles, but his dick was tiny. No wonder he had to rape inmates; he probably couldn't get a woman on his own.

When Dr. Clemons came over to the bed, he was smiling evilly. I started bucking again, but it was useless once more. He was clearly amused at my efforts to get out of the restraints. He laughed. Standing over me, he bent down and put his face on top of mine.

"Agh!" I screamed, and started squirming, but that was a big mistake.

As soon as I opened my mouth wide to scream, Dr. Clemons stuck his tongue into my mouth.

"Mmmm," I grunted, trying to fight to move my head.

He was holding my head in place, and the harder I fought, the more pain shot through my neck. He kissed me so deeply, I felt like I would swallow his tongue. He was pushing it practically down my throat. I was gagging and felt like I would throw up.

When he finished, I could smell the stink smell of his saliva on my upper lip. I was racked with sobs by then and my body shook all over.

He was breathing hard, like an animal, clearly excited by his sick acts. As he continued his assault, I screamed loudly and bucked my body so hard that I became dizzy.

Again, he seemed amused. He started laughing hard, like he'd been told a joke. Dr. Clemons got so turned on that he reached down and stroked himself. Then he got up off the bed and got a long black whip from his torture table.

"Please! No, please. I will do anything!" I pled, pulling my arms and trying to lift my legs. I could feel the arm restraints cutting into my wrists as I continued to fight hard against them.

"Don't worry. I don't care if you scream," he said. He picked up the whip and slapped me across my bare thighs with it.

"Arg!" I belted out in sheer pain.

He hit me again, and this time, I could feel welts rising on my skin. My legs shook from the sharp pain.

"Please!" I was sobbing and begging him for mercy. I screamed and begged countless times. But I quickly realized that the more I screamed and pled, the more turned-on he got, so I stopped. I didn't want to give him the satisfaction anymore, so I just bit down into my jaw and took the pain.

When his sick ass realized that the whip wasn't doing any more damage that would get a reaction out of me, he moved to his next form of torture. I saw out of the corner of my eye when Dr. Clemons picked up a huge oblong object. I couldn't tell what it was at first, but he brought it over to the bed and put the object between my legs. He forced it into me so hard that I had no choice but to scream out. Nobody that was human would've been able to take that kind of pain.

"Help me!" I hollered.

It felt like whatever he was using to abuse me would come through the top of my head. That's how far he was ramming up in me. I was in excruciating pain. My abdomen felt like it would burst. No amount of disease he could've injected me with would have been worse than this sexual abuse.

I screamed some more as he grinded the object, stretching my vaginal walls to capacity. He was smiling and grunting as sweat dripped from his body onto mine. He was clearly highly aroused by all of this. As he did everything that he could to bring me pain, I bit down on my bottom lip until I drew blood. But again, I muffled my screams, because the screams were fueling his satisfaction. He finally took the object out of me.

I felt relieved, but I knew he wasn't finished with me yet. By then, my thighs were shaking uncontrollably, and I just knew I'd go into shock any minute.

Dr. Clemons came and straddled me. I could barely breathe. He slapped me. It was so demoralizing. I think something inside me died forever. A piece of me that I can never get back died inside me. Dr. Clemons slapped me in my face again.

"This was more fun than I expected, Heiress," he said, and then he slapped me again.

My head was pounding. He slapped me, side to side, over and over again. Blood was on my nose and lips, and my legs and arms were burning with pain. I was so weak I couldn't even control my head. I felt like dying.

When Dr. Clemons was finished with me, he left me there. My wrists and hands were numb from being tied and my body burned all over. As hard as I fought it, I could not keep sleep from overcoming me. Within a matter of minutes, and before I knew it, I was knocked out.

I don't know how long I slept before I felt Lisa slapping my cheek softly to wake me up. When I opened my eyes, there were three people in the room. I moaned, which was all I could really do.

I could tell I looked a mess by the way Lisa gawked at me. She untied my hands and I immediately started flexing my wrists because they hurt so badly. She helped me sit up, and I swear I felt like I was a newborn baby. My back was just so slack and weak. I was too fucked-up to even think about getting that cell phone out of the pillowcase.

My mind was muddled. I didn't remember, but I believed Dr. Clemons had given me something before I went to sleep. I couldn't remember if I had been injected again.

"Are you all right?" Lisa asked the obvious question.

Of course, I wasn't all right. I was being tortured, abused, raped, and experimented on, with no hope for it to stop.

"Let me help you clean up a little before they move you," she said. She started washing me with some sort of sweet-smelling soap. She even brushed my hair back into a neat ponytail and put ointment on the cuts I had sustained. "You're going to be okay. I'll make sure of it," she whispered.

"What happens to me now?" I asked. My throat was so dry that the words came out sounding gravelly.

"You go back," one of the men in the room answered before Lisa could say anything. I guess he wanted her to know *not* to try anything funny to help me.

"Back where?" I asked. I looked at Lisa with pleading eyes. "Please don't let them keep doing this to me. I don't think I can take much more."

I didn't know if they were taking me back to the high-tech experiment room, the hole, or the other rooms where I had been moved through, tied down, and injected with drugs and diseases. It was all too much. My body was in a weakened state; it was so bad, even my teeth and fingernails hurt.

"Back wherever they say you go," the man told me.

Well, that didn't help. My heart sank. I'd been beaten and tortured in every way possible. I knew one thing for sure: I had to get out of there. Who would know if I got killed in this place? I really still couldn't believe this whole human-experimentation thing. It seemed more lucrative than the drug game. Woman after woman had been put into this unit by pretending to be suicidal or having some other psychotic condition.

After I was cleaned up, Lisa must've noticed how weak I was. She gave me some water and it hurt going down. It landed in my stomach like a ton of bricks. When I finished gulping down the water, I could tell it was time to go. Tears started coming out of my eyes. I was urgently thinking, *Misty, you have to get the hell out of this shit.*

I grasped the cell phone under the pillow and held on to it for dear life.

It would be a challenge hiding the cell phone. I knew I'd have to get creative, and I'd have to call someone before the battery died. I didn't know where my mother was, and wasn't sure if she even still had the burner phone I'd given her when everything was happening.

I had memorized Sandra's number, which she gave me when I was getting transferred. Thank God I had taken her advice and committed her phone number to memory. She was my last hope for some help. So, when I was left alone and they thought I had been drugged enough to be knocked out, I made the call.

As I dialed Sandra's number, my heart almost pounded out of my chest. I thought my hands were so sweaty that I'd lose my grip on the small device. I didn't know why I didn't just call the police first and tell them what was happening. I guess I had lost faith in the whole criminal justice system. Shit, imagine receiving a call from some crazy-sounding woman saying she was locked in a prison and they were experimenting on her with diseases and drugs and now raping her. The 911 operator would've probably thought it was a hoax and hung up on me.

My hands were trembling so bad, I could barely hold on to the phone. It started ringing on the other end of the receiver and I was praying silently that Sandra picked up soon. After the third ring, I started getting very nervous that she might not answer.

"C'mon! C'mon, pick up the phone," I mumbled under my breath. Finally, just as I thought I would hear her voice mail, I heard Sandra's deep voice come through the receiver, instead.

"Hello," she answered.

My shoulders slumped down with relief, and for a few seconds, I was at a loss for words. I still felt like my escape or any help was all a dream.

"Hello?" Sandra whispered into the phone.

I was crying so hard. I shed tears of relief and joy.

"Sandra. It's Misty. I need your help," I whispered in desperation.

"Misty! Where the hell are you?!" Sandra yelled.

I could hear the mixture of excitement and concern in her words.

"I've been waiting to hear from you. You a'ight?"

"Shush," I told her. I couldn't afford for anyone to hear. "I need you, Sandra," I said breathlessly. I was crying again so hard that I was out of breath. "I need your help now or I'm going to be dead. This is no joke. They're going to kill me."

"Okay, Misty, but I need to know what the hell is going on and where the hell you're at. The last time we spoke—" Sandra started, but I quickly cut her off.

I didn't have time for all of the small talk. I needed to deal with this present situation and the fact that I needed to get out of it.

"I am in a prison somewhere, and they are doing things to us here," I explained. The sobs wouldn't let me get my words out effectively, though. "They . . . they're doing things . . ."

"Oh my God! Things like what?" Sandra asked, urgency lacing her words.

"They're experimenting on us and raping us. It's the medical-testing unit. I'm going to die if you don't find me. Look up state prisons that may be contracting to private companies," I relayed as fast as I could.

"Fuck! I'm going to work on my end to come and find you," Sandra promised.

"You don't understand. I will die if you don't come soon.

I can't take much more of this. They will kill me," I cried. I knew to Sandra I sounded crazy.

"I am going to find you and send help for you. I promise, Misty. I won't leave you for dead," Sandra said.

"Please hurry. I don't have much more time," I said with finality. "I'll be dead soon."

"No, you won't. I'll make sure of that," she said.

With that, I ended the call and hid the phone again. My mind was going crazy with thoughts. I couldn't rest thinking about getting out of this place. I tried to use the phone to call my mother, but I couldn't get her. I started praying in earnest that she was safe and sound. But, with the way my life was going, I wasn't hopeful about anything good.

14

THE SECRET ROOM

Over the next few days, Dr. Clemons did it again and again. I always knew when he'd taken me back to his secret room, because that clock ticked loudly and I'd come to recognize the smell in that room. It was a mixture of medicine and sex. That led me to believe I wasn't his only victim.

It only took a few minutes before the thump of my heartbeat matched the loud tick of that wall clock. I shook all over and my vision was blurry. I moaned. It was a little trick I had learned to stay conscious whenever he drugged me up. I was being moved; I could feel myself being shifted around. My consciousness was becoming harder to hold on to. He'd used something much stronger on me this time, because I'd grown immune to all the shit they were putting in my body now.

Little squirms of light flashed through my eyes and I had to concentrate to make myself blink them away. My eyelids felt as though weights had been put on them. I knew this feeling always came right before I usually succumbed to the drugs.

I had been drugged so many times, I felt like a drug side-effects expert. I'd come to know that if I blinked and moaned and forced myself to move any muscle on my body, the medicine took longer to overcome me.

I moaned again; this time, I became painfully aware of a throbbing pain in my scalp. I lifted my hand in slow motion and attempted to place it on top of my head. It took a few tries, but finally I was able to touch the source of the pain. My heart rate sped up when I realized

Dr. Clemons had a tight grasp on a fistful of my hair. He was sick—that much I had learned by now.

"You won't remember shit," he grunted lustfully, clamping down harder on my hair.

Then I heard his zipper being undone. My head felt more wavy than it had in the past. It had to be a new and even stronger medication than I had been forced to ingest this time.

Immediately, the funky, musty smell of Dr. Clemons's dick caused the acids in my stomach to bubble up into the back of my throat. I gagged. I didn't know how long I could take the strong odor. I couldn't believe what was happening. This motherfucker was about to do some dirty shit to me. Thinking about it made me mentally and physically sick. I was tired of this. I wasn't going to stand for it anymore.

Forcing myself to swallow caused my head to spin a little bit. I gagged again.

"All you have to do is be a good girl. Don't fight or you'll make this worse than it has to be. Be a good girl and get it hard," Dr. Clemons ordered, a lascivious smile spreading across his face.

Then he swiped the head of his flaccid, nasty, moist dick across my tightly clenched lips, like it was the tip of a lipstick. The feeling of the moist, clammy skin on me caused another swirl of nausea to invade my stomach; this time, I locked my jaw tight.

Even with my head swimming, I felt emotional and tears

leaked out of my eyes. My entire body felt hot, like I had a fever. Darkness had tried to creep up on me several times, but I fought the effects of the medication by moaning and blinking. Dr. Clemons lifted his limp noodle and beat it on my lips this time. This was his sick attempt to get me to open my mouth and give in to his demands.

All I could think about was, where were Lisa and the other doctors? How could this bastard be getting away with this, over and over again, and they didn't know or didn't help? My eyes started to close again, and Dr. Clemons yanked on my hair to make sure my eyes didn't shut. He'd given me just enough drugs to make me too weak to fight, but not enough to put me completely out. This way, I could continue to complete his sick requests. I'd heard about rapes happening in prison, but never did I think I would be a victim like this.

"Open your fucking mouth," he whispered through labored breaths.

I still refused to open my mouth. My tears fell in streams. I don't know if that gave this sick bastard a thrill, but I couldn't help it. So much ill shit had happened to me, and it had become so regular now, that I had conditioned myself to go numb, but it hadn't worked this time.

I had been practicing how to fight against the effects of the medication they always forced on me too. This was a skill that had proven more valuable than anything else I had learned during my time locked up in that medical-testing unit.

It's mind over matter. Mind over matter, I chanted to myself. *Mind over . . .* But my thoughts kept slipping away.

Dr. Clemons dragged me down to the floor, and my burning knees were what let me know I had been on them for too long. He held my head in an awkward position and my neck ached from it.

"I said open your fucking mouth, you bitch! Don't act like you don't know how to do this. You ghetto bitches probably learn how to do this at ten years old," he hissed, forcing my face farther into his musty crotch. "Open your fucking mouth, I said," he grunted, frustration and lust lacing his words.

I grunted as my body jerked forward from the force of his shove, causing my face to scrape against Dr. Clemons's coarse pubic hairs. This time, vomit came into my mouth. I was forced to swallow the acidy fluid, because letting it out would've meant I would've had to open my mouth.

"If you don't open your mouth, you can guarantee your time here will be worse, and you won't be guaranteed to make it out of here alive," Dr. Clemons threatened, frustration evident in his tone.

Thinking about being injected with more disease, bound to a bed for days straight—left with no food or water for those days, left to grow sicker and sicker, and having those glaring, heated lights shining down on me as they injected me with ten different drugs that made me violently ill— finally prompted me to open my mouth.

Dr. Clemons smiled evilly. "I knew you'd come to your senses," he said softly, pulling my head toward his now-halfway-erect, tiny dick. "Prove to me you don't want to go back." He closed his eyes, waiting to feel my mouth on him.

I couldn't control the tears now. And these weren't the involuntary ones that came from the medicine either. These tears came from the white-hot ball of anger that sizzled like hot coals inside me. I was so angry, even that medication couldn't calm me down. It was a high that didn't last this time. Who knew that all I had to do to really overcome the effects of the drugs was to get angry enough?

I inhaled, closed my eyes, and, with the swiftness of a bear trap, I turned my head to the side and snapped my teeth down on a mouthful of Dr. Clemons's inner thigh. I bit down so hard, sharp stabs of pain traveled from my locked jaws up to the center of my face. I felt like a rabid dog on attack.

"Agh!" Dr. Clemons shrieked. "Agh! Let me go! Let me go! You bitch! Let me go!" he wailed, the shriek of pain streaking through his screaming insults.

I continued to clamp down with the force of a great white shark. Fueled by Dr. Clemons's cries for mercy, I ground my teeth into the thick muscle of his thigh until I tasted the sharp, metallic sting of his blood on my tongue. It didn't last long, though. Dr. Clemons not only beat me in my head and face, but he called in his helpers and they beat me too.

"You'll regret the day you did this" were the last words I heard him say before everything went black around me. This time, I prayed that the darkness was death. I knew in that moment, if someone didn't come help me soon, I'd be dead in no time. And maybe, just maybe, that was what I deserved, due to all the shit I'd done in my past.

God would have the last say-so.

15

USED AND ABUSED

Days and nights fused together in my clouded mind. I didn't really know how many days I was locked up in a different dirty dungeon-like cell, where there were no windows for me to see whether the sun was coming up or going down. I was living in hell, which was the only conclusion I could come to about my condition. I could tell you I definitely wasn't back in the high-tech hospital rooms, where I'd been taken before. I wasn't in Dr. Clemons's chambers either, because there was no clock ticking and no windows.

I moved my eyes around, although it was really painful to do it. My brain was mush by now, between the abuse and the constant injection of drugs. This shit was getting out of hand. The constant moving around was how I knew they were doing shit they had no business doing, and trying to hide it.

After the incident with Dr. Clemons, he'd beaten me in my head and face until I finally let go of his leg. Blood had leaked down my mouth and chin. By the time the nurses and orderlies and other doctors got on the scene, I had lost consciousness.

Over the next few days, I had awoken a few times to severe pain. I knew my lip was busted, my eye was swollen, and I had a gash over my other eye. He had beaten the shit out of me, but he also walked away with a chuck of skin missing from his leg. That's what his perverted ass got for thinking he could do that shit to me without any consequences.

Drugged or not, I still had a little street sense in me. I had been waiting for the right opportunity to show his ass that I was the wrong one to keep fucking with. Also, I started feeling like I had nothing more to live for, so I acted as such when I got the chance. I mean, what was the worst they could do now? Kill me? I felt like that would be my fate in the end, anyway.

I had no clue when the days changed into night, and I had slept so much that I wasn't tired anymore. I was starting to go stir-crazy. I had begun talking to myself whenever I was awake long enough. The mental deterioration was real, for sure.

When I noticed all of the little bugs that were living in this new dungeon with me, I almost lost it. There were huge hissing cockroaches, every type of spider you could think of, and even centipedes. I'd awoken to a centipede crawling on my face. I jumped up and panicked. I went crazy, running in circles and brushing it off of me, but there was really nowhere for me to run. I didn't even have on shoes to squash the bugs with, but at least I wasn't strapped to a bed or a chair like before.

I was back to square one in yet another solitary-confinement situation. I was going crazy. This treatment was cruel and unusual—something I knew was against the law, based on the stuff Sandra had given me to read over. I thought about Sandra every day and prayed that one day she was going to ride in with the cavalry and save me. She said she'd written everything down that I'd told her; now it was just a waiting game. Maybe if I called her again she would understand how life-or-death it really was, and she would help me out of this. I had lost hope on Anderson helping me. For all I knew, Terrell's family or Ahmad had already killed my mother and gotten to Anderson too.

Never had I lived in conditions like this. I was starting to grow increasingly paranoid and felt like I was losing my mind. I started seeing things and hearing voices. That had happened to me before, when I was on the drugs they'd given me; but this time, it was just my mind. Even when there were no bugs near me, I continued to feel like they were crawling on me. I just kept brushing off my skin and scratching it. I really felt like a mental patient locked up in an insane asylum. That is what that room reminded me of. This wasn't prison; this was torture. All I could think of was that the only way out of here was a body bag. *Period.*

I had tried screaming several times until my throat was raw, but I knew that nobody could hear me down here. This place wasn't like the one with the black doors and other inmates behind them. Here, there was dead silence, which was another thing that drove me crazy. I was alone. The sound of my voice just kept bouncing off the walls like an echo. That told me that the room was probably soundproof, so I really had no hope of anyone hearing me. The conditions I was being kept in were beyond inhumane, and I suddenly started to think that I would've been better off being given over to Ahmad and his crew. Once I started thinking like that, I knew I was delirious.

I was hungry as hell, and I felt like I had not eaten in weeks. I dreamed of all types of food. I dreamed of it so much, I thought I could taste a nice, big fried chicken breast with a lot of hot sauce. Who was I fooling? I would probably never get another chance at having fried chicken in my life.

After what seemed like an eternity of lying on the horrible, thin-ass mattress, I heard keys jingling outside of the door. I sat up when I heard the noises and I started feeling mixed emotions. On the one hand, I felt nervous that Dr. Clemons was coming back to kill me, once and for all, but on the other hand, I was feeling kind of happy to have somebody finally coming in there at all to see if I was dead or alive. I needed some human contact, and I was hoping that they would at least give me some bread and water to survive the days.

As the door to my new prison swung open, I sat up erect. When they walked into the room, I noticed that it was Lisa and two other people I didn't recognize. I backed up and sat back down on my bed. I had no idea what they were coming to do. I hugged my knees to my chest and began rocking; I just knew it was my time to die. I looked up at them helplessly. I wanted to say something, but the words wouldn't come.

Lisa finally spoke first. "Misty, are you all right?" she asked, her voice calm. She was back to the attentive, calm nurse I'd met before.

I swallowed hard as I tried to find the words to say to her, but none would come. I didn't trust one soul in that prison. *Not one.* I cowered on the bed, shaking.

"It's all right. We snuck down here to check on you. I got word about what happened and I'm trying to help you," Lisa said, following up. "He is out of hand, and we can't stand for it anymore."

I looked up at her through sad eyes. I didn't know whether to trust her or not. I shook my head no. "He— he's . . . going to kill me," I managed.

"Can you stand up so we can examine you? I need to make the case that this is not what should be going on," Lisa said, reaching out her hand to help me up.

I put my legs over the side of the bed and tried to stand up, but I couldn't. Lisa and the two men moved to my side. When they stood me up on my feet, my legs kind of buckled from being so weak. I had sat down or lain down for so long, my legs couldn't support me.

"What will happen to me now? Can you help me?" I asked in a raspy voice.

"I'm trying. But I need you to be on your best behavior so you won't bring any attention down here," Lisa said. "He put you here with no cameras so he could do what he wanted to you, but this works in our favor. We have to move fast," she said to me. Then she turned toward the other people and pointed toward me.

"As you can see, this inmate had been mentally and physically abused. I want this in the news story," Lisa whispered to them.

They were dressed like doctors, but clearly she had snuck them in, and they were reporters. My heart leapt in my chest. I don't think I had felt happy in so long, I didn't know how to react.

"Misty, I'll be back. I'm going to write it up so you can get out of here, and then we will work on everything else," Lisa said, getting ready to turn for the door again.

"Please! No! Don't leave me down here. I'll die! You have to help me get out of here. He will come back and kill me," I pled, panic taking over me.

"I will make sure you get out of here, Misty. I'm not going to let this keep happening to you," she promised. With that, she was gone.

I didn't believe her. I had thought about bulldozing her and pushing my way out of there. I knew that would just get me beat down and locked down for longer.

"Mmmm," I moaned as I came into consciousness a couple of days after Lisa visited me. I was immediately aware of every inch of my body, because everything was racked with pain. I slowly opened my eyes and painfully realized nothing had changed. The pain that shot through my skull when I opened my eyes forced me to snap them shut.

"Mmmm," I moaned once more, quickly feeling a fire

raging in my throat. It was because my mouth and throat were so dry from not eating or drinking.

As I lay there in pain, waiting for Lisa to come give me something to knock me back out, I heard a different set of footsteps coming toward me. I began to shake, with fear gripping me tight. In this prison, you just never knew who worked for whom, and what kind of crazy shit they were going to do. I swallowed hard, which was painful as hell.

I started saying a silent prayer in my head. *God, if You just let me make it through one more night without being taken back to Dr. Clemons, I'll never do anything wrong again.* I'd said many a prayer, but I meant this one. I was at the end of my rope now. Suicide was sounding really good to me, but I had already promised myself and God that I would never try that again.

Suddenly I felt a cold hand touch my arm. I just knew I was about to die. I couldn't bring myself to open up my eyes and face death like a woman. Then I heard a voice.

"Misty, I'm here, like I said I would be," a man's voice filtered into my ear. The voice was kind of soothing and didn't have any hints of evil behind it. It was also familiar. I felt relief wash over me. I opened my eyes slowly and my heart leapt.

"It's me . . . Anderson . . . you remember me?" he whispered lightly. "I finally got to your mother and did what you asked me to do," he said. "It wasn't easy. There are a lot of people after her, and then they came after me, but I was smarter than them. She is okay, but really upset they are not allowing her to see you."

A jolt of excitement flitted through my stomach, and even that caused me pain.

I finally calmed down a little bit and struggled to keep my eyes open. I could tell by the look of terror etched on Anderson's face that I must've looked like shit. I moaned and motioned for him to help me up.

"Lisa told me everything. We are going to get you out of

here," he said, looking around nervously every time he spoke.

"How do I know I can trust you? It's been so long, and you left me here for dead," I rasped, on the verge of tears. "I didn't think you were coming back. You were just gone."

Anderson looked at me with a serious look on his face and let out a long breath. Something about his look caused a flash of panic to go through my chest, but I ignored it. He was the person I had been putting all of my hope on since I'd been locked up. He and Sandra were my only hopes.

"You can trust me. I just needed time. But I must tell you, it's not going to be easy. We have to do this in steps. You will have to follow all of our instructions, or you risk being caught. If that happens, we are all doomed," Anderson said seriously.

I began shaking at what he was saying. It was the different steps in this place that I was afraid of. "No, please. Just take me out of here."

Anderson lowered his eyes and shook his head, as though I had given him an impossible task. I felt my stomach drop and it began somersaulting again.

"I will help you," he said flatly.

I shook my head in understanding and closed my eyes as tears began to leak from the sides. All I could do now was pray that Anderson wouldn't disappear again.

My prayers were finally answered. It was the middle of the night when Anderson and Lisa came together at the change of shift. They led me out of the dungeon cell and down another darkened, long hallway.

When we were finally out of the dungeon, I was happy to see light. I couldn't move as fast as they wanted, so they began helping me fallen-soldier style. I had one arm around Anderson's neck and one around Lisa's neck and they moved fast.

"We have to put you back into the dorm, but it won't be for long. I put you on the list so that the COs there won't be suspicious. But, I promise, it won't be for long," Anderson said. "I will come back for you. It was too long before, but it won't be like that, this time."

After we made it back to the dorm-style bunk area, which I had been in before, I was placed in a bed, like I'd been transferred there officially. I looked over and saw the same CO that was always there. He always turned a blind eye to everything. He was the same one that had let that strange man snatch me from my bed and carry me away.

The CO wore a serious look on his face and ignored the glares I was throwing his way. I guess he didn't care; he was there to do a job and obviously to turn a blind eye to the illegal shit that was going down inside the prison. A lot of employees inside that prison turned a blind eye. It was the norm rather than not.

I can't lie: I was never so happy to be in a room full of women in my life. I glanced around, but I didn't see Shanta. I figured, once she realized I was back, she'd come over and see me.

I stared at the bed and longed to just climb into it and get a decent night's sleep. That was just a dream, though. I knew that it was still prison, and at any moment, anything could change. I did the best I could to get some rest, but it seemed like the breakfast call came so fast.

As weak and shaky as I was, I almost ran to the chow hall. I was so hungry that I bent over a bowl of prison oatmeal, which doubled as slop, and devoured it like it was bacon and eggs. I did not even take a minute to breathe.

I saw a girl staring at me and I could tell she was looking at the bruises on my face and arms. I instantly felt self-conscious and a little embarrassed. I tried to cover the marks with my hands. She sat right next to me. I must admit she was bold. I hadn't had a lot of luck trusting chicks, so I instantly shot her a dirty look. I let her know with just the look on my face that I wasn't about to put up with no bullshit.

"It's all good," the girl said sadly. "You don't need to hide them. I know all about it. I've been there. Just be lucky you made it back," she said. She really looked like she felt sorry for me.

The look on her face made me push my food away and break down into racking sobs. I started crying instantly. I was kind of mad at myself for showing weakness, but I couldn't help it. The tears and breakdown came so fast and furious, I couldn't stop it, even if I wanted.

"They tortured me. They beat me and slapped me. I have been used and sexually abused. I have been put through some sick stuff and I just can't take it anymore," I cried, putting my face in my hands. "And God only knows what kind of shit they put in my body that might have long-term effects." I was really at my breaking point.

The girl looked around and moved a little bit closer. She started speaking to me quietly. I was surprised, but I listened to her closely.

"Sh . . . you are lucky to be alive. There are many women that don't make it out of there alive. They let you live for a reason, because if you were anyone else, you would be dead," the girl told me gravely. "I was one of the lucky ones too, but I think they can come back for me any minute."

"I don't even care if they kill me. They should've killed me," I said through my tears. I was shaking all over. "Look at me now. I want to die! I am never going to get out of here and I'd rather die than let these people keep on using and abusing my body." I continued to speak through racking sobs. I meant it too. I really felt like I had nothing to live for. I continued crying. The girl looked at me sympathetically.

"Sh," she hushed me. "You don't want them to hear you crying and saying that you want to die," she said.

"They will kill you and think nothing more of you. I've seen it done before, and it was like nothing to them," she told me.

"You heard what I said, I don't really care anymore," I sobbed.

"You have to live. You have to survive for the others. You are probably the only one that can help all of us now," she said.

Her words struck me as strange. Why would she say that I was the one that could help them? Where would she get that idea? I looked at her with a very confused look on my face. I didn't know what she meant by her words. I started getting paranoid that she'd overheard that I might be getting help to get out. Maybe she'd heard something about my plans. A cold chill shot down my spine. I looked at her sideways. She noticed the look.

"Shanta told me who you were before . . . ," the girl said.

I sniffled back my tears and looked at her then. Just the mention of Shanta made me put my guard down a little bit. "Before *what*?" I asked, my voice cracking.

"You don't know?" she asked, looking over her shoulder like someone might've been watching us.

"No. Now tell me what you're talking about," I said with urgency.

"Shanta is gone," the girl said, then hung her head.

"What? What are you telling me?" I demanded.

"They came and got her, just like they did you, but she never made it back. We heard days ago that she didn't make it," the girl said sadly.

A lump immediately formed in my throat. "How? What happened to her?" I croaked.

"The rumor is that she was stabbed to death trying to free herself from those bastard doctors. None of the other girls in with her had dared to step up, but they said Shanta had tried to save them all. She got hold of a scalpel, but she had no wins, and they turned it on her. We heard about it from another girl that made it out. She said they really did a job on Shanta. That evil Dr. Clemons did all kinds of stuff to her. It was a shame, because I found out that she had kids on the outside," the girl relayed.

My heart sank and I felt cold all over my body. I had really liked Shanta. She was genuine. The news of her death depressed me to no end. Shanta had been so nice to me. No one deserved to die like that. She was a victim of this corrupt system, just like me.

After I heard the news, I couldn't eat anymore. I lay in my bunk for two days, refusing to leave for chow or to shower after that. I kept picturing Shanta's face and all of the things she had done for me while I was on the dorm with her.

I could've never imagined that she would've given up her own life for others like that. It made me feel even weaker that I hadn't tried to fight for myself like she had. The depression had hit me so bad that the prison psychologist came by to speak to me; even that soft-spoken, mousy-faced woman couldn't get me to utter a word. She kept whispering my name and asking me if I was okay or if I thought I needed to see a doctor.

What the hell did she think? I had been tortured. I had lost a friend to this shit. I hadn't heard from my mother. Anderson hadn't come back yet. I was feeling helpless and hopeless. Every time I thought a little help was coming, it seemed like a fantasy. When it was all said and done, I would leave this fucking place dead or with all of the injuries plaguing me.

So far as I knew, I had endured broken ribs, a small fracture in my skull, hematomas, both eyes swollen two or three times each, a couple of cracked and missing teeth in the front, a fractured nose, a fractured cheekbone, and at least one broken finger on my right hand. I had been drugged up so much that I had pissed and shitted on myself numerous times. I had been injected with a sickness that had caused my body to swell up like I was pregnant and still made my lungs feel like they were on fire every time I did any kind of rigorous activity. I had been sexually abused at whim for weeks.

It was really a wonder that I was still alive. I chalked it up to God wanting me to get my revenge—or why else would I have made it through all of this alive. I was all messed-up and I refused to look in a mirror to see just how ugly I had become, but I was still alive. I could feel the raised scars still on my neck and left cheek—remnants of the slicing I had taken from those first chicks that jumped me and started all of this shit. It was apparent without even looking in the mirror that I was no longer pretty Misty Heiress. I felt the scratches and scars on my face. I even felt the lumps too. I would never be considered pretty again, and that was final.

The girl came back almost every day to check on me. "I wanted to make sure you were okay, Misty. You haven't been yourself, and I overheard them saying they might transfer you back down. You have to perk up," the girl told me. "You can't let them take you back down there. I'm so scared for you."

I was hanging on her every word, trying to find out what she knew. I realized that I needed to get to know her better.

"What is your name?" I finally asked her. "You've been talking to me for days now, and I don't even know your name."

"Lena," she said. "I remember when you first got here, they were taking me away. I never forget a face."

"Tell me what happened to you—if it's not too hard for you to talk about," I said.

"When they first took me, it was just to give me injections. Then I'd come back sick and they'd test out medicines on me. But that quickly changed when Dr. Clemons came around. Under him, they did unnatural things to me sexually and abused me with all types of objects. Sometimes when they brought me back, I couldn't even recognize my own face because I would fight back every time they touched me. The man behind all of this got upset because it caused him to lose a lot of money when the doctors wouldn't take me anymore. He told them he would make an example of me for the other girls, just in case they tried to do the same thing. So, one day, he gathered all of the girls in the dorm, stripped me in front of all of them, and . . ." Lena started crying hard as she told me exactly what happened to her.

I was crying too; her pain and sadness was getting to me. I could only imagine how she felt.

"He beat me like a slave. When I could not stand up anymore, he beat me on the floor. My body was bloody, and I screamed from the pain. All of the girls watching were crying. I was the example of what they'd get. After he got tired of beating me, he left me in a bloody heap and forbid any of the girls there from helping me. I stayed like that for two days, lying in my own waste, until a nurse finally came and helped me," Lena spat out. She was crying, but I could tell she was very angry and wanted revenge for what had happened to her.

"Oh my God. I'm so sorry," I said in a low voice.

Lena started wiping her face quickly, like she didn't want me or anyone else to see her crying. She started looking around frantically and her voice went lower. I figured out that she must've known they were watching us and didn't want them to hear her telling me her harrowing story.

"Misty, I know you have people helping you. I saw it when they brought you in here. I know that CO doesn't work this unit. I picked up on it. I'm just asking that if you get out of here and get some help, don't leave us all for dead. Make sure people know what is going on in here.

Make sure you try to save us and remember the things you've been through in here. If no one ever knows, we will never get saved," Lena told me.

I immediately felt guilty that I had Anderson and Lisa to help me. I couldn't think like that now. I had to think of self-preservation first, and then if I saved myself, I could help someone else. Right now, my first priority was getting out of this place.

The next day, Lisa showed up without Anderson. She woke me up as if she was there for the regular stuff she did as part of her job. My heart started racing, because I could see in her eyes that this was going to be the day. It was just a glint, but I caught on quickly.

Lisa led me into the bathroom and turned the water in the shower stalls on, full blast. All of a sudden, she was acting like she had before whenever she just bathed me and got me ready for whatever unit I was moving to. My high feeling suddenly crashed. I couldn't afford for Lisa to turn on me now. Not again. I was confused at first about her change of attitude, but she gave me a look with her eyes and then I kind of caught on to what she was doing.

Lisa had to play it off like we were going through the official motions. She had turned on the water so whoever was watching us on camera would not hear us talking. I had been wondering why Lisa was speaking so closely in my ears. I quickly caught on and just started playing along with her. Lisa kept the water running as she spoke to me.

"We are going to help you get out of here, but we are risking ourselves, so it's important that you get the story out right away so that nothing happens to those of us who are left here," Lisa said. "I want every doctor and every person involved to be held accountable. I don't care if we have to burn this place down. It *needs* to be done. I can't stand by and watch all of this disgusting shit any longer. I was forced to be a part of it, but no more."

I stood with my mouth wide open. I couldn't believe

what this lady was saying to me. She was really hell-bent on revenge if she wanted to risk helping me again. I was sure that she knew they were watching us with their eagle eye.

"How will you be able to get me out? They are watching me, and you will get yourself killed. That doctor is a sick person and he kills people," I told her.

Although I was very concerned for real, I was also growing kind of excited inside as my mind immediately started racing with thoughts of me making a run for it and getting to my mother on the outside.

Lisa put her fingers up to her lips to shush my questions. Then she signaled me to get into the shower. Once again, she was watching me take a shower and had turned back to being all business.

Lisa was silent for a long while as she and I both went through the motions to make it look like official business was going on. I took her cue and did as I was told. I didn't want to mess up any chances with her and make it where she wouldn't help me. When I was done, she returned me to the dorm.

"I'll be back later. It is going to happen tonight," Lisa whispered.

"I'll be waiting. Please don't let me down. Mentally, I might not be able to survive it if you do," I said meaningfully. I was dead serious too, because I needed her more than she knew.

16

MOTIVATED TO MURDER

"*Hold her legs open!*" *Dr. Clemons demands. Two of his orderlies rush over and hold me down. I am writhing and flailing, but I am no match for them. Then Lisa comes over with a wicked smile on her face.*

"*Lick that pussy. Turn her out,*" *Dr. Clemons commands right before Lisa plants her head between my legs.*

"*Anything for you,*" *Lisa groans.*

I was jolted out of a nightmare by a frantic voice and my body being shaken roughly.

"Wake up! Misty! Wake up!" a girl named Dana cried frantically. She was one of the inmates on the dorm.

I jumped out of my sleep, covered in sweat and unaware where I was at first. "Wha-what the hell . . . ," I grumbled, my mind completely fuzzy with sleep.

"She looks dead!" Dana said in a panic. "I think she's dead!"

"Who? What? What's going on?" I asked, my heart racing. My head immediately started pounding from being jolted awake like that. I felt dizzy and off balance, and the room started spinning a little bit. That was one thing I hated, being jolted awake violently like that. I was convinced that could make me have a heart attack and die.

"Come with me," Dana said, grabbing my arm and practically dragging me out of the bed. "I don't know if she's going to make it. I'm so scared right now."

"Who? Who are you talking about?" I asked, my voice going up a few octaves. She wasn't telling me anything, but she kept repeating the same thing. Dana didn't say shit; she just held on to my arm and dragged me over to the person she was talking about.

My eyes popped open when I saw Lena lying on the bed. Her body was limp; she was bleeding a little from her nose; and, honestly, she looked halfway dead. I immediately felt sick. I had had enough of seeing dead bodies in my lifetime. I had just talked to Lena, so seeing her like that made my blood run cold.

"Shit," I gasped, and threw my hand up to my mouth afterward. I didn't know shit about CPR. I couldn't even help her if I wanted to.

"Lena! Wake up! Please wake up!" Dana cried. This time, she shook Lena's body.

"What the fuck?" I asked, moving to Lena's other side. "How did this happen? What's going on?" I asked frantically. "Do you know CPR? Is she breathing? We have to help her." My words were rushing out of my mouth in rapid succession, fast like how my mind raced.

"How could he do this to her and just dump her in here like this? She's unconscious," Dana said, exasperated. "I want this motherfucker to die, I swear. Somebody has to stop this shit. He is getting away with murder . . . literally. I can't stand it anymore. All of these fucking CO and nurses and administrators just let him get away with all of this bullshit."

"She's still breathing," I said, after I had put my hand on Lena's stomach and felt faint movement up and down.

"We can call for help. They have to help her. They can't just leave her to die like this. Let's call someone." I went to move, but Dana grabbed my arm violently.

"No!" Dana exclaimed. "Are you crazy? These mother-fuckers don't care about us at all. They'll kill her this time. Just like they did Shanta and Carrie and Sheila. We have to help her ourselves. I don't trust those bastards! We have to take turns sitting up and watching her until she wakes up. At least she is breathing and her heart is beating," Dana said. She grabbed Lena's hand and gave a soft squeeze. "C'mon, girl. C'mon. You have a lot to live for."

I moved over and grabbed Lena's left hand. I kneeled by her bedside. "Just make it through this, Lena, and I swear we will get our revenge on that bastard, Dr. Clemons. We will fucking get him back. We will go after everyone in here who has ever hurt us, but you have to make it through this," I spoke to Lena softly as I held her hand tightly.

It was as if Dana and I looked over at the same time and noticed another girl named Fiona watching us intently. Fiona sat on her bunk across from where we were and she had a pen and a legal notepad. Dana looked over at her like she was crazy.

"Our friend is in a fucking coma and dying, with no way to get her real help, and you're writing a story?" Dana snapped. "I will fuck you up if you're planning on snitching. Put that fucking pen and paper away. There is nothing for you to write about, you dumb bitch." Dana was losing control now.

"I'm writing a plan," Fiona said evenly. "We need a plan of revenge. We need to study and plan it out. Nothing can be done without a plan. We can talk all we want, but if we don't plan it out, it's just talk," Fiona said, tears streaming down her face.

That seemed to calm Dana down a little bit. "Just write a plan on how we are going to help Lena," Dana said, her voice going softer.

"She will wake up," I said with feeling. "We don't need to write no plan. We just need to pray. She's going to make it through this, and everything is going to work out fine. Trust me," I said, but I didn't even believe it myself. My heart was hurting for Lena. This was all too much. This prison was too much. I had a hundred thoughts on how I could take the whole shit down.

I got chills when I heard footsteps tramping toward us. Dana's eyes went wide too.

"Hey! Inmates, get back to your bunks, now!" a burly CO shouted at us.

"I'm not leaving her side," Dana shot back.

When I saw several more COs arrive and start closing in on us, I touched Dana's arm.

"Let's move for now. We can't afford for them to take us out of here. She won't stand a chance if they do," I said. "As soon as things die down, we can come back over to her. We just can't afford to make waves right now. For her safety and ours."

Dana listened, but reluctantly. She let go of Lena's hand and eyed the COs evilly. I did the same. Those COs were just as complicit in all of the abuse as the doctor and his flunkies. Everyone knew that Lena was unconscious after she had just been returned from a "session" with Dr. Clemons. They'd dumped her in the bed like a dog.

What I didn't understand was, why hadn't they hidden her in those dungeons like they had done me? The only conclusion I could make was they wanted to send a message to the rest of us once we saw Lena's condition. This had been done on purpose. Maybe they had found out Lena was talking to me about what had happened to Shanta. There were a million and one thoughts crossing my mind.

We might have been forced to leave Lena's side, but it didn't stop us from sneaking to check on her and making sure she was still breathing every time the COs turned their backs for even a minute. Finally, during one of the times I went over, I saw Lena's eyes flutter open.

"Lena? Can you hear me?" I asked excitedly.

Lena's lips parted into a small smile, which made my insides warm up with happiness. She looked like shit, but that smile was worth a million dollars in my eyes. She lifted her hand weakly and extended it toward me.

"Where have you been? That must've been an awesome dream. I thought you would never come out of it," I asked, trying to make light of a serious situation. I held on to her hand and squeezed it reassuringly.

Dana rushed over too. We didn't care about those COs and their rules at that moment. We were just happy to see that Lena was alive and back to reality. I seriously thought we might have lost her forever.

"He will die," Lena croaked in a barely audible voice. She closed her eyes again and I saw small tears coming from the corners. "He can't get away with this. He has to die."

"Who? What?" I asked. My face was folded into a deep frown. That was an odd thing to say the first time you woke up after being out of it.

"Clemons. All of them will have to die. We will kill them all. I saw it in my dreams. I know it," Lena said, her voice becoming a little bit stronger. "He's going to die," Lena said with more fervor. She tried to sit up, but she immediately fell back down onto the bed. Her body was in too much of a weakened state.

I knew exactly how she felt. I'd been there numerous times since they'd started on me.

"Don't try to sit up. Just relax," I told her.

"No, I have to get out of here. There's a car waiting for me. I have to leave so that I won't be here when he dies," Lena said, the tone in her voice weird.

I looked at Dana strangely. We exchanged looks that said Lena was bugging out. It didn't change the fact that we were just happy that she was alive.

"Listen, you've been out of it. You must've been dreaming," Dana said, smiling. "It was all a dream, Lena, but trust me, one day it might be a reality if he keeps it up. Somebody is going to get their payback one day. Karma is not to be messed with," Dana continued.

"Yes, if there is one thing I know, it's that karma is a bitch that serves revenge with fire and fury. Everything comes back and in full circle," I said, speaking from experience.

Lena blinked rapidly and shook her head a little bit, trying to get herself right. She touched my hand and smiled. "You're going to be karma and get it done for all of us. I have faith in you, Misty. It's your purpose . . . to save us," she said. Her voice was almost like a prophecy and it scared the shit out of me.

Lisa returned in the middle of the night during the change of shift. It was the perfect time, because the COs were basically absent while new COs came on board.

"Misty," Lisa whispered.

My eyes shot open. I had been sleeping very lightly— partly because I was waiting for her or Anderson to return. But mostly it was because I was prepared to fight to the death if Dr. Clemons sent for me again.

"It's time," Lisa said.

My heart sped up and I sprang up in the bed like someone had put springs on my ass. Forget the sleep cobwebs in my mind; I was tasting my escape before it even happened. It was a good adrenaline rush like I hadn't experienced in a long while.

"Listen to me. Someone is going to come from facilities. Do what he says, exactly and to the letter, or this won't work. I am giving you a stun gun, just in case you have to use it at some point. Do not lose it," Lisa whispered.

My eyes grew wide. *In case I had to use it? Ain't your plan solid?* My nerves were bad from her saying that. It didn't sound like she was too confident I'd get out of there, or why else would I need a weapon?

"Why would I need that?" I asked. "Isn't this plan foolproof?"

"Nothing is foolproof, Misty. I can only make a plan, but anything can go wrong. You need to cooperate and be smart. I can lead you, but just so far. Now I am giving the stun gun to you, but you have to follow my plan closely. We are going to pray for the best and that you'll get out without using it. But, if not, don't be scared to use it to protect yourself," Lisa told me.

My heart was racing as I thought about the possibility of getting caught and having to use that stun gun. Not only would I probably get killed, but Lisa would surely be murdered for helping me. Lisa continued to act like she was just doing her rounds. I can't front; she was smart. I didn't really fully understand why she was risking it all to help me, but in any case, I was grateful.

Once Lisa had told me what she had in mind, I started getting myself mentally prepared for it. A stun gun would fucking certainly work out—if I had to use it and make a run for it.

Lisa told me one last thing: "If you happen to get caught or seen, you have to fight to the death to get out, Misty. We will have to destroy this place in order to stay alive, or else you will be dead and this torture and experimenting will go on for more years to come."

Lisa didn't say much more to me after that. It was just understood that I knew what the hell I had to do. We heard noises of the COs coming on duty and both of us were really nervous, but we hid our nervousness well. Then I saw the guy with the laundry cart pushing through really quick. He exchanged a look with Lisa. Then she pulled the sheets and blankets over my head.

"She's ready to go?" the man pushing the car whispered.

Lisa nodded and she remained silent.

"Let's do this, quick," the man said. "She's going to have to wrap up in the sheet—no jumpsuit, no hospital gown—just the sheet. If anything looks off, we will be caught."

I peeked and gave Lisa a look that told her I was ready to do this. Before I knew it, I had stripped, wrapped myself in a bunch of sheets, and folded myself into the oversized industrial laundry cart like I was a ball of dirty laundry. Lisa looked down really quick and I peeked up at her one last time. Nobody needed to know that Lisa and I had a plan in our heads. That smile and our eyes meeting was our little signal that shit was about to happen.

Thank you, I silently mouthed to her. I was about to make sure that I pulled out all of the stops to save myself and all of those girls in the prison that were suffering at the hands of the sick staff.

I knew I was evolving, thanks to the horrible experience I'd endured. The old selfish Misty would've just promised to help the other girls, but once I got what I wanted, I wouldn't have looked back. It would've been all about self for me, and I probably would've turned my back on everyone and just saved myself.

Something inside me had changed. I silently told myself that as soon as I was far enough away from the danger of getting caught, I would definitely notify the police and bring down these bastards. I also told myself that if I made it out of this in once piece, I would expose the entire scheme they had going on with using poor helpless inmates as lab rats and sex slaves. I definitely wanted Dr. Clemons to suffer for what he had done to me.

The only thing I had to do now was make it through the maze of buildings in the prison and fight my way to freedom.

17

THE ESCAPE PLAN

I was utterly shocked and surprised at how small I was able to fold my body into the prison's rolling laundry cart, where I was lying on its bottom. I can't lie, though. As bad as I wanted to get out of there, I was still disgusted that I had to hide under loads and loads of disgusting, dirty jail sheets, towels, and dirty rags that inmates had used on their nasty bodies. The heap of dirty linens stank to high heaven. I gagged at least a thousand times at the stench coming from the filthy laundry.

The facilities guy had told me that I was not, *absolutely not,* to come up out of the huge rolling laundry cart until he gave me the signal. Even if I thought it was quiet and wanted to see what was going on, I wouldn't dare move. Whatever it took to get out of that prison, I was going to do it, step-by-step. It seemed to be taking forever, though. I had cramps in my back and legs, and my neck ached like crazy. It didn't matter; I had no choice but to agree when this idea was hatched.

From what I understood; it was Anderson who had made it happen. He told me he had already collected half of the money he had asked for from my mother. I knew that I owed him the other half, but I had to get to it first. Most important, I had to get to my mother. I could only fantasize about our reunion and how happy she was going to be that she didn't have to be out in the world alone anymore. The thought excited me to the point where I wanted to scream, but, of course, I didn't. I knew better than that.

As the cart moved, I felt a big thump and then I could tell that it had stopped moving. Anticipation was creeping in and I wanted so badly to peek my head out. The long pause was causing me to grow increasingly curious, but, more so, suspicious. They hadn't said we would stop at all. It was supposed to just be smooth sailing through the prison and to the doors, where someone would be waiting for me. I was going to get the rest of the instructions when I got there.

I'm still inside. I know it. I'm not fucking out of this place, I thought.

My stomach fluttered with fear. Then, after what seemed like forever, I heard metal clanging and muffled voices. Sweat beads ran a race down my body. I was covered. My own perspiration and the stench of the dirty laundry were really doing a number on my senses. I held my breath in one-minute intervals, hoping that would help. It was all I could do to keep myself from vomiting.

"I am transporting laundry. So, why are you stopping me?" I heard the raspy-voiced facilities guy say. "You don't need to search shit. I been working here twenty years and I ain't never been stopped or suspected for shit," he said more frantically.

"Move the fuck out of the way, old man. If you ain't got shit to hide, then why are you arguing?!" a male voice barked. It was a CO, and I recognized his voice as one of those that worked with Dr. Clemons.

Shit! My eyes popped open in horror.

My heart sank. I couldn't believe my ears. We were being stopped, and that was not a good sign. I was dripping with even more sweat. I swallowed hard and let out a long, exasperated breath. I grabbed onto the stun gun and gripped it tightly. I finally remembered I had it.

"I ain't letting you search me or my cart," the facilities guy continued to argue.

"Nigga, I ain't asking, I'm telling you. I'm about to search it, and you'd be lucky if I don't strip-search your ass," the CO barked.

This was not going to end well; I could tell that already. I heard a physical scuffle happening.

"Get off of me! You can't do this to me!" the facilities guy hollered. I could hear the CO's fist connecting with the guy's body. I could actually hear cracks and crunches. I knew then that I had no wins. I was going to be found and I needed to mentally prepare myself to fight.

I closed my eyes and prayed. I listened intently to see if I could tell what was going on. It just sounded like chaos. I had already been in the cart for what seemed like hours. I knew it hadn't been that long, but, damn, if it wasn't too damn long. Now with the fight going on, I didn't know how much longer I would have to wait or if I would be busted.

Once I was found, the entire facility would be notified. Lisa had warned me that this would be my one and only chance to get out of there. I immediately put myself in a going-to-war mind-set. I waited, but I knew the time would come shortly.

"Shut the fuck up and move," the CO barked. I heard the facilities guy whimper, which meant he had lost his fight to protect his laundry cart from being searched. That also meant I was about to be found out.

"Now I'm real curious, you fucking asshole," the CO growled, then he chuckled and I could feel his presence hovering over the laundry cart. I squeezed my eyes shut. I was immediately thrust back to the last time I had to hide for my life.

Fear and anxiety had consumed my body all at once that day. Confused and scared to death, I had run into Mrs. Mabel's walk-in closet and closed the door. *Boom!* The sound of the bedroom door after it slammed the wall behind it had terrified me.

I had jumped then, and I jumped now when the laundry cart was jostled roughly. That quickly brought me back to reality. I realized I was in the same exact position again. Hiding out and about to get busted.

"So you say there ain't nothing in here I should be worried about, huh?" the CO asked as he jostled the laundry cart again.

I hugged myself tight and held my breath. I thought if I let out even a small puff of air that CO would find me.

"I'm telling you, man, ain't no reason for you to search," the facilities guy continued to plead. I couldn't front—he was really putting himself on the line to save my ass. I recognized that he didn't have to do that for me. Whether or not he was getting paid didn't make a difference. Once they thought they were caught, a lot of guys would start snitching right away.

"Then why the fuck you going so hard? All you had to do was let me take a look inside. You're being really suspicious, and I don't like it. I know all too well how a sneaky motherfucker looks when they are up to no good around here," the CO said.

"C'mon, man. You already beat me up for no reason. Just let me go so I can get my job done," the facilities guy said pleadingly.

"I will . . . after I look inside this cart and make you take out every piece of linen inside it and shake it out in front of me," the CO said flatly.

I gagged like he had gut-punched me. Sweat rolled down the crease between my breasts and ass crack. I was about to be found. My time was up.

"What? You really going to do all of that right now? I have a laundry truck to meet, man," the facilities guy said.

"You heard me. You will shake out every piece of laundry, and if you have nothing to hide, we will be all good here. But if there is something you're smuggling, you're going to be booked on more charges and housed in a cell under the jail. I know what my gut is telling me, and it's telling me that you're lying and you're hiding something, and I'm not budging. We can do this all alone, or I can call for a mass of backup that will take your ass down so fast, you won't know what hit you," the CO said in an unmoving tone.

How could the facilities guy argue anymore? If the CO decided to call more people onto the scene, I would be assed-out for sure. At least I felt like with the way it was now, it would be two against one—the facilities guy and me against the CO. If he called more COs, we wouldn't stand a chance.

I closed my eyes and took small, quiet breaths in an attempt to calm myself down. I wanted to jump up and shove that stun gun up that CO's ass so badly. *But that would be counterproductive,* I thought. *If I surprise him with my presence and then use my weapon, I might stand a chance.* That was how I convinced myself to remain calm.

"Suit yourself, but all you're going to find is shitty laundry," the facilities guy said one last time.

"Then show me. Maybe I like shitty laundry," the CO replied, being a smart-ass.

Suddenly I felt the sheets and towels and things being moved off of me slowly. My stomach swirled with nausea. *Fuck! This is a definite setback.* I didn't want to get caught lying down, so there was only one thing I could do. I had to get my ass out of there and fight.

I painfully unfolded my body and stood up. I felt like I

didn't have any legs because my circulation had stopped flowing from my contortions, which had made my legs numb. The facilities guy and the CO both looked like they'd seen a ghost when I popped up out of the cart. I kind of turned my body sideways. My secret weapon was right there, just like Lisa had instructed. I wrapped my hands around the stun gun. I knew this was my last chance. My heart was racing like crazy.

"What the fu—" the CO started, and his eyes went as round as dinner plates.

I quickly pressed that fucking stun gun up against the CO's neck and pressed the surge button.

"Ah!" He let out a pained sound and his eyes popped open. His body started bucking and, all of a sudden, he went limp. Before he could reach for his radio or anything, I hit him with another jolt from the stun gun.

"Ah, you bitch," he said weakly before he buckled to the floor in a heap. When he fell, he grabbed the side of the cart, causing it to spill over and causing me to tumble down with it.

"Shit," I cried as my body crashed to the floor. I was all the way out of the cart and my legs were back in working condition, but that didn't make me feel better. I looked over and he was still moving.

"Come here, you little bitch," the CO snarled, scrambling on the floor to get to me.

"Get the fuck away from her," the facilities guy said, rushing over. He gave me a look that said to run. The CO had gotten to his knees. He reached for the little, skinny facilities guy and pulled him down to the floor. The guy hit his head real hard and I heard a cracking noise.

"You're not getting away with shit. I got something for your ass, you little bitch. Wait until I turn you over to the doctor," he growled, moving toward me, but still holding his neck.

"Stay away from me. I'm warning you! I will light your ass up. I am not even kidding," I said, holding the stun gun out in front of me as I backed up.

"You can't do shit. Look at you, stupid ass. You're coming with me," he hissed, trying to struggle to his feet.

I exhaled and looked down at myself. I forgot that I was butt-ass naked because I had to be wrapped in the dirty linens to make sure I wasn't seen. "I'm not going, and I don't want to hurt you again, but I will. I swear to God, I will," I warned. The stun gun crackled as I hit the Surge button as a warning.

The CO didn't take too lightly to the warning. He lunged toward me and I jumped aside. His cumbersome body stumbled sideways and he fell. I took full advantage of the moment and hit him with a longer and more powerful jolt from the stun gun. His body jerked and he made a sickening grunting noise and then blacked out. That's the result I needed.

"Help me move him," I said frantically to the facilities guy who was still partially dazed from being punched.

"If we leave this area, we take a chance on being seen by cameras," he warned me. "Why don't we just run, since he's out of it. We can just get out of here."

"No. We have to take care of him or he's going to wake up in a few seconds, and even if we are gone, he will warn the others and we won't make it very far. I can't take that chance. Besides, you don't understand the types of shit this guy was party to and participated in," I stressed, panting.

"Put this on," the facilities guy said, handing me an extra shirt he was holding in his hand. I quickly slipped into it.

"I know you don't understand what this is about, but for me, it's a need. I need to take care of this one. He's one of the perverted orderlies and one of Dr. Clemons's flunkies. He did some unspeakable things to me and some of the other girls, but nothing was worse than the day I saw him piss on one of the female inmates who was too helpless to fight back," I said. "That shit sickened me."

The facilities guy scrunched up his face. I could still remember seeing this bastard CO's hot, acidy urine splashing onto that girl's face and soaking her hair. After that day, I had prayed daily that I would have the opportunity to get each and every one of the bastards that did shit like that to helpless inmates. I guess my prayers were answered. Not exactly how I wanted them to be answered, but this would work.

Now, as I stood over the bastard in a position of power, I was feeling a mixture of emotions. I knew it wouldn't be long before this CO would be missing from his shift and someone would start looking for him. I touched the stun gun and thought about hitting him again with another jolt, but something inside me said I wanted him to be looking into my eyes when he got what was coming to him.

"I know where we can take him, but we have to be fast. There's a staff utility room off the hallway. We don't have much time. I'm telling you, they're going to start looking for him and you and me, and all the alarms are going to be ringing," the facilities guy mentioned.

"Then let's do it. Help me drag his ass," I said.

We worked together to move the CO, but he was starting to come back into consciousness. He was moaning and groaning. Finally, after what seemed like forever, we got him to the room.

"Now what?" the facilities guy asked nervously. "I didn't sign up for all of this. They said transportation out of the building in the cart, and after I load you into the laundry truck, I have to drive for ten miles to a spot where there would be a black SUV waiting for you. They said you would know the person inside and you'd know what to do. They didn't say shit about all of this," he said, his voice shaking.

Shut up, weak ass! I thought.

"You didn't ask for it, but we are here now, and for both of our sakes, we have to take care of him or we will both be fucked. Not only will they take me back to the torture chambers, but they will have your ass locked up and they'll throw away the key," I snapped. I needed to make sure he saw this for what it was. We had no fucking choice in the matter.

Once we were tucked away in the utility room, I stopped for a few seconds and took three deep, cleansing breaths. I was once again in the tight situation where I was going to have to hurt someone for my own self-preservation.

"You can do this by yourself, Misty. You have to do this," I spoke quietly to myself. The stupid facilities guy was looking at me like I was crazy.

"What tools are in here? Is there any tape? I need to secure his mouth, hands, and feet," I said. I was all business now. Fuck the pain racking through my body and the consequences I might be facing. I needed to get out of there. I needed to put in the effort to get free. There would be no more lying down and taking abuse at this point. I had done that for too long.

The facilities guy went about finding stuff for me to use. I was silently praying that he hurried up before we got caught. I felt sweat running a race down my back. I shifted my weight from one foot to the other. Suddenly my bladder felt like it was going to bust. My nerves were on edge. I'd felt this unstable feeling so much over the past two years that it was becoming normal to me now. That wasn't good.

After a few minutes, he returned with the stuff that I needed. The hairs on my neck and arms stood up. *Yes!*

I swallowed hard and silently rattled off in my head what I needed to do. I had to keep my head in the game. I had to think back to some of the things I had heard Tedo and April say that day they were disposing of Terrell's body.

I had to put myself in a survival mind-set or I would lose the nerve to do exactly what it was that I needed to do.

Then I had a thought: *Did this dumb nigga secure the door?*

"Go secure the door to make sure no one comes in here," I instructed. "That's the last thing we need right now. Bad enough that before long they're going to be looking for this guy."

Finally, I heard the locks click. The door was secured and I would have to set about doing the deed. I walked over to where the CO lay.

"What the fuck are you doing? How the fuck did I get in here?" the CO murmured as he came into consciousness. His eyes locked with mine and I could see the shock registering on his face. "Wha-what are you doing with that?" he asked, nervousness dancing in his voice. He could see me holding the thick black tape and a wrench in my hands.

Suddenly, I couldn't move. I blinked wildly for a few seconds, but I was paralyzed, stuck. I don't know what the combination of emotions was that took hold of me. Looking at the CO's face, my mind reeled back to his actions, not only against the other girls, but against me too.

It had been another day when I'd been violently dragged out of a cell. As I had stood in the middle of the medical-testing facility room, I looked out into the crowd of doctors, orderlies, COs, and medical techs. I hated all of them. Some of them were dressed in their scrubs, some of them wore their uniforms, and some were in suits and ties, like this was their executive jobs.

As I had darted my eyes from face to face, I could definitely tell the difference between the ones that were there for actual work and the ones that were there for their sick proclivities. The bastards had huge lust in their eyes, and it seemed to be oozing out. I had listened as the doctor said all sorts of things about my vital signs, my health history, and the past tests they'd run on me. It was like I wasn't even human to them anymore.

"Misty Heiress, here for murder. No family visits. Weight, one hundred fifty-one pounds. Breasts, thirty-six, D-cup. Waist, twenty-nine inches." Everything about me had been rattled off like the stats of a sporting event. It was a demeaning and humiliating process.

I had been growing angry inside by the minute as I watched all of them look at me and write notes about me like I was a lab specimen. I had kept seeing this CO lick his lips as he watched me.

"Several more tests are needed to determine viability," one of the doctors had said. "As such, we will take a look at her closer. Isolation is necessary."

I had been so busy listening and trying to figure out what they were going to do to me, I hadn't realized just how preoccupied this CO seemed with me. When it was time for them to strip me for the testing, the doctors usually made most of the guards and COs leave the room. This day, though, they got to stay.

I had seen him. I had known then that it wasn't going to be a good result if I was left alone. I had been correct. I had been left alone, and the CO didn't hesitate to take advantage of it.

"What are you doing?" I had asked when he returned alone. "You're not supposed to be in here."

The CO had laughed at me. "Don't ask so many questions," he had said, then grabbed his crotch.

I had started to cry. "Don't do this. Please," I had begged.

"It won't take long. It never does," he had replied. "You bitches turn me on so much." He had been breathing heavy and sweating. Clearly, he had been excited by his dirty thoughts.

I had tried to scream, but the CO had grabbed me by the neck and put his huge hand over my nose and mouth.

I had realized if I didn't stop, he'd suffocate me. My nails were dug into his hands.

"Stop fighting and I'll move it," he had huffed, growing sexually excited by my fear.

Finally, I had stopped trying to scream. I just wanted him to take his hands off of me. He moved his hand from my mouth and trailed them down my body.

I had squeezed my eyes shut, realizing what was happening. I had lain there, my body stiff and rigid. I had held on to the sides of the sheets so hard, my knuckles had paled.

He had raped me, again and again.

I had felt a lot of anxiety, and had wanted to die . . . again. That had been the same feeling, over and over and over.

"You feel so good," the CO had panted in my ears, as if talking to me was going to change the fact that he was doing this against my will. "Tell me that it feels good for you too," he had demanded. "Say it!"

I had scrunched up my face and gagged.

Is he fucking serious? No, it wasn't good for me too! You disgusting bastard! You're abusing my body and you're asking if it's good for me too? I had screamed inside my head.

What came out of my mouth was much different. "Yes," I had whimpered the lie. If I hadn't, I think he would've continued until I did. I had just wanted it to be over.

Just like the rest of those bastards, the CO had groped my tits and had put his hands in every orifice on my body. There had been no way I could fight back.

I had tried really hard not to vomit on the CO and myself as he continued his assault for another few minutes. The longer it had gone on, the eviler I felt inside. I was having all types of murderous thoughts about the CO.

This is what these people had made me into. I was picturing myself doing all types of violent sick shit to all of them. In that moment, I'd told myself if ever given a chance, I would torture them all.

When the CO had finished, I let a wicked smile spread on my face. He probably thought I was excited by him, but I wasn't.

I had actually been thinking that this motherfucker had no idea what would be in store for him if I ever got my hands on him alone. He thought he could do sick, nasty, perverted shit to me, and get away with it forever. But he and the rest of them had no idea what I had in store for whichever one of them I got my hands on if I ever got out.

"Pl-please . . . what are you going to do to me?" the CO pled, snapping me out of my nightmare.

"I'm going to do to you what you like," I said, moving closer to him. "You remember all the sick things you liked to do, right?"

"It—it wasn't only me," the CO stammered, and I menacingly bent over him with my stun gun. He put his hands up in defense. "Please! I will do whatever you ask me to do. I'll help you get out of here," he begged, using his best acting skills.

I knew better than that. I didn't trust a soul. Not even the people who were actually helping me. I'd already learned that everyone in this world had ulterior motives. Everyone.

"Wait, now you want to help me get out?" I asked, tilting my head to the side and folding my face into a confused frown. "I was just listening to you tell this guy that you were going to turn us in."

"Um . . . no . . . I won't. I'll help you . . . I swear," the CO lied. "Please don't kill me. I have a wife and kids. I'll do anything!" The CO continued to spill lies out of his mouth, one after the other.

The CO could see my eyes glistening with fire and evil thoughts about what I had in store for him. "Please. Don't do this," he begged.

"All right, but what should your punishment be for the bad things you've done?" I asked, teasing him as I bound his feet with black tape. A mixture of excitement and fear flitted through my stomach, causing a wave of cramps to stab through my abdomen.

"Tell me what you think is fair?" I asked.

"Nothing. I'll help you get out of here and I won't tell anyone about this," the CO answered, watching me carefully.

"But remember everything you did to us? We suffered. If I just let you go, then you won't ever know the pain you caused us. There will be no consequences for your actions. Plus, I don't fucking believe you, asshole," I growled. With that, I grabbed his face and went around his mouth with the tape.

The CO shook his head, left to right, begging with his eyes. I smiled to myself as I walked around him, bounding his hands. I noticed that he'd peed on himself. It actually gave me sick satisfaction to have someone else in this helpless position.

"We don't have a lot of time. You're dragging this out too long," the facilities guy said to me as he paced around the door.

He was right. I was taking too long. We really did need to get the heck out of here, but it was like I couldn't hear him because I was taking so much satisfaction in exacting my revenge on this CO.

I could tell the facilities guy was thinking that I was no better than those abusive doctors and officers, but I didn't care. Maybe he was right. Maybe I had a level of evil in me that surfaced at times like this. I didn't care anymore, really. I needed to do this.

"I have to do it my way," I whispered to myself. I looked around the utility room for anything else I could use as a weapon, just in case I felt crazier than I did in that moment. The CO was a pretty big guy, so I couldn't be too careful.

"Damn," I whispered as my eyes lit up.

There were a lot of things I could choose from. There were tools and sharp objects and saws and even sandpaper. I picked up a pointed-end pickax and rubbed my hands over it. Then I picked up a hammer and thought about all the pain I could inflict with that. It was a torturer's dream to be in a closet full of tools. I smiled a little bit. It was the first hint of satisfaction I'd felt in months. I looked over and I could see the facilities guy's eyes stretch.

"Listen, I don't want no part of this," he mumbled nervously. "We don't have time. I'm telling you the cavalry is going to be looking for him any minute now. You're being stupid."

"Just keep watching the door and do what I tell you to do," I snapped. "At this point, whatever happens, happens, but I'm not giving up my chance on this revenge."

I stepped closer to the CO and took in a lungful of air, blew it out, and moved in for the kill.

"Look at you now. Not so tough—raping people and pissing on them, or beating them for no reason," I snarled.

The CO's eyes darted around frantically, and he moaned through the tape. He started moving his body and it reminded me of an inchworm the way he moved in and out, trying to get away from me. There was nowhere for him to go. I'd been in that position many times since I'd been locked up, so I knew the fear and angst he was feeling. I loved to see it dancing in his eyes. I was completely overcome with vengefulness in that moment. All sense and sensibility had disappeared.

"There is nowhere to run, you bastard," I gritted. My eyebrows dipped on my face as I looked at him lying there, helpless—like a sloppy, fat, beached walrus—with tears coming out of his eyes.

"Now you know how this feels, don't you?" I asked, squinting at him. "Not knowing what to expect. Not knowing what will happen to you, minute by minute. Not having anyone to help you or save you. Having your life and limb dangling in front of you in the hands of a sick person. How does it feel?" I felt my nervousness and fear hardening into a fiery nugget of fury, which spurred my actions on.

"Mmmm," the CO groaned, shaking his head.

"You want this one first?" I asked slyly, holding a pair of oversized pliers out in front of me. I wanted to see all six-foot-three and three hundred pounds of him suffer.

"Yes, I think these will do the trick," I said, my jaw stiffening and my eyes flattening into dashes. I straddled over the CO with evil dancing in my eyes.

The CO began breathing harder and harder. I could see all the veins in his temple and neck cording against his skin as he strained from pure fear.

"That's what I wanted to see," I said excitedly. "Remember what you said to me one time when you raped me? Remember your words? You said, 'This is no fun if you close your eyes. Let me give it to you, while you watch and act like you love it,' " I said, repeating some of the words he'd said to me, in the same cruel way he'd said them.

The CO inched his body some more, snapping his eyes closed.

Suddenly another quick memory of him forcing his wide body between my legs and his slimy dick into my desert-dry vaginal opening flashed through my mind. I remembered how he'd forced his chunky, sweaty palm over my mouth and nose, cutting off my air supply until I'd finally given up fighting. After the rape, I could barely walk or take a comfortable piss for days.

"Oh . . . what, you don't remember?" I asked, scowling.

The CO began wheezing like he was having a heart attack as I opened his pants and looked down in disgust at his shitty-brown skin and the layers of fat that made up his stomach. I felt my insides grind with nausea. I gripped the tool so tightly I left a dent in the palm of my hand. The adrenaline coursing through my body didn't allow me to feel the pain, though.

"Open your fucking eyes," I whispered in a low growl as I pressed my hand into his soft chest.

When he felt me touch him, he began panting and crying like the bitch that he was.

"Yeah, that's what I'm talking about," I snarled, getting ready to do the deed.

"We are going to get caught," the facilities guy warned.

I ignored him. Nothing or no one was going to stop the maniacal thoughts running through my mind. I wished I had way more time so I could really drag it out and make his ass suffer.

The CO tried to move so that he could get away from me.

"Uh-un, un. You can't go anywhere now," I scolded. "Now, do you remember the first time you raped me?" I asked, my voice hoarse with anger.

The CO nodded his head up and down in the affirmative.

"Whose idea was it?" I asked. "Yours?"

The CO shook his head side to side, frantically indicating no.

"Oh, so it was Dr. Clemons's idea?" I asked, taunting him.

The CO nodded his head up and down, frantically indicating yes.

"So it was all Dr. Clemons's idea. You didn't ever just feel like doing it on your own?" I repeated the question in a different form. "What about y'all torturing my friend Shanta and leaving her bleeding from her vagina? Or, what about hog-tying several of the girls and fucking them in the ass until they bled? You didn't like none of that?"

The CO shifted uncomfortably, but I pressed my weight down on him. His chest shuttered like he was struggling to breathe.

"Well, I hope you enjoyed it, and I hope there are girls for you to rape in hell," I growled, raising the pliers and clamping them down on the CO's balls with all of the force in my body until I drew blood.

"*Grrrr!*" the CO squawked from behind the tape on his mouth. His eyes shot open in shock. His body began writhing in pain.

I moved and quickly picked up the pickax.

When the CO saw me change tools, he really started going crazy then. He gagged, his bound hands instinctively moving up and down trying to get to me.

I drove the pointed end of the pickax into his neck and hit the main vein. Blood spurted everywhere.

"Holy shit!" the facilities guy yelped. "You're fucking crazy, and I'm out of here."

"Do not move until I say to move," I growled.

I stood over the CO and watched as his body bucked wildly. He tried to roll around to remove the blade from his neck, but I could see that he was getting weak as blood gushed from his neck and soaked the entire floor.

I remembered the doctor I used to work with telling me that it took about two minutes for a person to bleed to death if the internal jugular vein is cut, which is larger than the external jugular vein. It was more effective if the victim was lying down, like the CO was. I was hoping he would bleed to death in one minute.

"You might as well stop fighting. It'll only be a few more seconds. I hope it was all worth it. You and Dr. Clemons ruined me. Y'all turned me into a fucking monster that can't go back to being anything else," I said to him, my voice suddenly going eerily calm.

The CO let out a few more ghastly choking noises. I gagged a few times as the smell of the piss and shit that leaked from his body got to me. A smile curled on my lips as I took a sick sense of enjoyment watching the life leave his body. When the CO finally went completely still, having asphyxiated on his own blood, I went to work, making sure we didn't leave any traces of ourselves behind.

"Shit," I cursed, registering that I had cut my finger. I couldn't be sure that I hadn't mixed my blood with his, but I also knew I couldn't focus on that now. "Let's get the fuck out of here," I huffed, and raced over to the door.

"I've only been saying *that* for the past twenty minutes! Now you have blood all over my shirt," the facilities guy complained.

I stepped back, looked at the dead man in front of me, and smiled like a lunatic proud of my handiwork. I was quickly realizing that murder was easy when it's for the right reasons.

"These motherfuckers ain't ready for Misty Heiress," I mumbled under my breath.

18

FREEDOM, OR NOT

When I was finally pushed out of that prison, and I could tell I was outside of those walls, tears sprang to my eyes and would not stop falling. I was thanking God in all kinds of ways, although I knew I would need to pray really hard after what I had just done to that CO.

After the facilities guy got me outside in the cart, I was loaded into the back of the linen truck, just like it had been planned. We were about an hour late for the planned meet-up times. I didn't know how that would affect things, but I prayed it wouldn't.

The facilities guy left me in the hands of another man, who was driving the linen truck. I heard them mumbling about where I needed to be taken and what needed to happen. I thought I even heard them mention something about me having a lot of money. That made me a bit uneasy. Too many people in on a plan wasn't good. And them thinking I was sitting on some paper wasn't good either.

"You the one being busted out of here?" an old white man with a huge, round belly wheezed before he closed the door and locked me in the back of the truck. I coughed because inside the truck, it was fucking filthy and it smelled like a mixture of shit, musty armpits, and cheap cologne. I guess the cologne came from his ass; the other odors were from the dirty laundry. I didn't think I'd ever be that acquainted with dirty laundry in my lifetime.

"That would be me," I managed to say, wanting so badly to cover my nose with my hands. But my hands were dirty too, and covering my face with my sweaty, blood-stained shirt wouldn't help. Everything was foul.

"Alrighty, we on our way," the old white man huffed, pulling out.

I immediately started praying we made it through the guard station without a hitch. I heard voices as we rode through. I held my breath the entire time. I didn't speak much during the ride because I simply didn't want to open my mouth in that stink-ass truck.

The ride was miserable and seemed to be taking forever. We were definitely taking the most scenic route. Some of the roads we drove down had nothing but cornfields surrounding them. At one point, we passed a police car sitting off to the side and my heart drummed up in my chest.

After what seemed like forever, the laundry truck turned onto a long, dusty, one-lane road, with nothing surrounding it but trees and bushes. The scenery made me think of some deserted campsite in a movie like *Friday the 13th* or one of its sequels. Jillian and I used to watch those movies as kids. We would watch scary movies and then be scared as shit for weeks afterward. I smiled as I thought about the fun times with my cousin.

"We made it, finally," the stinky, beer-bellied white man announced as he slowed the truck to a halt.

I looked through the dirty windshield of the truck and squinted my eyes. *What the fuck? This can't be right?* I was screaming in my head, but I kept my cool.

"A farm? Lisa and Anderson told you to bring me to a farm?" I asked the man incredulously. My eyebrows were dipped low on my forehead and my lips were twisted into almost a snarl.

What the fuck is going on? I need to be in the city to get to my mother! I was thinking.

"Mmm-hmm, that's right. Someone else will get you on the next leg of the trip. Now, they said you wasn't going to give me no trouble. Said you just wanted to get as far away as possible, so they said for me not to worry. I don't want no trouble now. I expect to collect my money and be done with this. I risked a lot to help you out," the man said, hints of annoyance underlying his words.

He could tell I was none too pleased with my current surroundings. I snapped my mouth shut and eased the look on my face. Shit, I was a beggar and damn sure couldn't be a chooser.

"No, I'm good. No problem at all," I lied. I could tell lying and faking were going to be huge parts of my repertoire while I worked to get to my mother and as far away as possible.

I was led around the back of the farmhouse to another waiting truck. It was the type of truck I had seen on the highways that had closed-in animal crates hitched to the back. I could tell by the small holes in the truck's back cabin that it was, in fact, an animal transport truck. I looked at the man strangely, and he looked at me with amusement in his eyes.

"Yeah, this is your ride to freedom. Might be a little uncomfortable for you, but you won't have to worry about nobody finding you. Nothing but some chickens on the way to slaughter up in there," he said. There was an amused tone to his words; then he nodded toward the back of the truck. "Smells will keep even the most gung-ho police away from you." The man laughed.

I was growing wary of him because he seemed to be taunting me on the low. I didn't know what the man meant when he said something about the smell, but I would soon find out.

Another man stepped from around the side of the truck, nodded at the big-bellied white man, and unlatched the back.

"Go on, climb in," the man told me, nudging me forward.

I did as I was told. It wasn't really an option to decline at that point. I couldn't question any parts of this crazy plan; all I thought about was seeing my mother.

"Oh God! What the fuck is that smell!" I shrieked as soon as I climbed up onto the truck. "It smells like pure shit in here," I complained, gagging slightly. "Is this some sort of joke?!" I called out to the men.

Neither one responded, but as soon as the truck doors were closed and locked, I could hear them snickering. I eased down onto the truck floor between two crates. The sawdust on the floor pricked my legs and I felt like I was being stabbed with a thousand needles. It didn't help that my body was already in bad shape from everything I'd been through. The sound of chickens fighting in the crates was crazy. I could hear their nails scratching against the wood and they made a crying sound, which hurt my ears.

"Oh my God! What the fuck?" I shouted, hoping maybe my voice would scare the chickens into keeping still. "I can't believe this!"

My talking just made it worse. The chickens began reacting and shrieking because of my presence. Some of the crates moved violently from the chickens flapping their wings. I could barely move left or right because of the cramped space, but I was able to put my hands up to my ears. It didn't help. I started praying in earnest that this wouldn't take much longer.

The second truck also didn't go toward the highway, which made me think they were still purposely taking back roads so we didn't run the risk of getting stopped by police. After driving for a while, we finally got to another place. I hoped this was going to be it.

I immediately got nervous because when I was going over my escape plans in my head, I had anticipated being in the city when I got away. Now shit had changed, which meant I had to change my plans. My mind started racing with different scenarios about my escape. My thoughts were broken when the driver looked up into the rearview mirror and smirked at me. That caused a cold chill to shoot down my back. I wasn't up for no more bullshit.

"You ready to face the music?" he asked.

That's when I noticed he had an accent that sounded like Ahmad's. "Who are you?" I asked, my voice rising.

"We finally got our hands on you, Misty. You ran right into our trap," he said.

I scrambled up off the floor to try to open the back door to jump out. But when I did that, his foot mashed down onto the gas and the truck sped out of control. My body lurched forward and I went barreling into the chicken crates. One fell over and at least ten birds escaped and started going crazy. One of the chickens tried to fly and attacked the driver.

Now the truck was really out of control. I screamed when I saw the driver just miss crashing into a huge tree. He drove the truck onto a patch of grass. The truck swerved all over the place and I just knew I was about to die. I struggled to open the back door; the truck's jumpy movement and my own pounding heart made grabbing the door handle difficult. But finally, I was able to get the door open and jump from the truck. I rolled onto the grass and took off running. My legs were burning and my chest felt like it would cave in. All I could think of was that Anderson had to be working with my enemies. But that didn't make sense. They could've just killed me.

As I ran, I saw a lady in the park. She had just taken her baby out of her car. I ran straight for her, pushed her down, and hopped into the driver's seat of the car. I peeled the fuck out of there.

"Oh my God! Oh my God!" I screamed out in joy as I raced the vehicle down the road. My fucking hands were trembling so badly, I could barely keep them on the steering wheel. I was so excited inside. Lisa's plan had worked, but not exactly how it was laid out. At first, I didn't know if I should stop or keep going, because I needed to get in touch with my mother or Sandra or somebody.

I stepped on the gas and kept checking the mirrors for any cops or any followers. I looked down and saw that the woman had left her cell phone in the cup holder. I kept following that one road, but I was growing very anxious to find a spot to stop and call Sandra and let her know that I had gotten away. I was going to need her help, for sure. I knew explaining this to Sandra would be difficult. I knew she would want me to just keep on running as far away as I could get until she could come and get me.

Finally, after driving for a few, I decided to stop. I called Sandra.

"Sandra!" I cried into the phone. At first, I was dealing with such a big rush of emotions I couldn't get my words out properly. After I calmed down a little bit, I was finally able to tell her a quick version of the entire story about Lisa getting me out, but how one guy had turned on me and I was now lost.

Sandra said she was part of the plan; she'd been contacted by Anderson, but she grew worried when she didn't hear from me. Sandra told me she was supposed to meet me on a back road in Norfolk. She gave me the location.

"Sandra, if for some reason I don't make it to you, please make sure you send the authorities back to that prison to save all of those women. If I get away and meet up with you, I have to go back and help the others. It is the least I can do for them . . . I made promises, and they are suffering," I told her seriously.

"Misty, just get out of there right now. Let me get you in the clear first. This is too risky to worry about right now. Hang up and drive," Sandra said with feeling.

Sandra told me to hang up the phone because the woman whose car I'd stolen probably already had the police pinging the cell phone towers to triangulate my location. I hadn't even thought about that, and she was right. I couldn't risk keeping the phone, although that meant no more communication with Sandra. I was out there all alone, and all of law enforcement was probably looking for me right now.

I did like she said. I hung up. And as I drove, I threw the phone out of the window and sped away from it. I followed all of the landmarks I remembered passing, until I was up the street from the location where I had arranged to meet Sandra. My heart was beating really fast and I was sweating. I was very nervous that someone would jump out on me before I could get to her. Luckily, the windows on the woman's car were tinted so dark that you couldn't see inside.

I drove past the location first, so I could make sure everything was legit before I exposed myself. I just prayed really hard that as I passed, Sandra would see me and give me some signal that it was her. Even though I drove by slowly, I couldn't tell. I saw people eyeballing the vehicle suspiciously, so I knew I had to go around the block and stay back before they started to investigative further. I worried they'd realize that the car was stolen—or worse, that it was an escaped inmate behind the wheel. Just being on the street had me hella nervous. All I could do right then was hope that Sandra could piece together the clues and get there as soon as possible.

Suddenly a tap on the window almost made me lose my heart through my mouth. I whipped my head around and saw Sandra standing outside the car. Relief washed over me like a warm wave.

"Open the door," Sandra whispered.

"Oh my God," I gasped, happy as hell to see her. I scrambled out of the car and rushed into Sandra so hard and fast that she stumbled back a little bit.

"Whoa, whoa," Sandra said, chuckling. "I'm happy to see you too, Misty."

At first, it took me a minute to catch my breath because I was crying so hard.

"Oh my God! You have no idea what I've been through. I can't believe this day is here, and it almost wasn't. Ahmad sent someone and they infiltrated the plan. I don't know how he always finds out everything," I said through my happy tears.

What if I didn't get away? What if they were waiting for me in the back of that truck? These were the thoughts running through my mind.

"Oh my God. I can't stop saying how happy I am to see you," I said.

"I'm happy too, but we need to get out of here. This area probably is hot as hell now," Sandra said.

I can't lie. I was still kind of dazed by the way everything had happened. I was shaking all over, and my heart was beating like a drum. I knew that the prison realized by now that I had escaped. It wouldn't be long before they would be on a mission to find me, and on an even bigger mission to keep me from exposing the things going on in the prison. That meant they were going to be trying to shut me up . . . permanently.

I started thinking about Shanta, Lena, Dana, Fiona, and all of the other inmates that were subjected to the abuse of those sick people. I knew that once Dr. Clemons realized he might be exposed, it wouldn't take them long to figure out who helped me get away. All fingers would point back to Lisa and she would surely be killed. I could just imagine them pulling her down to the bowels of the prison and beating her, torturing her, and then executing her in front of all the girls so they could make an example out of her. It didn't matter if she worked there; I believed they were ruthless enough to kill her in there. Lisa was on my mind like crazy.

But I also had bigger problems on my hands. Terrell's family and Ahmad were still trying to set me up for the downfall, and now I was sure they knew I had escaped.

As I settled into Sandra's car and contemplated my next move, I suddenly saw three black cars with dark tinted windows barreling past us. My stomach jumped. I knew right away they were law enforcement vehicles that were probably on my case. I also knew that they'd be setting up search perimeters soon. They would probably be riding around with some of those bloodhound dogs trying to find me. All they had to do was spot the car and I would be done. I'm sure they wouldn't spare my life, especially after what I had done. After I saw the cars whizzing past me, something snapped inside me.

"I have to get to my mother, but after that, I need to do something about that prison. I can't let women continue to be tortured there," I said.

I went into superhero mode in my mind. I just said to myself, I had to take things into my own hands. I wasn't about to let an opportunity for revenge slip right through my fingers and I wasn't going to let the girls down.

No matter how dangerous the mission was, I was hell-bent on bringing Dr. Clemons down and getting revenge for all of the abuse I had suffered. I couldn't just let them all get away like that.

19

REUNITED

"Baby girl?!" Her familiar voice was like the sweetest music to my ears. The excitement of hearing it was indescribable.

"Mommy? Mommy, is that you?" I called out, the glare of the sunlight hurting my hypersensitive eyes.

Sandra and I had been driving all night, but when the sun came up, I had to get into the trunk, just in case. Being in that dark trunk, I felt like I had been riding for days when the car stopped abruptly, jarring my cramped body. My stomach was churning with a mixture of extreme hunger and nausea from the motion. Finally, I heard that voice.

"Mommy!" I called out again.

"Yes! Baby girl! It's me . . . in the flesh!" my mother called out and opened the trunk of the car.

I had never been so glad to see my mother in my entire life. She leaned down and I threw my arms around her neck and squeezed her like I never wanted to let her go.

"I'm happy to see you too, Misty," my mother said, barely able to breathe. I was squeezing her so tightly.

"You have no idea how happy I am that you're safe and sound," I cried.

"It hasn't been easy. I'm not even going to lie, Misty. You got us all into some dangerous stuff out here, and then when you just disappeared and I couldn't find you even in the system, I just knew they had gotten hold of you," my mother said on the verge of tears. "I just knew my child was dead and that I would be dealing with another death all alone."

"No, Mommy, I'm alive. They used the system to punish me. It has been a horrible experience," I said. "I don't even know how I made it through that, but I am here. Like Grandma told me once, when I saw her on the other side . . . I have a bigger mission, and God won't be satisfied until I fulfill that mission," I continued.

"Well, for now, let's savor this moment together," my mother said.

She handed me a department store bag. I looked inside and couldn't believe my eyes—she had a disguise ready for me. My eyes almost popped out of my head when she pulled out the wig, contacts, and clothes. I knew my mother had definitely learned how to be street savvy after everything she'd been through because of me. I was glad she was thinking on her feet.

My mother looked around before saying, "Scrunch back down and put on those clean clothes. You need to put this on so we can check into the hotel for the night. Just in case someone's looking, push down the back seat and exit from there instead of jumping out this trunk. We will have to figure out a plan after that. But right now, you look like you need a good night's rest and some good food," my mother mentioned. Her eyebrows were raised as she took in an eyeful of my old and new cuts and bruises.

This was why I loved her so much. She never let me down.

* * *

"This shit is not bad for a girl who broke out of a prison with nothing and no one being able to find her for months!" I beamed as we all entered our hotel room.

"Shit, you're a genius for this one. I've been locked up a ton of times and only ever used legal defenses to get out. I swear, I don't think I'd have the balls to convince anyone to help me actually escape," Sandra said, rushing over to check out the wet bar.

"It would've been even better if there was a big steak, some fried chicken, some fresh designer threads, and some damn foundation in here waiting for me. I'm so tired of looking like shit, it ain't even funny," I said.

"Just be happy we got into this room without any suspicion," my mother said, shaking her head. "Tomorrow we can think about all of the other stuff, like clothes and food."

When we checked into the hotel, we sent my mother to the front desk to check in. My mother looked like an innocent older woman, and none of us wanted to draw suspicion. Sandra, with her manly features and her masculine swag, and that little hint of attitude that traced through all of her words, would've been memorable. Her description might stick with the front-desk clerk in case anyone came snooping.

My mother was perfect for the job. I would've been, once upon a time when I was pretty, with my perfectly straight white teeth and my blemish-free skin tone with its beautiful glow. I was quietly upset that I might never look the same again after everything I'd suffered through.

"I need a shower and sleep," I huffed, kicking off my sneakers and unzipping my hoodie. All of the bending, ducking, and running in the past twenty-four hours had me aching all over.

"Yeah, I feel you. You can go to sleep. I'll be up. I want

to watch the news and see if they're saying anything about you," Sandra said.

"You know we can't stay here long, right? A few winks and we gotta go," my mother chimed in.

"Yeah, I know," I grumbled. I couldn't stop thinking of my promises to Lisa and to Lena and the girls. It was so hard to let that go. I felt like I had to do something more.

"Don't sound like that, Misty, we have to do what we have to do," my mother said.

I didn't respond. I just shook my head and walked into the bathroom. I saw Sandra pick up the television remote and she clicked it on.

"Damn, I knew this shit would be all over the news," I heard her say.

I rushed back out of the bathroom and stood at the threshold, watching the television. My heart sank as I listened.

"Police and correction officials report that a convicted murderer, Misty Heiress, escaped from a maximum-security prison in Virginia today. In the brazen escape, it is suspected Heiress had inside help. Staff members at the facility are all being interviewed so officials can determine who inside assisted. Officials report that at least one prison staff member was found dead. Investigators say they cannot confirm or deny whether the staff member's death was caused by Heiress or another staff member, at this time," the journalist reported. "Police are scouring the area for Heiress. For now, the facility is locked down and the FBI has been called in to the prison to launch an investigation."

I listened to the reporter's words and waves of nausea rolled through my stomach. I didn't know if it was the excitement of knowing I had actually pulled off an escape or if it was the fact that killing the CO had exacted at least some revenge so far. My mother would've never approved of me killing anyone, even if it was to get away.

I was so transfixed with the news that I didn't even see the look I was getting from my mother.

"Did you kill someone to get out of that prison, Misty?" she asked, her face folded into a confused frown. "I would hope not. We all have to answer to God one day."

"Look! Don't ask me no questions about that. I had to do what I had to do. Would you rather I be dead and you never see me again? Sometimes things are inevitable, so don't blame me," I snapped as the knot of anger and anxiety in my chest finally unraveled. I hung my head as a quick pang of guilt came over me like a dark hood.

"*Blaming you?* It's not about blaming you. It's about what's morally right," my mother fired back.

I sighed loudly and shook my head. I looked over at Sandra and she just raised her eyebrows to let me know she wanted to stay out of it. I quickly shook off the feeling of dread and guilt that had trampled on my mood.

Fuck it. What's done is done, I thought.

But then, I could hear my grandmother's voice in my head: "*You have a mission down there, Misty. There is something you have to do, so you need to go back and find out what it is.*"

She was right. The guilt of leaving Lisa and the girls behind was still gnawing at me. I know I needed to be careful, but I couldn't help feeling like I had more to do.

I lay awake in the hotel bed in silence and hardly able to sleep, although I should've been extremely exhausted. When the digital clock on the hotel nightstand finally read 4:00, I sat up in the bed like I'd been jolted with a shock of electricity.

"Sandra, you asleep?" I whispered.

"Mmmm," Sandra moaned, and then sucked her teeth and turned over.

I don't know how Sandra and my mother slept so soundly, when I couldn't get one minute of sleep. Worry, fear, anxiety—you name it, I was experiencing it.

I got up from the bed and stretched the kinks out of my still-aching limbs. I wanted to make sure my mother and Sandra were sound asleep before I left the room. I knew it was a risky undertaking, and probably crazy as hell in a sane person's eyes, but I couldn't shake it.

I had to do it, just like Lisa and I had planned. With me gone now, and no one to expose Dr. Clemons, or get the other girls out of there, all hope would be lost if I didn't do something. Plus, I still felt like I had scores to settle back at the prison. It had taken months to put all of this in place and we did it, but there was still a huge void inside me.

"I'm going to keep my promise," I whispered under my breath with feeling.

I still had everything in my head, just like we planned it. Once I could see Lisa's face on the outside, it would go down how we wanted it. I had my head back in the game.

I didn't really want to part ways with my mother again, but I knew this time would be different. I smiled as I looked at her sleeping peacefully. She was going to be mad when she awoke and I wasn't there, but that was okay. In the end, she would be proud of me when I did what I needed to do, which was to save a bunch of women from being used and abused.

"I will be back, and I will make you proud," I told her even though I knew I was playing Russian roulette. With all the things I'd done wrong in my life, I wanted to do something right. Something that could balance out my Karma.

Then, as quietly as I could, I stepped out of the hotel room. I sucked in my breath because my nerves lit up as soon as the air hit my face. I surveyed the surroundings and then gave myself a quick pep talk.

"Stick with the plan and this shit will all be over soon," I told myself out loud.

I was being crazy, I know, but I had a mission on my

mind, and, honestly, nothing else mattered. I needed to make things right within myself and for those girls. The old selfish Misty had been replaced by a new person—a person who was going to end up as a hero. A person who was not going to let people like Dr. Clemons get away with murder . . . literally.

20

CARRYING OUT THE PLAN

Icranked up the engine of Sandra's car and I pulled out. I started toward where Lisa told me to rendezvous. I knew this was probably a bad idea, but after all of the risks I had already taken, it was just one more. Deep down inside, I was feeling like, *What did I have to lose now?*

I looked over at the gun I had taken from Sandra and took comfort that I had the weapon at least. I wasn't afraid to use it. What did I have to lose? The entire nation had already pegged me as a murderer, anyway. So, why not run with the myth? All that mattered was that I knew who I was and what I represented.

I followed the road, making sure I played it safe. Shortly after I left the hotel, I pulled onto the highway, but I was paranoid. I could've sworn someone was following me. I had to make a quick, calculated decision and I did. I detoured because something inside me told me I was being trailed. I drove for a while and did a few jumps on and jumps off of exits, so that if someone was following me, they'd lose me. A few times, I really had to maneuver the car to make sure I was not seen. It was crazy. My nerves were frazzled as hell as I weaved in and out of traffic.

Finally I exited the highway. I really had to keep letting other cars get in front of me to stay inconspicuous. I made it to the road Lisa had told me to get to. It appeared to be a private road. I had to actually stop and look around to make sure I wasn't in the wrong place. The little private road led the way up to a house. The house was huge and it was nice from what I could see of the outside.

I pulled onto a small road at the side of the property. I pulled close enough to see if Lisa was there, like she said she would be. I pulled over and stayed out of sight for a few minutes. A car stopped and I saw someone getting out, but I couldn't tell if it was Lisa or not. I kept on watching. She tapped on the window. I jumped so hard, I hit my hand on the steering wheel. I got so scared, it made me sick to my stomach. When the door to the car opened, Lisa jumped inside.

"Oh my God, you almost gave me a heart attack," I huffed.

"You did so good, Misty. I was so happy when you called me from Sandra's cell phone to say you'd made it. Things at the prison are crazy right now," she said. She was back to nice Lisa, which was good. While I was inside, sometimes I didn't know what to expect from her.

"What is this place?" I asked.

"Dr. Clemons's house," she said stoically.

"What?" I asked, sucking in my breath.

"Yes, and you'll see why I brought you here in a minute. I needed you to see what he's doing now," she said.

Within a few minutes, I looked up and almost swallowed my tongue at what I was seeing. There was a line of girls being brought out of the house. They were all chained together so there was no way they could get out. They looked like animals being taken for slaughter. Some of them were staggering from the drugs they had probably been given, and the ones that were sober were being forced to keep the other girls on their feet.

"Are you serious? He sneaks them out to his house?" I asked incredulously.

"No, the prison sells them to him! He takes the ones he wants and does this, and others he does what he did to you," she relayed.

I was so fucking mad; I bit down on my lip until I drew my own blood. Dr. Clemons was a sick bastard, even on a level I had no idea about. He deserved to die, for sure.

With my hands shaking, I immediately turned to Lisa and asked her a serious question. "Did you bring what you were supposed to bring?" My anger was coming across in my words.

"Yes, I did, but we will be risking other lives if we do this," she said, sounding concerned.

"We knew this, though. We knew in order to get rid of him, someone would be at risk," I said. As I was saying that, I saw a van pull up. I looked on with my eyes wide as the girls were loaded into the van. I could only imagine where they were taking them, but at least that meant those innocent girls would be out of the house when we exacted our plan on Dr. Clemons.

"I'm glad he took them out. We have to hurry and then we have to get as far away from here as possible. It could all go bad. We just need to be swift setting things up," Lisa said.

"What are you talking about?" I asked. "I'm staying right here until I see it all go down, Lisa. Call me crazy or whatever you want. You can leave and go get help for the girls at the prison, but I have to see him die," I said with feeling.

"I think the feds are down with Dr. Clemons, so I don't know how I'm going to get help," she said.

Her words hit me like a ton of bricks and my stomach immediately began cramping up.

"These crooked-ass feds are the ones who sold me out

and got me into all of this bullshit in the first place," I muttered.

"Listen to me. We will get this done and we can handle that part afterward. We have to do this, or there will be no other opportunity," Lisa continued.

"But I thought you said we had to wait for a certain time or something?" I asked. I couldn't even think straight. All I could think about was my promise to Lena and Dana. That was going to be a thing of the past now. They would think I betrayed them if I didn't send authorities to the prison. But what choice did I have? I couldn't trust it. State agents had already turned on me once. I wasn't letting that happen to me again.

"Misty, are you ready?" Lisa whispered, elbowing me in the ribs. "Wake up. Wake up."

I blinked rapidly and shook my head a little bit. I couldn't even believe I had fallen asleep waiting. I touched my face.

"I feel out of it," I said. I whipped my head around to remind myself I was no longer trapped inside the prison. "But I'm up now," I whispered back, getting my bearings. "This guy is taking mad long to come out, though. I'm sick of waiting, for real."

"I know, my nerves are on edge," Lisa confessed.

"Well, we are here now, so don't get nervous about shit, and we will wait for days if we have to," I said.

Lisa nodded in agreement.

The sun had come up in Dr. Clemons's neighborhood and the area was alive with people. Lisa and I were getting nervous that someone would spot us parked in the shrubbery between Dr. Clemons's house and his neighbor's. The expansive backyards of the estates gave us some cover, but we knew if we got spotted, it would be all over for us. It was bad enough we looked like two burglars dressed in all black; all it would take is one nosy neighbor and our cover would be blown.

Another hour passed before I saw any movement in front of Dr. Clemons's house. I was the first one to notice.

"Look," I whispered, urging Lisa to pay attention. "Do you see what I'm seeing?"

"Yes, that's him," Lisa said, like it was so obvious.

"Yeah, but look," I said, my words breaking off.

Lisa's jaw dropped slightly and her brows furrowed. My body stiffened and my breath caught in my throat. I swallowed hard and Lisa's eyes went as round as saucers. For a few seconds, neither of us said anything. We just stared at what was unfolding in front of us.

"He's not by himself," Lisa said, panic stringing through her words.

"I can fucking see that," I snapped, my lips turning white while my heart hammered against my chest bone. "I thought you said he didn't have a wife or a family," I spat.

"I didn't think he did. What are we going to do?" Lisa said, her voice forceful but shaky. "We can't go through with it. Not now. Not like this. Could we?"

"Argh! We gonna need to call this off. But I'm gonna get this bastard, just not like this!"

Lisa glared at me. "It's too late now. We can't run out there and say, 'Hi, Dr. Clemons, don't get in your car because we rigged that shit with dynamite!' " Looking unsure, Lisa continued, "But the trap is laid. We can't turn back or else everything we've been planning for is over. Our lives will be fucking over. It's either us or him."

"You're wrong, Lisa. We just gotta find a way to make sure he's by himself when the car blows. We can't let an innocent person just die like this," I whispered back harshly, putting my hand on the door handle, preparing to open it.

She grabbed my arm and pulled me back from opening the door. Pissed that Lisa had turned on me, I wasted no time getting in her face.

"Lisa, you can't be that fucking weak. We can't go back on the plan now. We just gotta find a way to get that kid away from the car before it blows. No matter what, we are all in. You helped me and I could've kept it moving, but I came back and risked it all for this reason, and this reason only. You have to be smarter than this. You think this shit is just that easy? Just as hard as it was to plan, it's even harder to stop it now. We didn't just plan to blow some random nigga up. This is the fucking Devil. This the nigga who did unthinkable shit to me that we talking about here. What the hell? You act like you can't fucking re-member. Think about all the shit he did and then went home at night like he ain't do nothing. Think about the sick acts you watched him perform on us, with no pain medication or anesthesia, how you watched girls bleed to death, pigs," I gritted. My head swirled from a rush of adrenaline.

"You can't feel sorry for a piece of shit like him, Lisa. He didn't give a fuck about you or me or them girls and still don't," I preached.

"I know all of that, okay! But . . . ," Lisa said, a hot stream of tears suddenly falling from her eyes.

I sighed and shook my head. "I feel the same way, but I'm not gonna let this chance get away from us. Instead of worrying, let's just hurry up and figure out a distraction so only Clemons is in the car." I hated that she was wavering and showing any weakness, because it reminded me of just how cold I had become inside.

"I know Clemons deserves to die, but I ain't never de-liberately killed no one before. It's a sin and the karma will come back on us," Lisa continued to press.

I sucked my teeth. "I know. But I'm not leaving here until he's dead," I said flatly. I had told myself to take the emotion out of these actions. "I'm not going to let you fuck this up. This shit is going down. If you can't stomach it, then don't watch," I said, turning my face away from Lisa.

Lisa slumped in the car and turned her face away so she

couldn't see the front of Dr. Clemons's house any longer. She put her hands over her ears in an attempt to drown out the sounds. I knew that what was about to happen was suddenly tearing Lisa up inside, but I also knew we had no choice now.

"Lisa, it's his fault this shit had to happen," I said softly. "He did some unforgivable shit to us. We didn't know someone else would be here, but if we go back on it now, I will end up locked up again and then he will do some cruel, animalistic shit to me again," I reminded Lisa.

She nodded her head in agreement, but she still didn't turn back around to watch. I turned my attention back to watching Dr. Clemons, and tried to figure out how I could make sure he was in the car alone. The nervousness I had felt when I first saw him had faded into a burning vengeful hatred. Family or no family, Dr. Clemons had to die for everything that he'd done.

Suddenly Shanta's face flashed through my mind and my anxiousness to get the deed done increased. My chest heaved up and down now.

Find a distraction. Don't let the kid and wife get in the car, I chanted in my head; my fists were clenched tightly. I was so close to exacting revenge that I could feel every nerve in my body coming alive. But my revenge wouldn't be right with a kid dying.

I watched Dr. Clemons through squinted eyes as he threw his head back and laughed out loud. Even from a distance, his laugh sent chills down my spine.

What man who is a father would do the things he did to us? I thought. *A sick bastard like him don't deserve a child or a wife or any family, for that matter.*

The little boy seemed happier than I could ever remember being in my life. The small kid ran around, baiting Dr. Clemons to catch him. The woman looked on at them, smiling.

"Got you!" Dr. Clemons called out playfully, grabbing

the boy in a playful football hold. This was definitely a different side of the perverted doctor than I was used to seeing.

Dr. Clemons bounced the boy, giggling and kicking his legs, as he carried him to the back seat of a red Chevy Tahoe. My heart throttled up in my chest; I had to act now if I was going to save the kid. My eyes searched the surrounding yard, looking for anything that could help. As I grabbed the car door handle, I heard the child say, "I gotta go potty. Now!"

The woman laughed and moved to pick up the boy. "All right. Let's go back inside and handle this. Honey, why don't you warm up the car?" Without waiting for an answer, she walked back to the house with the boy.

Thank God! "He's getting in the fucking car, Lisa. They went back inside, but he's getting in the fucking car," I whispered almost breathlessly, my legs trembling now.

Lisa closed her eyes tightly and shook her head from left to right and started to mouth a prayer, but before she could complete one sentence—

Boom . . . Boom . . . Boom . . . three huge blasts made us jump almost out of our skins.

"Oh my God!" Lisa gasped out.

My ears were ringing from the loud blast. The force of the blast sent dirt and soot flying all over the car.

"Ouch," Lisa winced, covering her ringing ears with her hands and rocking back and forth. Dirt covered the car and made it hard for me to see out of the windshield, but I knew we needed to get out of there and fast. The blast also made my head feel like I'd been hit with a sledgehammer, but I still had our escape plan at the forefront of my mind.

My hearing was slightly impaired and my back ached from sitting so long, but I was ready to get moving.

"We gotta go! C'mon! The cops and the bomb squad will be here any minute," Lisa huffed.

"Is it done?" I asked. "Is it really done?! Is he really gone?!" I screamed out.

"Sh!" Lisa scolded.

"Oh my God!" I said, hitting the steering wheel. "We did it!"

I reached over and shook Lisa's arm. "We fucking did it! Thank you so much," I cried out.

"Shhhh. We need to go!"

I wanted to sob from relief and happiness and all kinds of emotions, but I knew we did have to leave. "It was either him or us. Him or us," I reiterated. "Now we just have one last thing to do and our plan will be done," I said.

"Misty, I am suggesting that you run, drive, and never look back. The way shit looks, you will not only be blamed for the CO's murder, but you will also be charged with this now. They will send you to prison for the rest of your natural-born life. You know how the feds are," Lisa said to me sincerely.

I could tell she was serious and sad when she thought about everything that had happened. I felt the same way. "Look, Lisa, I have to go. I don't know what I'm going to do or how I'm going to get away. If I never see you again, just remember that I'm grateful for what you did for me," I told her. I meant my words too. I was really feeling like I would die at the hands of the police or the feds at this point.

"Everything you did brought the attention we needed at the prison. I am going to make sure the girls know you got rid of that monster for them and kept your promise," Lisa said.

My heart just melted hearing her say she would let the girls know and that they wouldn't have to suffer anymore. I was a wreck. Here I was thinking I was going to bring in the cavalry to those other girls. That plan was out of the window and now I wouldn't get to see it come together.

*　*　*

I sat in that vehicle crying hysterically and sick to my stomach. I suddenly felt dizzy. I opened the door, leaned out, and threw up. After I did that, I realized that I just needed to get back to my mother and Sandra and really get the fuck out of Dodge now. Another wave of panic came over me. I knew it wouldn't be long before my enemies or the cops would come to my location and put my mother back at risk, and now Sandra too. Too bad I wasn't going to be around to see all of the rest of the bastards at the prison being led out in handcuffs.

I made up my mind that I was taking Lisa's advice and getting the fuck out of there. I reached over into the passenger seat and picked up the gun. I placed it in my lap, just in case I needed it right away. Then I looked around suspiciously, made sure there was nobody watching me, and I pulled the car back onto the road and started to drive the hell out of there. I planned on getting far, far away. Wherever I ended up, I knew it would be a better life than I had now.

As I got out of there, I was flying down that little road, trying to hurry up and get to the highway. When I got almost halfway up the road toward the highway, just like I suspected, I started seeing a bunch of black vehicles speeding down the opposite side of the street toward Dr. Clemons's house. I knew right away it was the ATF and bomb squads.

They were really flying by, so they didn't even notice me. I had the car headlights turned off. The vehicles had lights on the tops of them, but no sirens were blaring. They were trying to make a sneak attack. They just didn't know that I had fucking spotted them before they spotted me. *Those bastards.* Little did they know when they got to the house, they wouldn't find me there. All they were going to find was a dead doctor who deserved to die.

Lisa was right. Those bastards were coming, but they were coming for me.

"Damn, I really have to get out of here!" I said out loud as I watched them flying by me. It was like my worst nightmare as I watched those cars. Not before long, they would figure out the whole thing, and soon they'd really be looking for me. Now they could really say I was a fucking armed-and-dangerous fugitive, because they had made me one.

I swerved the car off onto the side of the road so they wouldn't notice me. It was a long line of vehicles flying by; and so far, they weren't paying me any attention, but I had to make sure. When I pulled the vehicle off into the bushes, I ducked down in the front seat. I couldn't take a chance that any of them would recognize my silhouette in the vehicle. I knew they couldn't see me because of the dark tints, but I couldn't risk it.

It was about ten minutes until I saw the last set of lights fly past. I was gripping the gun I had in my hand so fucking hard, my hand started to hurt. I wanted to wait a good amount of time before I pulled out of there, just in case. Finally I took a deep breath and decided that I was finally ready to make a move to get my mother. I sat up in the seat and looked around nervously. I didn't see any more cars on the road, so I pulled out of the bushes and started for the highway and toward my escape. I drove for a few feet and, all of a sudden, a car flew out of the side of the bushes in front of me.

"Oh shit!" I screamed, slamming my foot on the brakes. The tires started screeching; that is how short I had to stop. I just barely missed hitting the vehicle that had pulled in front of me. My chest was heaving in and out. All I could see was my life flashing before my eyes if I would've slammed into that fucking car. My nerves were even more on edge now.

"You fucking dummy! What are you doing?!" I screamed at the strange car.

They had almost caused me to hit them and, oddly, they

had pulled their car horizontally into the road. I was blocked so I couldn't move.

"Get the fuck out of the way!" I screamed, but all of my windows were up and I knew the person driving the car couldn't hear me. I couldn't see inside the windows of the strange car. It didn't look like one of the FBI cars. So I figured it was probably somebody who had gotten lost on that little road.

"Move!" I screamed, finally rolling the window down a little bit. I didn't want to call that much attention to myself, so I couldn't blow my horn for fear that I would attract the attention of all of the state and FBI activity, which was now going on up the street at Dr. Clemons's. As I sat there and waited for this car to move, I suddenly noticed headlights approaching from behind me. "Oh fuck!" I screamed. The headlights were not relenting. They were coming toward me, full speed ahead, and I knew right way that they were going to slam into the back of the vehicle. I was being trapped in. These motherfuckers were ambushing me.

"Fuck this!" I screamed. I mashed down on the car's accelerator so hard, I could feel the floor of the vehicle. The car barreled into the stopped car and pushed the car a few feet, but not before the other vehicle slammed into me from the back. My body jerked and I hit my head on the back of the seat. I was dazed and in pain for a few minutes. As I tried to get myself together, the next thing I heard were loud bangs and glass crashing all around me.

"Oh my God!" I screamed. Whoever was in both cars was shooting at me. Bullets were flying at me from the front and the back.

Just as I lifted up my hand to return fire . . . *bam!* A bullet hit the inside of the car.

"Agh!" I screamed out. It had just missed me.

More bullets started flying over my head and I got down low. I was scared; I could feel urine leaking down my legs. I was starting to feel dizzy from the fear. *Bam!*

Then another one of the wild shots licked off; this time, it hit me somewhere on my body. Fire lit through my veins.

"Help me!" I let out a bloodcurdling scream. I felt like my heart was beating in my shoulder. That's when I realized the shot had hit me in the shoulder. I was in severe pain. I was trapped—a car in front of me and one behind.

I lifted my opposite hand and let off a few shots from the gun I had. But I couldn't see if I hit anybody. Finally the shots stopped raining down on me and I didn't hear shit for a few minutes. I said a silent prayer, and just as I did, the driver's-side door to the car flew open. I could see body silhouettes, but the faces were blurry. The gunshot wounds I had suffered were making me real dizzy. I must have been losing a lot of blood. Still, I managed to get off a kick, but it was all for nothing. I was snatched out of the vehicle. My body was way too weak to fight.

"Get her into the other car," I heard the voice say.

I knew right away it was the voice of one of Ahmad's men. I couldn't mistake the accent anywhere. He had climbed out of the car that had stopped in front of me.

"I thought . . . I thought you were in prison," I rasped. "I didn't know you got out!" I was barely able to get the words out of my mouth. I was in shock. I looked at his evil face as he contorted it into a wicked smile.

"Misty, you are not smarter than me. You just don't know how many connections I really have. You have to be taken out, once and for all," Ahmad said.

"You might as well. You and a whole bunch of people are after me," I said weakly, and let my head droop to the side.

"Let's get her out of here. I have to take care of her and get far away from this place," he said to his men.

There was another car way up in front waiting for us. I was forced into the back seat and handcuffed. One of the guys tied a handkerchief around my arm and leg to stop my gunshot wounds from bleeding.

"I need a doctor, or else I will bleed to death," I said.

"Well, if you bleed to death, it was all your own fault," the boss said to me.

Just as the car started to pull out, I heard them start speaking in their language rapidly.

"Go, go! Hurry up!" Ahmad screamed out in English.

I couldn't figure out what the panic was all about, at first. Then I heard a loud noise outside. It was the sound of helicopters hovering over the area. Then I heard the distant sound of sirens wailing too. I knew then that the police and the feds had finally caught on that I was in the area. Ahmad just didn't know what he had walked into with me being with him. I knew they weren't coming to save me; instead, they wanted to take me down too. The police cars started gaining on the car I was in. They were all panicking. Ahmad's henchmen started shooting at the cop cars.

"Oh shit!" I screamed out.

Once again, bullets were flying everywhere. The helicopter overhead was now shining a bright light on the vehicle we were in. Ahmad had never anticipated that whenever he got his hands on me, I would be a fugitive from the law—with every law enforcement entity on my ass and his at the same time. More bullets were flying, and all of a sudden, one of Ahmad's men in the front seat got hit in the head.

"Aggh!" I screamed. My yell was so loud, I could feel the veins in my head and neck pop up. The henchman's body slumped over, and the driver started swerving because the other guy's body fell on him.

"Drive! Get us the fuck out of here! Now!" Ahmad screamed out, and he held a gun to the driver's head now.

At this point, I didn't care either way. This shit was a lose–lose situation for me. Either Ahmad and his men were going to kill me, or the feds would kill me or take me back to prison for life for the crimes that I actually did do this time. We kept driving and now I could tell there was more than one helicopter in the sky trailing the car.

The helicopter got really low toward the highway. It was so low that I could see it from inside the car. That was the first time I had seen something like that, but I also remember Terrell telling me that the DEA sometimes used snipers in helicopters to take down fleeing drug dealers. I had a feeling this was one of those instances.

Just as that thought entered my mind, I heard a loud *bang;* then the windshield shattered and the driver of the car slumped over. Blood splattered all the way into the back seat and got on Ahmad and me. The car was out of control and I just knew we would die.

"Oh my God!" I screamed at the top of my lungs. Even with our impending deaths, Ahmad wasn't giving up on his mission. He put his gun to my head. He was about to shoot me, but he wasn't fast enough. Suddenly another shot whistled through the vehicle and Ahmad's head just exploded.

"No! What the hell is going on?!" I screamed out again.

All of a sudden, the vehicle slowed down and crashed into a tree. The fucking fed had thrown out a spiked strip on the highway, which punctured all of the tires on the car, stopping it instantly. There was only one other guy alive in that car with me. He pointed the gun at me and told me to get out of the car.

"I'm scared. They will shoot both of us," I said, trying to buy some time.

He wasn't trying to hear me. He grabbed me and we exited the car together. He was using me as a human shield. He had the gun up to my head and was screaming something in his language. The state agents had surrounded the car and there were guns drawn all over the place.

"Please! I'm not the criminal here! Please believe me! I was kidnapped and forced . . . ," I started screaming. With his broken accent, the man holding me told me to shut up.

"Release her or you will die! She is a fugitive from justice!" I heard some of the agents yelling.

I felt like I was dead already. He was choking the shit out of me and he was crying. He knew that his life was over. He knew that this shit had all come to an end. I also knew my fucking life was over, because those state agents had fire in their eyes. As far as they were concerned, I had killed three people now.

"I said let her go!" the agents yelled again.

But the man just pressed the gun to my head even harder. The next thing I heard was a bullet whistle past my head. I even felt the heat from it up against my face. Suddenly the man's arm was released from choking my neck and his body collapsed on the floor. It was a sniper from the bushes. At that point, I knew I had nowhere to run or hide. I threw my hands up in surrender. My bullet wounds were killing me. I was ready to face whatever came next for me.

Those state agents descended on me like I was holding an arsenal of weapons. They wrestled me to the ground and roughly handcuffed me behind my back. I was screaming out in pain, but they didn't give a fuck about my injuries. One of them started reading me my rights. I kept trying to plead my case.

Finally, I told one of the agents they needed to speak to Lisa. I told them she would be able to tell them everything that had happened to me and how things went down in the prison.

21

IS IT OVER?

I was taken to the hospital and my wounds were treated. I was locked down at the hospital and chained to the bed. There was a bunch of girls there from the prison. Obviously, my plan had worked, after all. The feds were having them treated for injuries they had suffered at the hands of Dr. Clemons. So all of my work wasn't for nothing; at least the girls had been saved.

As I lay there and thought about how I was going to spend the rest of my life behind bars, I noticed Lisa walking by. My heart jumped. She winked at me. I let a smile spread over my face.

"Lisa?" I whispered.

She stopped walking and looked in my direction. She put her fingers up to her mouth as if to tell me to be quiet. They couldn't stop her; she was dressed like a nurse who worked in the hospital. The agent that was guarding me wasn't happy when Lisa told him he had to leave the room.

"I need to see this patient in private, sir," Lisa said to the agent. "Maybe you can take your break, and I should be done in about fifteen to twenty minutes," she told him.

"Okay, but keep your eye on this one. She may be injured, but she's a crafty one," the agent said. He looked skeptical about leaving, because no one could take the chance of me escaping again.

When I was alone with Lisa, her eyes lit up. "Misty, thank you for keeping your word. I am sorry for what happened to you," she said.

I started crying. I knew that I had to do it. There was no doubt in my mind that if I had gotten out, I'd have to save the rest of the girls.

"Lisa, I need your help. I just need you to make sure my mother remains safe. I probably will never see the light of day again, but she doesn't deserve to keep going through this with me. Tell her I said to take the money, pay Anderson even though our plan failed, and then move to an island somewhere," I whispered to her.

Lisa nodded her head in agreement. I whispered Sandra's phone number to her and she told me she already memorized it from before.

"There are a few more things that need to be done, and, in your honor, I will do them. I will also see to it that this time you have a proper defense," Lisa said.

"You finished, Nurse?" the agent called, and knocked on the door. Damn, they were not playing with me this time. "Ms. Heiress is still a prisoner. Let's go," one of the agents finally said to Lisa.

I was glad I had enough time to give her the information she needed to help me. I knew she wouldn't let me down because she recognized that I had really risked my life to save her and the other girls.

Those bastard feds took me from the hospital down to their cells, all over again. They continued to try to question me about the murder of the CO, but this time, I was smart. I wasn't speaking to them without first speaking to a lawyer.

So they kept me sitting in jail for an entire week. Finally, on one of the days I was sitting there, I heard feet coming toward the cells. I just figured they were coming back to harass me again. But when I looked up, I couldn't believe my eyes. I had to actually rub my eyes because after all I had been through, I just knew I was dreaming.

Standing in front of me, dressed to death and looking sexy as hell, were Sandra and my mother. I threw my hands up to my face and just burst out in tears. The guards opened the cell and I jumped into my mother's arms. I couldn't breathe, she held me so tightly.

"What are you doing here?" I said through my sobs.

"You have a real good friend and she was looking out for you," my mother told me.

I knew right away she was talking about Lisa. Then I noticed a man there with them.

"Oh, Misty. This is Mr. Schwartz. You know, the lawyer I promised you before," my mother told me.

I couldn't stop crying from being so damn happy. The man extended his hand to me for a handshake and then he handed me a couple of documents.

"What's that?" I asked softly.

"This is your entire defense, and maybe some information for that lawsuit you will be filing against the criminal justice system," Mr. Schwartz told me.

All I could do was smile. I was about to face the music, but now at least I had a good lawyer and I could point out all of the injustice I suffered my first go-round.

"You won't be here for long if I have anything to do with it. Because not only were you sentenced unfairly, there are a lot of holes in your case files." Mr. Schwartz said to me. "In addition to that, a lot of women wouldn't even have a fighting chance. You're a good person, Ms. Heiress, and that will come out during your trial. I won't let them discount what you did and everything that happened to you. Besides, they have a flawed case. I hear you were like a ghost . . . just moving and dodging death," he said.

"I don't know about that. I just know my grandmother told me that I had a purpose and I couldn't tell what she was talking about then, but now I know," I said.

Mr. Schwartz was a beast. Within two days of meeting him, I was out on bail and awaiting meetings with the feds and state prosecutors.

Even though my situation was looking better, I still felt dead inside. So much had happened, and I knew I'd never be the old Misty again. I had so much anger inside me. I wanted to kill everyone that had a hand in my ordeal at the prison. And I still had promises to keep to the women I'd left behind.

It took about a week to get my mother settled and the supplies I needed. But now revenge was about to be served. My heart rate sped up with anticipation as I watched the COs being shuffled out of the prison and toward the waiting police cars. To finally face justice. But I, too, had justice to dispense. I got low to the ground and moved downhill until I was sure I was a safe distance. I stood up to get a better look at the cars in the distance.

"Shit!" I cursed when I saw Anderson walk over and knock on the window of one of the vehicles. "You better get the fuck away," I whispered. Lisa had told me today was his day off, so why was he here?

Anderson walked away and started toward another vehicle, which was five cars away. There was nothing I could do for him. I quickly ducked down and covered my head with my arms before the . . .

Boom! Boom!

Even from my safe position, the blast sent me reeling backward. I uncovered my eyes to see a cloud of dust that resembled a huge tornado rise into the sky.

Even with my ears ringing, I could hear the screams erupting from the prison complex and from the people in the cars who weren't instantly killed by the blasts. The force of the explosion had sent Anderson face-first into the dirt, and several other people were knocked down. Car windows were shattered and car horns wailed. Cars, torn from the ground, were flipped over. The police vehicles holding all of those evil-ass COs were completely engulfed in flames. The entire place erupted into massive chaos, with people running and screaming.

I got off my back and raced down the hill on the far side of the prison, where I was to meet up with Lisa. My head pounded from the sound of the blast, but my mind and soul felt vindicated and satisfied. I was too busy to even care if there were any eyes on me. I finally collapsed when I was far enough away. I then realized that I was bleeding from somewhere.

This didn't deter Lisa from trying to lift me up from the ground.

"Misty, come on and stay with me. We can get out of here," Lisa begged me.

"It's okay, Lisa. You can let me go," I insisted. I could see everything around her was fading away. Even the light was dimming.

"No. I can get you to a hospital. The wound isn't that bad," she said, refusing to listen to me.

Her cries were fading in and out of my ears. That was okay. I had come to do the job and now it was done all the way. Everyone had been taken care of. Things around me were fading fast; this time, I wasn't afraid. This time, I embraced it.

I moved toward a bright light. That's when I saw my grandmother, Jillian, and Carl—everyone that had died.

Jillian was smiling at me, and I was smiling back at her. My grandmother came over and grabbed my hand.

"You did good, my child. You did good."

After that, I knew I had fulfilled my purpose. I was dead. There would be no more running, hiding, suffering, or prison.

I was no longer *property of the state*. I was now property of God. Not a bad place to be, if I do say so myself.

Connect with

Us

Visit us online at
KensingtonBooks.com
to read more from your favorite authors, see books
by series, view reading group guides, and more.

Join us on social media
for sneak peeks, chances to win books and prize packs,
and to share your thoughts with other readers.

facebook.com/kensingtonpublishing
twitter.com/kensingtonbooks

Tell us what you think!

To share your thoughts, submit a review,
or sign up for our eNewsletters, please visit:
KensingtonBooks.com/TellUs.